The Concrete Angel
Concrete Angels MC series, Book 4

Siobhan Muir

DEDICATION

Dedicated to Lisa Benedict. Thank you for your greatness.

ACKNOWLEDGMENTS

Writing a book is never really a one-person job, and writing a series is especially difficult alone. Keeping track of details is so much easier when you have help. Not only does it take a great deal of hard work, editing, and research on the part of the author to get things correct, but without my compatriots, there'd be a lot more mistakes.

Great thanks to Lisa Benedict, Paula Wyant, and Maranda for refining my understanding of witches and their craft. Huge thanks to Mary Decker and Rose Sogioka for beta reading this bad boy and catching inconsistencies. And great thanks to Kris Norris for designing the perfect holiday biker cover. Thanks to Paul Henry Serres, and Alex B for being the face of Flint.

As always, great thanks to my readers for cheering me on. Y'all make my writing worth the detailed effort..

CHAPTER ONE

Flint

I sat on my bike at my favorite overlook in the Colorado Rockies and looked down on the twinkling lights of Fort Collins. Snow fell like feathers on the ground as if someone had engaged in a massive pillow fight and their weapons had broken apart. The temperature had dropped near true zero keeping most of the human population inside, but I didn't mind the cold. I actually preferred this time of year.

The season shifted people's awareness back toward hope and kindness, even if only briefly. The cold forced most of them indoors and that meant I could move around more freely. And the cold really didn't bother me. Gargoyles rarely noticed it. The changes in weather didn't often catch my attention. I could ride my bike rain or shine, snow or fog, blistering heat or brutal cold. Ice was always tricky, but even then, I didn't really have to worry about injuries.

But tonight, the cold had penetrated deeper than usual. I rubbed my chest to massage away the ache.

Must be the time of year.

I could just pick up the strains of holiday music rising

up in the windy air from the shopping centers below. Some of it was pretty, filling my chest with feelings of nostalgia and memory. Others sounded like dirges and were best left ignored. I preferred to sit above the comings and goings of the human world when they got into their celebratory moods because they could become so manic. Either deliriously happy or miserable depending on who and why.

I'd lived long enough to find the extreme highs and lows exhausting and frivolous. Such emotions seemed a waste of time. I preferred the calm beneath the thrashing of human existence. It let me see things more clearly and not get swept up in their brief excitement. I enjoyed humans for the most part, but there were times I needed my space away from them.

Like tonight.

Loki had declared it a night of revelry at the Concrete Angels compound though the actual holiday was still a few days off, and I wasn't in the mood. There'd be a lot of drinking and fucking and general partying, but my awareness had grown contemplative as the days grew shorter and I just needed some quiet. The celebrations seemed damn near desperate this year, like the humans were trying to sugarcoat shit and be happy about it. I wasn't willing to buy into their false frivolity and I'd bolted out of the compound to find some peace.

So I'd cleared my absence with Quan-Yin and Nessie, jumped on my bike, and headed out into the dark foothills of the Rocky Mountains, trying to find peace and quiet. This spot always settled me when the world threatened my serenity. I took a deep breath and let the snowy silence fill my soul.

Until the two 4WD SUVs came roaring up the quiet road and skidded to a halt, spraying snow and gravel ahead of them.

Oh for the Goddess's sake.

They left the lights on as several male humans piled

out of the vehicles, laughing and shouting in drunken revelry. I swallowed a growl. So much for quiet and solitude.

I sat no more than fifty feet from them, but they were too focused on their festivities to notice me in the falling snow. I prepared to kickstart my bike to find another quiet spot when a new sound reached my ears.

Is that a frightened woman?

Two of the males dragged a protesting female from the car, her body language screaming fear and anger. It felt as if someone had thrust the end of an electrical cable to my body. A low rumbling growl emanated from my chest and I rolled to my feet, stalking through the snow to the vehicles before I realized what I was doing.

"You been writing about shit you shouldn't, little girl. The boss-man doesn't like witches and says we can do what we want with you, especially if you come back dead." The guy holding the woman around the throat squeezed as he shook her.

It was weird she never said a word. *Could be that the hood on her head is muffling her screams.*

"Think she'll turn us into toads if we let her talk? Good thing we gagged her. Right, boys?"

Well that explains her silence.

A chorus of drunken predatory assent ricocheted through the air as the men converged on the woman. She squeaked, unable to voice her protest, and my lips pulled back from my canines. I didn't suffer bullies in the MC, I definitely wasn't putting up with them at the overlook.

I slammed my fist through one of the passenger windows, the glass shattering inward on impact. All the men whirled to face the new threat and I scowled. I pointed at the woman and shook my head, gesturing for the men to let her go.

Being mute always made conversations tricky, and most people didn't know American Sign Language. But body language often spoke louder anyway. Oh sure, I could make grunts and growls, but enunciation was beyond me. ASL worked better.

"Who the fuck are you?"

I raised an eyebrow. *Yeah, like I'm going to answer that.* I signed in ASL, "Let her go."

"Oh lookee here, boys. We got a deaf guy trying to defend her honor." The guy sneered as the others laughed. "Beat it, punk. She's our prize for the night. But because it's the holidays, you can have her when we're done."

I rolled my eyes. *They always travel in packs of idiots.* "Let her go now." The energy of my hands was emphatic.

"Look, dummy, I'm gonna say this slow. Get. The. Fuck. Outta. Here."

I shifted my gaze to the woman. She'd backed away and seemed to be working on the bindings on her wrists. That she wasn't panicked surprised the hell out of me. Still, she couldn't beat those odds. *Go time.*

The men thought I'd given them my answer so they weren't expecting me to grab the first one, and throw him bodily into the others. They were so light it was always fun to see how far they'd go, like a stone skipping over a still lake. I braced for battle when the leader scrambled to his feet and threw himself at me with snarl.

Bring it, bad boy. I grinned. Fighting an angry gargoyle never worked out very well for humans. But then, my human disguise worked so well, most didn't know it until too late. They'd find out now. *Come on, boys. Let's dance.*

****

Rochelle

I'd been minding my own business, enjoying the lights and the snow around the Holiday Depot as I sipped my hot chocolate. The other ladies of the Triple C – Colorado Covens Co-op – had wanted to take pictures with the hot Santa on the old-fashioned train engine with brass accents and a big FC on the front. I wasn't interested in the guy— he seemed a little too handsy for me, but I took some shots for my blog, The Better Bitter Brew: The Witch's Guide to Fort Collins. Mostly, content to watch the festival.

But someone grabbed me, gagged me and threw a bag over my head, before dragging me into a vehicle tall enough they had to lift me. It smelled like male sweat, cigarettes, and cheap alcohol. Combined with my panic, it damn near made me puke.

"Boss-man says she's got magic, the real shit, not sleight-of-hand crap, but it ends at sundown."

I almost laughed, but I didn't want to give them an excuse to question me. My magic never ended with the time of day. I'd been an earth witch since puberty, particularly of hearth and home, and my power was that of defense and protection, not offense and destruction.

"Tonight we're gonna end her. But first I think we get to play. I've never seen a witch's tits." Someone leaned close to my head. "Hey, little girl, can witches fly?" He chuckled as my heart sank. "Guess we'll find out. It'll be like the Chutes and Ladders without the ladders."

I gritted my teeth against the fear. More than likely the sexy Santa had distracted my companions enough that they hadn't seen anything and I was on my own, between a rock and a hard place. Good thing I liked rocks.

"You been writing about shit you shouldn't, little girl. The boss-man doesn't like witches and says we can do what we want with you, especially if you come back dead." The guy holding me around the throat squeezed and shook me like a dog.

Panic bubbled up but I gritted my teeth harder and tried to think around the clawing fear. Who did I know that hated witches and yet could hire the scumbags taking me now? I couldn't see the dude speaking, but I could smell his over-use of Drakkar Noir. *Damn, I thought that stuff went out with the 90s.*

"Think she'll turn us into toads if we let her talk? Good thing we gagged her. Right, boys?"

I protested around the gag before everyone froze when an explosion of glass punctuated their laughter. Everyone turned, at least I thought they did, and the guy released me. I took a deep breath against the urge to scramble away, but I didn't know which direction to go. Were we close to the cliff they'd been talking about? I tried to still my racing heart and listen to figure out where everyone was until Drakkar Boy growled.

"Who the fuck are you?"

Silence met his question and I wondered why. Didn't guys like the tell the story of the ass kicking they were going to give? *I'd really like my eyes back.* My voice would be nice, too, but I'd settle for my sight.

"Oh lookee here, boys. We got a deaf guy trying to defend her honor." Drakkar Boy's voice held derision while the others laughed.

That explains why I haven't heard the new guy speak.

"Beat it, punk. She's our prize for the night. But because it's the holidays, you can have her when we're done."

The hell you will. I took two steps back from where I'd felt air movement and I hoped I'd gotten out of view so I could work on breaking my binds. If I could get free, I might be able to escape while the men were distracted by whoever had joined them.

"Look, dummy, I'm gonna say this slow. Get. The. Fuck. Outta. Here."

Apparently that had set the new guy off because someone grunted in surprise and landed on the ground nearby with a heavy thud. A low snarl answered Drakkar Boy's shout of anger and the hair stood up on the back of my neck. *What the hell kind of creature makes that sound?*

"Grab him, you fuckin' idiot!" Voices rose in anger and fear.

"What for? It's not like I can hold him now, can I?"

"Help!"

"You catch him. Creighton doesn't pay enough for this shit. I'm fuckin' outta here!"

There were meaty thuds and cries of pain, but the truck I'd arrived in didn't move or start. I yanked and tugged on my hands until the bindings finally broke. I ripped off the hood and pulled the gag out of my mouth before I looked around.

Bodies littered the ground near the SUV, but I couldn't tell if they were only unconscious, or dead. And one man stood in the beams of the headlights.

Broad shoulders, bald head, and exposed abs of solid stone.

Sweet glory.

Despite the snow swirling around him, he wasn't wearing a shirt. But he looked like a total badass. The leather cut, denim jeans, and biker boots helped, too. I waited for him to say something, but he just stared at me, a look both hot and feral. I shivered and hoped he wasn't like the others.

I expected him to say, "Are you all right?" or the equivalent, but he simply stared and I had to clear my throat to find my voice.

"Thank you."

He nodded and did this odd rearrangement of his lips as if his teeth didn't quite fit behind them. Again, I expected words from him, but he didn't speak at all as he turned and started picking up bodies. Like they were nothing more than sacks of grain.

Holy shit. His strength made me realize I might be in real trouble. *If you're gonna go, Rochelle, now is the time.* But the snowstorm had picked up. I could easily get lost in the Rocky Mountains and die of exposure without the SUV. What the hell was I going to do?

So I stood there in the snow and watched the badass biker dude collect the bodies and shove them in the SUV without a word. I felt kinda stupid, like a dumb damsel in distress who couldn't save herself, but I didn't know what to do. *Maybe I should start walking down the road and hope for the best.* Yeah, that was a good way to get lost or dead or both.

The man turned after he slammed the doors shut and lifted an eyebrow at me just standing there. Hell, I would've too. He paused, tilting his head, before he approached slowly, stopping about three feet from me. Then he pointed at me before curling his index finger into the "OK" symbol and raised his eyebrows.

Are you okay?

The question was easy enough to read from his expression, but why hadn't he said anything?

I shook my head. "I don't know."

He grimaced. He pointed at me again and did some motion with his hands.

Wait, was that ASL? It looked like he'd signed "hurt."

"No, I'm not hurt, but I don't know where I am or how I'm going to get home." I wrapped my arms around myself and shot a look into the increasing snow.

He sighed and took another step closer to me so I could clearly see his hands. Despite his rough appearance, his hands looked strong, supple, and well maintained though the nails were a little longer than I expected.

He pointed at himself then at me and back to his bike.

"You'll give me a ride?"

He nodded. The question was could I trust him to get me home? *And do I want him to know where I live?* But why wasn't he speaking?

"Can you speak?"

He sighed again and shook his head, annoyance

clouding his expression.

"Can you hear?"

He nodded, motioning me toward his bike. I hesitated a little longer, but what choice did I have? I could stay up here on the edge of a cliff in the snow, or I could take a chance on this guy to get me closer to home. Taking a deep breath, I followed him to his Harley parked off to the side of the gravel overlook, slowly accumulating snow.

We stopped at his bike and I tapped him on the shoulder. His skin was warm, but hard, the muscles taut. When he looked at me, I used my hands to sign at him, "Can you read sign language?"

Surprise and relief filtered over his face and some of the fierceness receded. *Yes.*

I pointed at myself and nodded. "Me too."

"Good. I'll give you a ride." He pointed to the bike.

"Thank you. I live in Fort Collins."

He gave me a thumbs-up as he straddled his bike and those thick, hard thighs damn near took my breath away. What the hell? I was stranded on a mountainside in a snowstorm with a badass stranger, and my libido decided to make an entrance? *I'm gonna need my vibrator tonight.*

I shoved my attraction out of my thoughts and straddled the bike behind him. Settling against his body was a little like finding a heater. The heat from him permeated my jacket and I let out an involuntary sigh. A deep rumble rippled through the air and I realized he was laughing at my relief.

He wrapped one hand around mine at his waist and squeezed gently before kickstarting his bike and rolling us toward the road home. Bikers weren't good guys, not that I had heard. It all was a jumbled mess of lies and innuendoes that had very little basis in truth. But this guy had not only saved my life, he laughed when I cuddled up to his warmth and it didn't creep me out. *Yeah, I'm in so much trouble.* Hopefully, it wouldn't end badly for me.

CHAPTER TWO

Flint

For the first time in my long life, I was actually speechless. Not because I couldn't enunciate words, but because the woman sitting behind me on my bike had stolen coherent thought. If anyone could listen to my mind, they'd find me rather verbose. But she settled everything down to quiet and pleasure.

Her happy sigh when she snuggled up to me had made me chuckle and I couldn't help squeezing the arms around my waist. All humans had an energy to them and most of the time I found it frenetic. But this woman felt as quiet and solid as a mountain cave left to the seasons. And she had spoken with sign language, making our communication a helluva lot easier.

She didn't say anything more until we'd come down off the gravel road leading to the overlook, but I was strangely content with her silent presence at my back. The snow flying past my face felt good, cooling some of the heat generated by the adrenaline rush of the fight, and I sped up. The woman behind me snuggled closer and ducked her head behind my shoulders. My wings tingled and I grinned into the wind.

Until I realized neither of us were wearing helmets, it was damn near zero degrees Fahrenheit, and she wasn't even wearing leather.

Shit, fuck, way to go, numbskull.

I slowed the bike down and sat up straighter to block more of the wind and snow. Hell, I didn't even know where I was going except generally into Fort Collins. I usually wasn't so careless or disorganized. I almost always had a plan. But put one human woman on the back of my bike and I lost all focus.

We got down to the bottom of the hills and I stopped at the light. I turned and tapped her on the shoulder so she'd look up.

Her hazel eyes met mine and I forgot what I needed to ask. Gargoyles usually didn't covet much. We didn't need more than a place to roost, a nice view, and adequate hunting grounds. Oh yeah, we were definitely carnivores. But we all were guardians of one kind or another and we defended treasure. Sometimes it was books or knowledge. I had quite a few friends who'd once guarded libraries and universities. Sometimes it was sanctuary like on mosques, churches, or temples. Other gargoyles loved treasure of the more traditional sorts and hung out on museums or banks.

I'd never had something to guard until Loki found me and asked me to be security for his biker club. He said I'd be the original Concrete Angel and the way he'd grinned told me he thought himself pretty funny. I wasn't actually made of concrete, but my skin was damn near impenetrable by wood, steel, or another kind of stone. Made me very tough to kill and a great security guard for the club.

But the woman on the back of my bike made me want to chuck it all and guard only her. She was a treasure I'd never encountered and I didn't even know her damn name.

"What?" She raised her eyebrows aware that I'd turned for some reason.

I blinked. Then raised one hand. "Where going?"

Signing with just one hand made the question truncated.

"Oh, uh, my shop's on the corner of north Taft Hill road and Laporte Ave. That way." She pointed to the right.

I nodded and turned the bike to head down the snowy street. It wasn't far from where we were, which was both good and bad. Good because she needed to get warm. Bad because soon she'd be off my bike and away from my body. And that made me want to turn around and haul ass the other way.

What the hell is wrong with me?

I'd known this woman all of thirty minutes, and I was already thinking kidnapping? I mentally shook my head and headed for her shop. We stopped in front of a stand-alone brick building with a Tudor-style wood addition to the second floor. It had a sharp A-shaped gable over the door and a weathered wooden plank sign that read *The Herb Cabinette.*

Cute, a play on herb cabinet. I parked the bike on the curb in front of the shop and paused, reluctant to let her go, but knowing she couldn't stay outside.

She cleared her throat and swung her leg off the bike to stand on the sidewalk. "Thanks so much for the rescue and the ride. I appreciate it."

"You're welcome." I dipped my head along with my hand. "Have a good night and be safe."

She nodded and took a few steps toward the alley between her shop and the next building. But she stopped and turned, biting her bottom lip.

Hey, that should be my job.

I blinked. Where the hell had that thought come from? I didn't even know this woman's name or her pseudonym. It wasn't like she was a prostitute used to meaningless sex meant to scratch an itch.

"Um, would you like to come up for a cup of tea?"

I didn't know who was more surprised at her question, her or me, but it felt like she'd just given me the Apple from the Tree of Knowledge. A forbidden fruit that was too good to pass up. I turned off the bike and yanked the key out, swinging my leg over the seat. Hell yeah, I'd like some tea. And maybe a little more of this pretty woman who'd captured my attention.

****

Rochelle

I'd invited him in. What the hell was wrong with me? I must've had a serious "white knight" complex to invite in this burly, hard, badass biker who'd tossed men around like firewood. But it was the holidays and cold outside, and everyone deserved a hot cup of tea after something like that.

He'd been surprised and didn't seem to mind the snow, which was weird, but some guys just have that massive internal furnace and wear shorts in a blizzard. This guy could've been like that. But I'd invited him in and I didn't even know his name.

"Would you like some tea? My name's Rochelle Stone, by the way. I figure you should know who your host is."

He looked at me like his world suddenly made sense and he gave me a devastating smile. "My name is F L I N T." His fingers moved with ease spelling out his name and I loved watching them. "Tea would be fine."

It was so strange talking aloud to him when his communication came in the form of body movements and hand gestures. It almost made me want to whisper though there was no one else around to hear our conversation.

"Make yourself at home while I get the tea started." I blinked. I never gave strangers this much free rein in my home. I needed my head examined.

I scuttled into the kitchen and shook my head. I'd

never been quick to allow my inner sanctum to be breached by anyone, much less a bold, bald, and brash-looking guy like Flint. But he had a solid, steady quality to him that pushed away some of my usual reservations. I put the kettle on to boil and set out a poppyseed roll I'd picked up at the local Hungarian deli down the road. I didn't know if he'd like anything to eat, but food brought people together and it seemed rude not to offer.

When I returned to the living room, I found him examining all the little treasures with which I'd decorated my home. The seashells from a beach in Florida. A sand dollar from Whidbey Island. Fossil bones from a cave in Nevada. Beeswax candles from a local apiary. Crystals from the Rocky Mountains. Most of the things were natural, offered to me by the Goddess along my travels. But I also had a small framed photo of my mom and me enjoying the river park in Golden, Colorado. The image was of me sitting on one of the fish statues while my mom stood behind me with her arms around me. I loved that photo, even more so because it was the last time we'd been together before she died.

Flint turned and gestured at the photo. "Is that your mother?"

I nodded, trying to swallow around the lump in my throat. "Yeah. She was killed a few weeks after that picture was taken. I still miss her."

"I'm sorry." His expression softened.

"Thanks, I appreciate it." I tried to smile but it probably came out a grimace. "I brought some poppyseed roll if you're interested, and the tea is almost ready. Would you care to sit down?"

He tilted his head and narrowed his eyes before he nodded and searched the room for a seat. Bypassing the couch and the armchairs, he grabbed one of my metal kitchen chairs, spun it around, and straddled the seat carefully.

"Are you hurt or stiff?" I stood there holding the plate like a deer in headlights.

He shook his head and signed, "Why?"

I shrugged. "You just moved so gingerly I thought maybe something had happened during the fight."

He raised his chin in understanding. "No, I'm heavy and I didn't want to break the chair."

"Oh." I'd never heard that kind of explanation before, but given his physique, I probably shouldn't have been surprised. Which reminded me. "Aren't you cold? I mean you're shirtless in zero degree weather. I'd be freezing."

He shrugged and reached for a slice of poppyseed roll, a secret smile curling his lips. The kettle whistled, distracting me, and I retreated to take it off the stove. I so wanted to know what that smile meant, but I'd promised him tea and never went back on my promises. I also never gave up when I wanted to know something.

"Peppermint, Ginger, Huckleberry, Green, Black or White tea for you?" I almost forgot to look at him, so used to people speaking, but I remembered at the last moment to turn my head to watch his hands.

"It's the holidays. Peppermint, please." His lips curled into a smirk and I couldn't help but laugh. For a rough and tough biker, he had impeccable manners.

"Peppermint it is." I brought him the steaming mug as I carried my own back to the table. "Definitely seems to fit the season." I handed him his cup and sat down, cradling my own. "I didn't get to really thank you for your help, and for the ride home. So, thank you." I used ASL along with my words to emphasize the words. Then I bit my lip. "Did you kill them?"

Flint took a few moments to answer, sipping his tea as if it hadn't been boiling hot. *The guy must have a cast iron mouth.* He set the mug down and shrugged.

"Only one, I think. The others were unconscious. I threw them in their vehicle." He shrugged. "They were threatening and hurting you." He shrugged again as if that explained why he'd taken on five guys alone for one stranger.

I wanted to ask him if this was a 'knight in shining armor' sort of complex, but I didn't want to sound ungrateful. I would've found a snowy grave that night if he hadn't stepped in.

"I appreciate it. I'll say blessings and prayers for the one who died." I shot a look toward my little *puja*, the Sanskrit word for altar, and thought about lighting a candle.

"Why?" Flint tilted his head.

"Why would I say blessings and prayers for the dead?" He nodded. "He was trying to kill you."

"I know, but I don't want his angry spirit to come looking for me and wreak havoc on my home." I rose and grabbed my matches. It seemed like a wise move to start the protection spells and wards. "Give me a moment."

I lit three candles, the large central pillar illuminating the rest of the *puja*, as I sank to my knees. I raised my gaze to my favorite image of the Goddess and lit a bundle of sage. I bowed my head, asking for blessings on the dead man and protections for my home. I waved the bundle back and forth and around a loop three times, allowing the sharp-scented smoke to fill my nose and the air around the *puja*. I also asked for protection on myself and my reluctant savior.

I pictured Flint in my head as I offered the sage, and felt a weird tug in my chest, as if someone had tied a ribbon to my heart and pulled it taut. I inhaled sharply. *That's a message.* I'd experienced enough of the Goddess's communications to know I was meant to pay attention to that one. But what was She trying to tell me? That Flint was a friend in need of defense? Was he a new guardian of my home and person? Or was he a threat to me?

The last one brought a sharp pain in my side. *Definitely not a threat.*

At least She'd given me that answer. The Goddess

liked me to figure shit out as I went along, but sometimes She'd give me direct responses. Whatever Flint was to me, he was definitely important, and I'd include him in my daily prayers and blessings.

I bowed my head with a prayer of thanks and rose to my feet. A solid, warm presence rested behind me and I realized Flint stood at my back close enough to wrap his arms around me and kiss my neck.

Why the hell am I thinking about that?

Because Flint wrapped his arms around my waist and drew me against his chest, kissing the back of my neck. The heat and sweetness of his kiss made me close my eyes and lean into him. *Oh glory, I want this.* I needed his hands on my body unlike I'd needed any other physical touch before. I didn't want to think or worry or analyze. I only wanted his heat, his body, and his sexual attention.

I was an earth witch, more attuned to rocks, crystals, and mountains than I was to life energy. But his touches and attention brought an affirmation of life, of survival, that I needed to make it through the night. When his rough tongue painted a path beneath my ear, I gasped and turned in his arms to meet his gaze.

"Come to bed with me, Flint."

He blinked down at me, some of the lust clearing from his eyes. "Right now? Tonight? Here?"

"Right now." I reached around him and grabbed a handful of ass. It wasn't soft by any stretch of the imagination, but it felt great in my hand.

He hissed and growled, the lust returning to his eyes. I let a seductive smile curl my lips and he growled again, tilting his head to take my mouth with his.

Slick heat engulfed my mouth as he slid his rough tongue between my lips and caressed me. He tasted like peppermint and smelled like petrichor, my favorite scent of rain on dry stone, and he kissed like heaven. Most of my coherent thought splintered in the face of his thorough kisses, but I had enough presence of mind to remember my wards and his bike outside.

I pulled back from his drugging kisses and rested my forehead on his broad, warm and smooth chest. His breath brushed my hair in an agitated rhythm, and a thick ridge pushed against the front of his jeans.

"Give me a minute." I raised my head to meet his gaze. Intense lust and need stared back at me with a dash of incredulity. "I need to reset the wards on the building."

He tilted his head with a frown. I read the question on his face.

"Someone tried to kill me tonight. I want us to be protected, including your bike." I shot him a rueful grin. "And someone distracted me before I was finished."

He snorted but still moved his hands. "Wards? As in energy protections?"

I bit my lip, debating if I should tell him I was an earth witch. Given how we met – men trying to kill me because I was a witch – I had reservations about telling people about my abilities. But if he knew enough to ask about energy protections, he might not have the same hang-ups about witches.

I nodded slowly. "Yeah. I'm an earth witch, attuned to the energies of ley lines and the Mother Earth Goddess. I use Her energy to protect my home and business from malicious attacks and destruction."

He tipped his chin up in understanding before a sultry smile curled his lips. "Still want to go to bed?"

"Hell yeah. Give me one minute."

I closed my eyes and sent my senses out to the wards and protective layers I'd laid around my home. I noted the places where the magical energy appeared worn or thin and reinforced it. *Looks like someone came by to test the waters.* Thank goodness I'd directed the ward energy into digital form so I could tell who'd tried to get in, but I didn't have time to check that now.

"There, all done." I opened my eyes just as he leaned in and brushed my lips with his. "Oh, that's lovely."

He growled and it set my libido on high. There was something wicked about the sounds he made and it revved up my heart, making me want to drag him into my bedroom and have my way with him. Fortunately, he didn't seem inclined to argue.

"Bedroom, this way." I tugged him down the little hall from my kitchen/living room and into the bedroom. I flicked on the lights. The warm, golden glow of the string of holiday lights gave a fairy wonderland look to the room.

His hand moved. "Pretty."

"Thank you. I leave the lights all year round but I particularly love them in the winter."

He nodded and stopped me next to the bed. "It matches you." He trailed one hand along the side of my face, pushing the hair behind my ear. "You're beauty and light together." Then he tilted his head and kissed me with banked hunger.

I loved the rough texture of his tongue as he slid it over mine and each stroke made arousal surge through me. I couldn't get enough of his taste and I moaned into his kiss as I tried to pull him tighter against my body.

The problem was he wore very little clothing and I wore too much. But hell, I didn't need to be naked to give him a blowjob, and there was something so tantalizing about that thick ridge behind his fly. I let my hands rest on his chest below the leather cut and the heat of his smooth skin seared them in delicious ways. I trailed them down his body, bumping over his defined abs until I reached his waist band and belt. I dropped to my knees and looked up at him as I grasped the buckle.

Our gazes met, his glowing with arousal and something else. Hunger and need flooded through me and I wasn't sure if it was my own emotions or his I'd picked up on. I pulled the belt through the buckle and slid it apart before unbuttoning his jeans and opening the fly.

Sweet Goddess, he's gone commando.

His cock pushed out of the denim with solid, smooth warmth, and I started to drool. He wasn't the biggest male I'd ever been with, but like Goldilocks, he was just right. Hard, healthy, and hot, I grasped his shaft and slid my lips over the head.

I don't know what I was expecting. I'd sucked cocks before, but he tasted like hot, sexy heaven. His skin was smooth and taut over hard muscle, but there was an erotic give to his cock that I couldn't get enough of.

I went to town on his shaft, licking and sucking with abandon while his hands fisted at his sides. I loved seeing the pleasurable strain in his face and body as I worked him. Deep rumblings came from his chest and I loved hearing them, knowing I was the cause.

I glanced up at him and found his blue-gold eyes narrowed in slumberous pleasure, and I moaned as my own arousal ramped up. He growled in response and I swear my pussy spasmed with a desperation I hadn't felt in a long time. But I *needed* to suck him to completion.

I slid my mouth down as far as I could go until he bumped the back of my throat, and swallowed. He groaned and hissed as I pulled back, raking my teeth gently over the crown of his cock. Flint growled and tightened his fists as he locked his knees. I whimpered at the flood of arousal and repeated the motion.

He growled louder and grasped my head in his hands as he pumped his cock into my mouth. All I could do was hold on until he hardened to solid stone against my tongue and filled my mouth with hot cum. It tasted like delicious petrichor, and I swallowed it down like an addict.

I licked him clean, wanting more, but he groaned and lifted me to my feet before he kissed me. His hot tongue branded mine as he scoured my mouth, teasing and tasting me as he clawed at my clothing. He pulled back long enough to look me in the eyes and gestured to my sweater.

"May I undress you?"

Who knew this guy could be so polite?

"Yes, please." I lifted my arms so he could tug the soft wool over my head, freeing my breasts.

He tossed the sweater aside and stopped, his gaze riveted to my chest. For a moment I wondered if there was something wrong because he froze, not even his breath moving his chest. As the moment stretched, I glanced down at myself and hoped he wasn't disappointed with my body. I had stretch marks on my breasts from when they ballooned during puberty. I even had a few on my hips. But when I glanced back up to his face, his expression told me nothing.

Sweet glory, does he find me hideous?

I almost twisted away from his sight when his hands moved. "You're very beautiful." He raised his gaze to meet mine. "Let me pleasure you."

"Okay."

Not my most eloquent of answers, but when a hot, badass biker guy wanted to make me feel good, I wasn't about to quibble. He nodded and unzipped my jeans before pushing them down my legs. I hadn't gone commando, but I had worn some red lace undies that covered nothing. While they were the dregs of my underwear drawer, Flint seemed to find them fascinating.

He inhaled quickly and his nostrils flared as he licked his lips. *I'm gonna take that as approval on his part.* He growled as he grinned and I caught sight of his long canines. Or longer than usual canines. They weren't vampiric long by any stretch of the imagination, but they gave him a feral and primitive look that really tripped my trigger. Cream filled my pussy with the thought of him biting my shoulder when he came.

Biting my shoulder? Where the fuck did that come from?

But the image wouldn't go away as he stripped me bare and laid on me on my bed. I swear his eyes glowed as he crawled over my body, his cock returning to the hardness I'd enjoyed in my mouth.

He settled his weight on me, grinding his hard shaft into my mound and I moaned as the erotic massage sent spikes of arousal through me. His eyes glowed in the dim light and he grinned with each sound I made. Those sexy canines flashed again and I arched into him as he dipped his head to kiss my neck.

Sweet Goddess, I loved having his body on top of mine. He was hard and strong, and so fucking sexy I couldn't wait for him to thrust into me. I grabbed his ass and rocked my hips, allowing my vulva to caress his cock.

He gasped and growled, pulling out of my grasp to search the floor for his jeans. At first I thought he'd changed his mind, but he'd scrabbled through the denim, throwing his wallet and keys and phone in his search for something. It took me a moment to realize he wanted a condom.

"Bedside drawer, Flint. Brand new box."

He snarled as he leapt for the drawer and yanked it open. He seemed to realize what he was doing because he slowed down and opened the box more carefully. *It would definitely suck to get a papercut now.*

He pulled out a condom, tore the package open, and sheathed himself before he crawled over me to line his head up with my entrance. He growled again to get my attention and met my gaze as he slowly shoved his hard shaft into my pussy.

Oh my glory, the stretch and heft of him. My eyes closed and I threw my head back as he came to rest, balls-deep inside me. But then he stopped and we both spent a few moments feeling the rightness of where we were. I opened my eyes to meet his, and the world shifted on me. Surrounded by the of glow of the twinkling holiday lights, the frightening, ugly world fell away and I lay cradled in the warmth and strength of Flint's arms.

Nothing could shake that perfect moment and the Goddess's presence filtered into my awareness. *This must be what it's like to sit with Her.* We shared that connection of perfection and I realized I didn't want just a one-night-stand with this man.

Which was weird because I'd never wanted anyone longer than a quick fuck before.

But Flint held the ancient wisdom and presence I'd been searching for since the loss of my mother, and I didn't want to lose it now that I'd found it again. I reached up and grasped his face, making him meet my eyes.

"Please."

He growled and moved, achingly sweet as he dragged his cock between my folds before sliding back in. He rocked with measured strokes, stoking my fire and igniting my desperation. I needed him to move. I needed him to lose control. I needed his heat and strength and erotic pleasure. I clenched my inner pussy muscles and it lit him on fire.

He growled and sped up his thrusts, his lips pulling back from his teeth. It was sexy as hell and I whimpered at him, determined to push him over the edge of lustful ecstasy. I trailed my hands down his chest and tweaked his nipples as I licked my lips.

"Oh glory, fuck me hard, Flint."

That did it. He let loose a roar that shook my windows and pounded into me so hard the bed creaked. My arousal bloomed brighter than ever and my orgasm threatened to overwhelm me. The slide of his cock against my clit ignited my release and I wailed as it crashed over me.

That must have kicked off his orgasm because his thrusts sped up and pushed me deeper into my pleasure. I flew ahead of his joy as he stiffened above me then dropped onto me and sank his teeth into my shoulder. The pain yanked me out of my first orgasm and threw me into another, pleasurable heat catapulting me back among the stars.

At last, we returned to awareness and I found him licking my shoulder and mumbling an apologetic noise, almost like the whimpers of a dog. He held me gently, his big body cradling mine, and rumbled a combination of comforting and worried sounds. I took a deep breath and relaxed completely before nuzzling him behind his ear.

"Thank you."

He froze then lifted his head to look at me. He raised his eyebrows in a worried, perplexed look.

"That was the best sex I've had in a long time." Hell, it was the best sex I'd ever had, but he didn't need to know that. I cupped his cheek and rubbed my thumb over his chin. "Whenever you're ready, I'd like some more, please."

A deep chuckle rumbled from his chest as he grinned, showing his long canines. My pussy spasmed with renewed need as I watched him retreat to the bathroom to dispose of the condom. He returned with his shaft hard once again as he grabbed another condom from the drawer.

"This time I want you to ride me." He rolled the condom on and climbed onto the bed. He settled on his back on motioned to me. "I want to play with those breasts while you rock my cock."

I shot him my own grin as I straddled him, stroking his hard shaft before lining it up with my pussy, already dripping with pre-cum.

"Wish granted." And I impaled myself on his cock.

CHAPTER THREE

Flint

Something buzzed incessantly in the room and I wondered if Rochelle had set an alarm to get up. I opened my eyes and looked around her bedroom with the fairy lights still glowing in the early morning darkness. Nothing moved. Not even Rochelle. She lay curled up on her side and just the curve of her hip made my cock stand up with enthusiasm.

But the buzzing started again and I rolled out of the bed to find my phone. I fished it out from under her sweater and read the notification.

Loki.

I wasn't surprised he'd texted. I usually didn't stay away from the compound longer than a couple of hours, being security. He must've been shitting purple bricks by the time he got around to texting. I unlocked the phone and read his message, snorting with amusement.

Where the fuck are you?

I tapped out a response with the same love and care he'd shown. **Getting laid. Why?**

I didn't expect him to respond right away so I set about getting dressed. While I didn't feel the cold, most humans had an issue with a rock hard, ripped naked man wandering around. They were too uptight in my opinion, but I'd lived around them long enough to realize they weren't going to change. I'd brought my cut into Rochelle's home, but my extra shirt remained in the paniers on my bike. I shoved my feet into my boots just as my phone chirped with another text.

Det er bra. I hope it was good because I need you down at the southside shop. Scott and Attila are packing up some product for distribution and I want extra security.

I nodded. Since Backlog started using us as scapegoats for their illegal shit we'd stepped up our vigilance. Not that we weren't into all sorts of illegal shit, but we weren't taking credit for theirs.

I'll be there in ten.

I made sure I had my wallet, keys, and phone before I took one more look at the woman who'd brightened my night. Rochelle's wavy terra cotta hair lay tousled over the pillow, the glossy deep auburn appearing more oxblood against the white cotton. The freckles across her nose and cheeks reminded me of the glorious specks of amphibole in a creamy pink granite, each one precious and unique. I wanted to map them with my fingers and relocate the ones on other parts of her body, like her full breasts with their pink areolas and her mound with its russet curls. My cock hardened with the thought of all the places I wanted to taste again and my phone chirped, reminding me I had to leave.

Fuck. I needed to say goodbye but I didn't want to wake her. I cast my gaze around the room, looking for pen and paper, hoping a note wouldn't be too chickenshit after the incredible night we'd shared. *When I bit her.*

Yeah, that was weird. I'd never done that with anyone before. Sex was fun and felt good, but I'd never lost control so much as to sink my canines into my partner's shoulder. I found a pad of paper in her living room and tried to find the words to express how much I'd enjoyed her, and maybe apologize for the bite.

Yes, gargoyles could write and read, though sometimes I had a tough time holding those small writing implements without breaking them. I wrote my note and folded it before returning to the bedroom to set it on her bedside table near her phone. I paused there to watch her rest and wonder if she'd let me see her again.

It was such an out-of-character thought, I hissed and turned away, heading for her door. I didn't have keys to her place, but I hoped her wards would keep out any unwelcome visitors. I headed down to the street and stepped outside, scanning the open area for lurkers. It was a habit I'd gotten into when Loki asked me to be security for the club.

I didn't catch anyone scoping the place out and climbed on my bike, kickstarting it and letting it warm up from the frigid temperatures overnight. It grumbled for having been left out, but the engine caught and I pulled away from the curb after a few minutes.

I don't remember much of the ride over to the shop on the south side of Fort Collins. It looked like a mechanic's shop from the outside with a human-sized door beside a set of vehicle doors. No one was parked outside, but I suspected that was to keep curious humans from snooping around. That, and police drones overhead. We'd learned that motorcycles often made the authorities curious and took pains to keep the bikes out of sight when doing anything important.

I clicked the garage door opener app on my phone and one of the doors slid up into the building, exposing Attila with a shotgun casually draped over one shoulder as I rode in. Despite his relaxed appearance, I could hear his heartbeat thundering from the doorway.

"Bloody hell, Flint. Warn a body. We were bracin' for the coppers to come rushin' us."

I shrugged as I parked the bike and signed, "Didn't Loki text you I was coming?"

"Och, the bloody bastard never said when to expect ye."

Attila scowled as he waved at the Scooters, our wannabe members, packaging up our "care packages" of designer drugs for the wealthy trust fund clients. Most humans believed the drug trade was kept alive through the down and out people living on the fringes, but there wouldn't be a drug trade if it wasn't for the rich-and-miserable. We didn't cater to the middle and lower financial classes.

I waved to recapture his attention. "I'm going to scout the perimeter and look for eyes."

He nodded. "Brilliant. We should be done here in another half hour." Then he leaned close, his expression serious. "And look for things that doona belong, eh? I smelled someone who isna member of the club here, but it was too faint to give me a good read on who they were."

I raised my eyebrows but nodded. "I'll check it out."

"Right. Thirty minutes."

I waved at him and started my search around the shop while they kept working. Attila was a werewolf and had a remarkable nose. If he said he'd smelled something off, there was reason for concern.

I searched the ground floor first, checking behind pallets of product while Scott and the Scooters packed it up into actual fucking gift baskets with bows and shit. It was the holidays after all. Scott nodded to me before he barked at the Scooters to get back to work. The wannabe members of our club often treated any trip away to the shop like a school field trip, using any excuse to fuck around when the teacher's head was turned.

I didn't find anything of note on the ground floor so I took the stairs up to the "loft" above the shop's offices. It was more like a storage space for old pallets, crates, and equipment that wasn't needed. Most of our crew didn't visit there much so it would be a great place to hide something like a mic or a camera where no one would think to look.

I stopped at the top of the stairs and closed my eyes, letting myself sink into the earth energy flowing through the building. I had to hand it to Loki; the man knew how to put his buildings on top of ley lines. Six thick ley lines came together in a large node below the shop, making it hum with energy. Not many people knew about ley lines, not even the Elder Races, but most of them could sense the lines, if only unconsciously. The building hummed with so much energy, it could easily hide the electronic signature of a little listening or viewing device.

Damn, Rochelle could definitely do some hard-core wards here. And if we had an intruder come through, it might be a good idea to have her build those wards.

I shook my head. Why the hell did I keep thinking about Rochelle? We'd only had sex once. It had been phenomenal sex, but it wasn't like we had a real relationship or anything.

A stab of pain shot through my chest at the thought and I gasped, bending at the waist with a hand between my pecs. A memory filled my mind's eye of my canines sinking deep into Rochelle's shoulder and the rightness of the action. She'd even thanked me for it. It seemed like the right thing to do with her and I hadn't ever felt so connected or grounded as I did after fucking her.

Except it wasn't really fucking. More like making love.

I shook my head and refocused on my task. Attila's nose had picked up someone new here and right now, Rochelle was the least of my worries. I shoved the memories of us together into the back of my mind and let my energy merge with those of the ley lines under the building.

I settled enough to open my inner eye, the one people

in India and Asia called "the Third Eye." I growled a little to get in tune with the lines and asked the node to show me the memory trails of anyone who'd come up to the loft in the last two months.

The images condensed in front of my mind's eye like smoky ghosts wandering around me. Mostly, the loft remained undisturbed with only the dust motes for company. But then Scott and his old lady Numbers had come up for a hot tryst against some old crates in the back corner. They moved around to another spot near one of the small windows the size of a 40-inch TV screen. They humped like rabbits for about twenty minutes before making out and returning downstairs with goofy smiles. I'd have to give him shit for that.

Next Loki and Attila had come up and rearranged some of the crates, taking a few away and adding others with the help of some Scooters. Most of the crates looked like supplies to make the trust fund babies' care packages. All pretty standard stuff.

But about a week ago, someone new ghosted upstairs. The person wasn't large, but they wore dark clothing to mask their appearance. Loose jeans covered the legs and a hoodie with the hood up finished the outfit. The person checked every box and crate upstairs, taking photos with their phone before creeping to the next pallet.

Someone must have come in downstairs because the hooded figure ducked behind some unused pallets for a short time. I couldn't sense what spooked them, but they hid for about an hour before tiptoeing to the railing and peering over just to the right of where I now stood. They affixed something to the underside of the railing overlooking the floor below before they skittered down the stairs.

I waited to see if any more energy ghosts appeared in the loft, but nothing showed up until I arrived twenty minutes ago. I pulled myself out of the ley lines and turned to the railing. Everything appeared normal until I crouched to look at the underside.

Bingo!

I pulled a bandana out of my back pocket and wrapped it around the little electronic camera pointed at the ground floor. I twisted the bandana tightly in multiple layers and shoved them in my pocket. The best part – the little mic wouldn't be able to pick up my voice, since I didn't use one. I stomped down the stairs to the first floor and looked for Attila.

I found him overseeing the loading of the care packages into the van. I waved to get his attention and signed, "We may have a problem."

I pulled the bandana out of my pocket and unwrapped it carefully, making sure to keep the little camera's lens facing the folds of cloth. "Someone has been watching and listening."

Attila scowled at my hand and signed back at me, "Could you see or smell who?"

I shrugged. "Smaller person, maybe a buck fifty or a buck sixty-five, moved quick and furtive, but with confidence. You want me to take the gizmos to Neo or do you want to?"

"Och, we're nearly done here, but I still have to get this shite loaded and packed up. We need to do something about this, but I havenae the time right now." He eyed me narrowly. "Do ye have a wee date or somethin'?"

I definitely wanted to get back to Rochelle's warm arms, but this was a priority and Loki would find ways of making my life miserable if I didn't bring this to Neo. Plus, the last thing I wanted was for Loki to focus on Rochelle. He had a way of making people's lives difficult for his own entertainment.

I shook my head. "No date, just wondered if you were headed back there directly. I promised Grub I'd pick up some eggnog on my way back." I'd promised no such thing, but it seemed like a good distraction to keep Attila off the scent of my love life.

"Yer still goin' back there faster than I."

I nodded. "Okay. See you at the compound."

"Right." He waved and turned back to his workers. "Let's go, you lot! There's no time for feckin' around."

I snorted and headed for my bike. I'd have to buy eggnog just to make it look good because Attila's memory was as good as his nose. And I wasn't ready to explain my night with Rochelle to anyone.

****

Rochelle

"Good morning, sunshine!" My best friend Joslyn didn't do anything quiet, particularly mornings.

I cracked my eyes open to find the clock and tried to make sense of the digital numbers. Was it really ten thirty? I never slept that late. I scrubbed my face with my hands and sat up, belatedly remembering I was naked as the covers fell to my waist. I hastily grabbed them as my nipples beaded in the cool air and I immediately looked around for Flint.

My badass biker lover had disappeared, but a folded note with my name written in an elegant cursive scrawl sat beside my phone on the side table. Before I had time to grab it, Joslyn strode into my room.

"Why are you still in bed? We have to go over the big holiday promo drive and wildlife benefit auction stuff." She frowned and narrowed her dark brown eyes. "You look different. Your aura is all over the place. Shitty night last night?"

I nodded with a grimace. "You could say that. A bunch of goons tried to throw me off a cliff."

She gasped and sat down on the bed. "Holy fuck! Did

you call the cops?"

"No. They had me hooded and gagged so I couldn't see them."

"Shit. Do you have any clue who sent them after you?" She looked me over carefully as if checking for injuries.

"Not much. They kept saying 'boss-man hates witches.'"

"Which could be any number of rich assholes in the United States."

"Exactly. So I'll just have to focus on my goal."

"Which is?"

"Shield Fort Collins from those kinds of mudfuckers."

"Oh, something simple then." Joslyn grimaced. "I thought you went out with the Triple C ladies."

"I did. They found the hunky Santa on the train and the goons found me."

"But you got away, right? I mean you're here and you're talking to me, so that means—what happened to your shoulder?"

I blinked at Joslyn's abrupt change of subject. "My shoulder? What are you talking about?"

"Here." She got up and headed for my bathroom to get my hand mirror. "This is what I'm talking about." She offered it to me.

I took the mirror and angled it to view my shoulder. Puncture marks, not unlike something from a vampire horror flick, marred the skin of my trapezius muscle on my left side. Despite the appearance of damage, the punctures didn't hurt that much as I ran my fingers over them.

"Holy shit. I have no idea what that's from."

She snorted. "You dating a vampire or something?"

I shook my head and shot her a dry look. "They're not on my jugular vein or my carotid artery. These are in my shoulder." I waved my hands vaguely at my shoulder. "This is more like a…werewolf."

I stopped and thought about Flint's longer-than-usual

canines. *Could he be a werewolf?* I'd heard the stories bandied about between my mother's more eclectic friends, and a few of my witch colleagues had told stories about the "Moonsingers" who could shift into their true forms at will.

Sweet glory, am I gonna shift into something furry when the moon's full? Damn, I don't want to invest in chew toys.

Joslyn wasn't buying it. Of course, she was newer to the witch community than I. "Did you encounter a werewolf last night?" She tilted her head, the beads at the end of her braids clacking with her puzzlement. "It does look like some sort of animal bite, but smaller than a wolf or a dog. Are you sure one of the thugs didn't bite you? If it was one of them, you need to get some Frankincense oil on that ASAP and go to the clinic for a Tetanus shot. Humans' mouths are filthy."

I turned my gaze back to the punctures and thought back to my night. Yeah, it had started out scary, but it had ended with the sexy heat of a man who'd taken me to sexual heights I hadn't achieved before.

All this from his bite?

I thought about the second time we'd fucked – though *fucked* wasn't the right word for our sexual endeavors. It was more like making love – and how much more in-tune we were. It made me think we'd connected on a soul-deep level.

I snorted at my own hokey romanticism. "I'll definitely get inoculated."

"Let me at least put some Frankincense and a bandage on it." Joslyn rose and headed for the bathroom.

I scrubbed my face with my hands and looked for my night shirt. Then I remembered it was still in the closet because I hadn't bothered to 'get ready for bed' with a hot, sexy, hard-as-stone biker who fucked me into exhaustion. I hoped Joslyn wouldn't mind seeing my naked butt as I scooted out of the bed and sauntered to the closet to find a tank top.

"Damn, woman, who the fuck bruised your ass?"

"What?"

I looked down at my hip, but couldn't see anything. Instead I opened the closet door and checked out my butt in the full length mirror. Two perfect handprints of fingertip bruises decorated both cheeks.

"Holy fuck."

"Yeah, I bet." Joslyn held out the Frankincense oil. "And as your best friend, I invoke the right to know all about it. I thought you were accosted by goons."

I laughed as I pulled on a long tank top and PJ pants. "I was. And then this guy came out of nowhere and rescued me."

"Awww. A knight in shining armor, huh? Was he the one who left the completely sexy hand prints on your ass?" She tilted her head to look at my butt even though it was now covered with PJs.

"He wasn't wearing armor." Hell he hadn't been wearing much at all considering the weather. "And yeah, they're his handprints. His name is Flint and he's a biker with the Concrete Angels."

She raised an eyebrow while I tried to get the Frankincense on in the mirror. "Here, give me that." She took the bottle and dabbed some oil on my shoulder. "You did the horizontal mambo with a biker from the Concrete Angels? Don't you know they're badass and dangerous?"

I couldn't argue that. Flint had been both badass and dangerous—to "boss-man's" thugs. But he'd treated me with respect and kindness, and he was a fuckin' accomplished lover.

"Is that some sort of trick question?" I shot her my own raised eyebrow. I knew about the Concrete Angels because the local covens who frequented my store and blog kept a wary eye on them. Most of the witches around town swore the members weren't human. "I know who they are, and I know their reputations. I didn't ask for him to rescue me, but I did ask for the sex and it was totally worth it."

Joslyn raised both eyebrows. "Really?"

"Hell yeah." I stretched luxuriously, but flinched a little as the wound at my shoulder pulled. "Best sex I've had in a long time, and I'd do it again."

She nodded slowly. "But you do know he could be something bad like a drug dealer or gunrunner. Good sex doesn't make up for that."

I wanted to defend Flint and say he wasn't into that sort of thing, but I didn't know enough about him. Eventually I would, it was inevitable if I remained connected to him, but at the moment I didn't know much.

I shrugged. "He was a great lay, frankly, and nothing he does will change that. I'll find out more about before I fuck him again. Will that make you happy?"

She shot a pointed look at my shoulder. "I might not know all the things that go bump in the night in this world, but that looks like a mating bite to me."

I snorted. "Come on. You've been reading too much paranormal romance."

"And you haven't read enough." Joslyn shook her head. "Let's just hope it was a love bite instead of something more permanent and binding or you might be shit-outta-luck."

I shook my head and pulled a sweatshirt on over the tank top. "Did you bring me some coffee or do I have to go make my own?" I detoured back to my bed to grab Flint's note and stuffed it in my pocket before heading to the kitchen

"You have to make your own because yours is better than anything else around here." She followed me and picked up a new bag of our favorite coffee off the counter. "They only had pre-ground today but that makes it faster brew this morning."

"Blessed be to that." I nodded as I took the bag and

opened it.

The scent of the grounds settled my soul as I scooped them into my coffee maker. Joslyn settled on one of my high chairs against the kitchen bar counter and dug around in her purse, as I thought about Flint's note. Excitement made my hands shake as I filled the reservoir in the machine and pulled out the crumpled paper.

GOT CALLED TO WORK EARLY. THANK YOU FOR LAST NIGHT. WOULD LIKE TO DO IT AGAIN WITH YOU. SORRY I HAD TO LEAVE, BUT DIDN'T WANT TO WAKE YOU. TEXT ME WHEN YOU GET THIS NOTE.

— FLINT

He'd printed his phone number below and my heart fluttered like a teenager with her first crush.

Get a grip. He's just being nice.

But despite my stern words, heat bloomed in my chest and excitement made me giddy. Joslyn had reminded me to be cautious, but I couldn't wait to text Flint the next chance I got. Just thinking about him made me happy.

I cleared my throat to talk about the holiday promo drive for the blog when an urgent feeling hit my gut. I periodically received what my Mom called 'Goddess Messages,' strong feelings or premonitions of some sort of action.

The first one I'd received when I was only six years old and I refused to leave a Chuck E. Cheese's after a birthday party. My mother had tried to get me out the doors, but I clung to the ugly plastic mascot with all my six year old strength. Her boyfriend at the time had been fed up with Mom's 'brat' and stormed outside to sit in the car.

Except he'd never made it. A meth-head in an SUV had used the sidewalk outside to try to evade the police and hit five people, three of whom had died including my mother's boyfriend. When things had calmed down, Mom asked me if I knew about the impending accident and I'd told her I had a bad feeling about a big car with shiny gold wheels. The SUV had been a stolen pimpmobile with gold rims.

After that, she paid closer attention to when I got 'Goddess Messages' and they'd saved us more times than I could count. *Too bad I didn't get one before the goons got me.* But then, Flint had been there to rescue me. I hadn't gotten a message before my mom got killed, either, so they weren't consistent.

But I had the same feeling now that I'd felt at the Chuck E. Cheese's, and the message was clear. I needed to move some of my things, precious and irreplaceable things, into my storage unit. A place I'd secured under a false name and ID due to another Goddess Message.

"Rochelle, are you okay?" Joslyn appeared in front of me, her face creased in concern.

I blinked. "Yeah, but we might have to put off the holiday promo drive a bit. I need to move a few things into my storage unit."

She frowned. "Are you moving?"

I shook my head and shrugged. "I don't think so, but my gut says I need to move some of my precious items out of here."

I had insurance for both the shop downstairs and my residence, but insurance couldn't bring back heirlooms or items of sentimental value.

"Let me get dressed for real while the coffee gets going and we'll take a few things to storage." I headed for the bedroom.

"You got a Goddess Message, didn't you?"

"Yeah, but I don't know when it's going to happen. Could be later today, could be in two weeks." I jerked off my sweatshirt and tank, and traded them for an underlayer and a sweater. "I'll need to do a backup of my electronic records and leave a copy there since I can't exactly store my computer."

"Do you know what's going to happen?" Her voice came from the kitchen.

"No." I pulled my socks on and grabbed my shoes as I returned to the main room. "But it's going to be destructive and if I want to save anything special, I need to move it today."

"Okay. Show me where your boxes or totes are and we'll get shit packed." Joslyn rolled up her sleeves.

The hard part would be choosing what to keep and what I could lose.

CHAPTER FOUR

Flint

I didn't expect much notice when I got back to the Concrete Angels' compound. I figured I'd bring Neo the electronic gadgets so he could trace their signals back to their source and that would be that. Then I'd be free to go back to Rochelle. But as soon as I stepped into Neo's Black Room, I found him, Loki, our VP Michael, and our private detective, Eric Marshal. I remembered him as someone else, but the memory was getting more and more difficult to access as time went on.

Rather concerning for a gargoyle. We were the guardians of memory after all.

"What have you got for me, Flint?"

Neo gave me his patented dark-eyed stare and it always made me feel like he knew a helluva lot more than he said. I was pretty sure he was human, but sometimes I wondered if he actually had some Elder Races in his heritage when he got like this.

I unrolled my bandana and showed him the little camera and mic.

Eric hissed in recognition. "That's the same kinds of gear the U.S. Marshals use. Where did you get this, Flint?"

I gave him a thoughtful stare. It wasn't that long ago that Karma, our Enforcer, had had me keep an eye on Eric. Of course, he was her Old Man now—he even wore PROPERTY OF KARMA on his leather jacket—but I was still hesitant to outright trust him. I felt like I was missing something about him and it made me cautious.

I pulled out my phone and flipped through the pictures in the gallery until I showed him a planter with "One Day You'll Die" painted on it that sat in the park across from the southside warehouse. He didn't know sign language so most of our communication had to be by text.

"It's the warehouse closest to where we did that raid on the prostitution ring." Neo brought up a map on the screen and I nodded.

"That makes sense." Eric leaned forward, scrutinizing the screen. "The Marshals got wind of that operation thanks to you guys. What's the serial number on the tech?"

Neo raised an eyebrow. "Why?"

"I still have some contacts in the local Marshals office. I might be able to figure out who put it there."

I rubbed my chin before I waved at Loki. "Tell him the person who placed the tech was smaller than an adult male, might weigh as much as one-sixty, but was definitely not a teenager. Had some skills at hiding and surveillance."

"Flint says the person who set up the tech wasn't big, but moved with adult confidence." Loki shot Eric a look. "And you shouldn't contact any of the Marshals. They'll suck the life right out of you, ja?"

"I can probably find the same info if you give me access to the Marshals' database." Neo tapped at the keyboard. "Shouldn't take me more than a nanosecond once I'm in."

Eric snorted. "I'm pretty sure my old…friend's login won't work. They've probably scoured the system by now."

Neo shook his head. "Depends on how on top of things

they are up there in IT."

"You can try. The login was cdeville at USMarshals dot gov." Eric didn't sound very convinced, but Neo was magic with a keyboard. And that's from a member of the Elder Races, where magic was our stock in trade.

"Password?" Neo's hands flew over the keyboard.

Eric rattled it off and instead of coming back with "no such account", the computer showed a "if you've forgotten your password" link. Neo chuckled as Eric shook his head in disgust, but at least we weren't down for the count. Neo had the new password sent in a text message and in about six seconds we were into this former Marshal's account.

Heh, with Neo, getting in was inevitable. Hell, he even seemed to have a way with women, though I hadn't seen him go off with any of them.

It didn't take more than a couple of minutes and he had the current database uploaded and emailed to a dummy account where he could peruse it at his leisure. I didn't get along with too many electronic devices – my phone was about it – but Neo made it look easy to manipulate them.

Note to self – update my personal protections. Not that it would do much good given his skills.

"Okay, it looks like the database hasn't been restricted yet, but they'll probably close access when they detect this account's perusal. Text me the serial number, Flint."

I punched the letters and numbers into my phone and sent them. Neo immediately typed them into the search bar and the database repopulated with all the information.

Eric stared hard at the names and badge numbers on the listing and sucked in a quick breath. "Aw hell. Anna."

The listing showed an A. Fitzsimmons and a badge number, but nothing else.

"You know this Marshal?" Neo asked.

"Yeah. She was my friend's partner. He didn't know if she was working with Backlog or not. And I don't know if this proves anything. She could be looking for him." Eric rubbed the back of his neck with his hand. "Anna Fitzsimmons was always tenacious and since it was an old boys club in some ways, she had to be. My buddy often said she had a good head on her shoulders but he still didn't know if she'd been corrupted by Backlog. From what I knew of her, though, she wouldn't have believed he was dead until she saw the forensics on the body."

"Bring up a picture of this Anna Fitzsimmons, ja?" Loki tilted his head with his signature half-smile.

Neo tapped the keys and an ID badge appeared on the largest screen in the center. The woman in the photo had warm tawny skin and dark hair pulled into a severe bun. Instead of the usual governmental pose, she'd raised her chin just enough to challenge the photographer. I suspected she wasn't a woman to be dismissed.

"Who is that wee lassie?" Attila's voice came from behind me and the humans in the group jumped.

"Holy shit, Attila, don't sneak up on me like that." Eric rolled his head on his shoulders to loosen them. "That's U.S. Marshal Anna Fitzsimmons. She was Marshal DeVille's partner."

I waved to get Attila's attention. "Seems like that was the person in the loft at the warehouse."

His eyes narrowed and his nostrils flared. "What was she doin' in the warehouse, do ye reckon?"

Eric shrugged. "Some sort of surveillance. She could've been looking for DeVille."

"Is she workin' for Backlog, do ye know?"

Eric shook his head as we all focused back on Anna. "No idea. DeVille couldn't be sure but he hoped she wasn't. How long ago did she check out the camera?"

Neo closed the ID window. "Looks like…about three months ago, around the Autumnal Equinox."

Attila growled. "I smelled someone about that time, but the scent was fleeting, barely there."

"That's not the only camera and mic set she checked

out. Apparently, she's been surveilling a few places around Fort Collins." Neo pulled up the list of equipment.

"Can you tell where she placed them?" Eric leaned forward.

"Not yet, but give me some time." He shot a look at Eric. "Unless you know your buddy's partner's login info?"

Eric snorted. "Yeah, no way she'd tell him that."

They kept hacking at things on the computer and my attention started to drift to red hair the color of the Vermillion Cliffs and skin like the Coral Sand dunes, my sexy earth witch. The scent of her hot pussy filled my nose and my cock lengthened in my jeans. I shifted back toward the door, hoping to make my way back to Rochelle. The brethren didn't need me now that I'd brought the equipment to them. They could figure out who Anna Fitzsimmons was and deal with her.

"Flint." Loki caught me just as I slipped out the door to the rec room. "A word if you please."

Not much freaks out a gargoyle, but when Loki asked for a word, even I swallowed hard and followed him to his office without argument. I suspected he wanted me to shut the door but I refused to do so without prompting as he settled behind his desk and put his feet on the surface.

"How was your night last night? Good lay?"

Unease surged but I shrugged with nonchalance. "Good enough. The lady was in trouble and I was in the right place at the right time to help. She was very grateful."

Loki's grin widened. "Det er bra. Will you see her again?"

I tilted my head from side to side. "Maybe. Why?"

He gave me a one-shouldered shrug I didn't believe for a second. "It's been a long time since you've spent the night away from the compound. It's not your usual, ja?"

I snorted. "I spend a lot of nights away from the compound, especially when the holidays get too frenetic."

He raised his eyebrow. "Once every month is not a lot.

And you're mostly alone. Of course, you could change that if this woman becomes more important to you."

I held myself still, not wanting to give the Norse God of Mischief any ammunition. I saw how he'd badgered the other members when they found partners and I wanted none of that.

Not that I was thinking about making Rochelle a permanent partner. Was I?

The thought stumped me and I sat there silently, mulling over the idea in my head. Was that what the biting had been about? Did my inner gargoyle know something I didn't?

I must have been silent too long because Loki shrugged as if he hadn't been watching me for any little reaction. "Just think about it, ja? You don't want to let a good thing go before you have the opportunity to enjoy."

He didn't say anything else, but the unspoken phrase, *Trust me on this*, echoed in the air between us. I shot him a sharp look. Did the prez of our club just admit he'd had someone he cared for and lost them? I wasn't terribly curious by nature, but I ached to know who'd stolen the God of Mischief's heart and took it with them.

I nodded slowly. "Something I should know about, Loki?"

His gaze sharpened. "Why?"

I shrugged. "Just doing my job as security. I need to know if I should expect anyone to crash our gates looking for you."

Loki smirked. "You should always expect that, Flint. I do."

I snorted. "Fair enough." My phone chimed with a text and I checked the screen, a little thrill of joy zipping through me at the sight of Rochelle's name.

Loki didn't miss a thing. "Ah, she texts, ja?"

I nodded and shoved the phone away for the moment. "Humans are good at that. In fact, they make texting an art."

Apparently my sarcasm came through my signs because he rolled his eyes and shook his head. "Invite her to the compound, ja? We should know this woman who texts our Concrete Angel."

I nodded slowly. "Sure. Just as soon as you share the combination to the Asgardian vault."

Brief surprise flashed in his eyes just before he laughed. "Be careful what you wish for, ja? I might just agree."

I shot him a dry look as I headed for the door, but my gut clenched with the idea of Loki finding out about Rochelle before I had safeguards put in place. That warning was well placed and highly regarded in our circles. Loki granted wishes all the time, just to see what would happen. I wasn't ready for that yet.

He let me go and I took advantage of my solitude as I pulled out my phone and read Rochelle's text.

Sorry it took me so long to text. Had something come up this morning. Thank you for last night. Any time you'd like to do it again, I'm game. Tonight is fine, too. She'd added wide-grin and heart emojis that warmed my stone-cold heart.

I took a few moments to decide what I wanted then typed my reply.

Tonight, 7 PM outside the Dodgy Leprechaun Bar. Please dress warmly.

This time I wanted her to be prepared to ride my bike in the snow. I needed to check in with Quan-Yin about that night's security rotations, but I'd find a cozy place to enjoy Rochelle without distractions.

****

Rochelle

It was like I'd recently moved and all my stuff was still in transit. The house and shop seemed so empty, but the Goddess Message had been emphatic. *Save the important things, irreplaceable things.* Something was coming and I needed to be prepared.

Joslyn had helped me move everything and now we sat down to get our holiday promo drive going. If anyone clicked on the page on our website, it'd show the 404 error, which considering I'd been home since Samhain and the winter holidays were fast approaching, was not a good thing for my business.

So I was trying to focus on work when all I really wanted to do was think about how delicious the sex with Flint was. The way he'd played with my nipples while I rode him brought happy flutters to my belly. He could do that to me anytime.

Of course, he won't if you don't text him.

Shit, I'd totally forgotten to answer his note. While Joslyn fiddled with the website, I rose and made some tea, giving me an excuse to type out a discrete text to Flint.

Sorry it took me so long to text. Had something come up this morning. Thank you for last night. Any time you'd like to do it again, I'm game. Tonight is fine, too.

I added a little wide-grin and heart emojis and hit send. He didn't respond right away and I wondered if my emojis were a little too over the top.

Swallowing against unusual nervousness, I tried to return my focus to the website.

"I think if we make a single large graphic and send them to the goodies page, it'll make things go easier."

"Uh-huh." I nodded as I stared off into space, worried that Flint might not be as interested as his note had suggested.

"Then we can decorate it with the holly and sparkly lights backgrounds, and add the writing in the brush font you liked."

"Yeah, sounds good."

Joslyn paused and tilted her head. "Plus, I think you'll get more takers if you added pink dildoes, a couple of naked women with huge tits and duck faces, and hot men in Santa hats and candy cane thongs."

"Um-hm—what?"

She threw back her head and laughed. "I knew you weren't listening."

"Sorry, I was thinking about last night."

She raised an eyebrow. "The good part or the scary part?"

"The good part." I hissed a sigh and licked my lips. "Definitely the good part."

And then my phone dinged with a text.

Tonight, 7 PM outside the Dodgy Leprechaun Bar. Please dress warmly.

I couldn't stop the smile curling my lips.

"Oh ho, what's this? A text from a hot guy?" Joslyn leaned over to look at the screen before I could jerk it out of sight. "Are you gonna meet him again tonight?"

The smile wouldn't leave. "Yup. But we gotta finish the holiday promo drive page or I'll have to cancel."

"Not on my watch, missy."

I put the phone away and we buckled down on our big sales push for the holidays. We posted BOGO sales on moisturizing creams and lip balms, 75 percent off summer time tan and burn rejuvenating oils and creams, 25 percent off gift baskets and sets specifically holiday related, and BOGO sale on blessed Solstice and Yule supplies.

We added graphics and bright colors with holiday motifs that made the page eye-catching and festive. Joslyn managed to keep her attention on the website instead of grilling me on Flint and our fun evening, but I didn't think her silence would last. We finished the website and the newsletter sale announcement just before 6:00 that night when my eyes started to cross.

Joslyn packed her phone into her purse before she leaned back in her chair and propped her head on her hand.

"So, you're going out with this guy again tonight. Is your phone charged?"

I rose and strode over to my kitchen counter. I'd plugged it in before we linked the BOGO sales. "Yup, all charged."

"Good because tonight I can't be your wingwoman." She sighed and rubbed the back of her neck as I returned to the table.

"Oh yeah?" Not that I needed one. "What's going on tonight?"

"It's the last city council meeting before the holidays and Tyler says this asshole named Earl Creighton is trying to push through some new bullshit ordinances before the new year."

I frowned, something sparking in my memory. "How can he do that? I mean, who is this Creighton person?"

"He's another council member, but he has some really weird hang-ups. The ordinances have something to do with 'non-Christian' and occult businesses in town bringing in the 'wrong element' or some such tripe."

I sat up straighter. "Occult businesses? You mean like mine?"

"Yup, exactly like yours. This guy is legit afraid of witches and healers that aren't wearing some sort of Catholic robes or something."

"Did you say his name was Creighton?"

"Yeah." She stood and looked for her coat, but paused to glance at me. "Earl Creighton, why?"

I scowled. "One of the punks last night mentioned that name before he took off. As in, Creighton didn't pay him enough to get beaten up. I think Councilman Creighton paid a bunch of goons to kill me."

"Shit. Are you serious? Are you sure it's Councilman

Creighton?"

I shook my head. "No, and I can't ask the goons. They're not coming back after what Flint did to them."

She swallowed hard. "Did he kill them?"

I shrugged. "I dunno. He said one might have died. They definitely weren't moving when he threw them back into their SUV. I didn't stick around to see if they were breathing."

"Shit. And you didn't tell the cops."

I shook my head as I headed back into my bedroom. "No. I didn't feel like they'd help me. But now that I know it was probably a councilman who ordered them to deal with me, I'm glad I didn't. Who would the cops believe? Me, a bohemian witchy woman who sells essential oils, or a well-to-do, rich, white councilman? I'll give you three guesses and the first two don't count."

Joslyn scowled and shook her head. "Yeah, I'm not gonna argue with you about that. I know how the cops operate when it comes to rich white men versus women."

Our eyes met and we nodded.

Joslyn had been set up to take the fall by her business sponsor. He used her business as a front for his drug distribution schemes. She had no idea he'd been wheeling and dealing behind her back, but a savvy detective caught wind of it. The way the paperwork had been doctored, the man's reputation as a stand-up member of the business community had weighed heavily against an honest and naive Black businesswoman and her friends, none of whom were as well connected. Only her lawyer believed her and managed to diffuse the situation. But she'd lost everything.

I'd gained, of course, by getting a fantastic business partner who knew all the pitfalls of the Fort Collins business community and how to circumvent the obstacles presented by the wealthy men who had everyone bamboozled. And she'd gotten street credit despite the assholes who'd ignored her warnings. I'd hoped she'd get together with her lawyer after the case concluded, but so far she hadn't made any moves toward him despite his kindness, savvy, and obvious interest.

"Speaking of rich men, are you gonna call Andre Kingston anytime soon?" I closed the computer and gathered up all the notes we had for our site. "I mean, it's the holidays. Give yourself an early Yule gift."

"As if." Joslyn shook her head. "As you said, it's the holidays. He's probably got a swanky girlfriend or family to dote on. The last thing he needs is some rando calling him."

I snorted. "Come on. You're not a rando, he's known you for over a year now. What's the best that can happen? He'll be lonely and want some company for the usual rigamarole of the holiday season. It could be a great start to your New Year." I grinned as I headed into my bedroom to change into clothes meant for being outside.

"Oh, like you are?"

I shrugged. "Well yeah. I'd say starting something with a hot biker is definitely new for the New Year."

"How do you know it'll last?" She leaned against my doorjamb with her arms crossed over her chest.

"I don't, but that's not the point. Kingston was really interested in you and now he's not your lawyer. You should give him a call." I turned my attention to donning a long chenille sweater over fleece-lined leggings and a turtleneck undershirt. "I'm getting ready for my date tonight and you have a city council meeting to go to. But call Kingston and invite him out for tea. What's the best that can happen?"

"The best? I ring in the new year with a thick cock and multiple orgasms."

I grinned. "Wish granted…if you call him."

I didn't tell her that I had a gut feeling about Andre Kingston. I'd had the feeling since I saw him interact with Joslyn. He'd kept everything very professional, but the way he spoke with her and listened to her showed more than he meant. There'd been no impropriety, but I'd seen the spark and wanted to fan the flames of that attraction.

She rolled her eyes. "Okay, okay, I'll call him, but don't expect miracles."

"Why not? It's worked for me so far." I winked as I pulled on my boots.

"Shut up!" She laughed and shook her head. "You're impossible."

"Nope, I'm possible. There's a difference." I headed out to the living room and grabbed my coat. "I gotta get going if I'm going to meet Flint."

"Are you really going to be okay tonight, Rochelle?" Joslyn bit her lip. "I'm a little worried you're getting into trouble with this Concrete Angels member."

"Thanks for the concern, but I'm going to be fine. I have a feeling about this guy."

"Like you have about Andre Kingston?"

I nodded and grasped her shoulders. "Yup. My gut says he's good for you. And you deserve to be happy, Jos. Seriously."

She sighed and nodded. "You're right. I do. I'll call Kingston and let it ride."

"Good." I paused as another Goddess Message hit me. "Why don't you take some of the product we still have downstairs for your brother and sister-in-law? Hell, take some for Kingston when you see him." I reached for my laptop bag and added both the laptop and tablet, my ereader, and the charging adaptors and cables for them.

She narrowed her eyes as she watched me. "Are you sure?"

"Oh yeah." We'd taken all the excess inventory to the storage unit earlier and I'd checked to make sure all my property and business insurance premiums were paid up. "Just lock up when you're done. I really gotta get going."

"Okay. Take care of you tonight, right?" She gave me a hug.

"Always."

I paused to take one last look at my home. It looked empty to me with all the important knickknacks and art gone, but the remainder I could lose. The shop had needed a makeover for a while and the insurance money would help with that. Sadness and resignation filled my chest as I locked the apartment and followed Joslyn downstairs.

We entered the shop and I helped her pick out some gifts for her brother and sister-in-law before taking my electronics and a few of my dried herbs and creams out to the car. I'd already taken most of my raw materials and brewing equipment to the storage unit, but a few extras would be helpful in starting over.

I sighed. My mother and I had started this business over twenty years earlier when I'd been a teen. She'd taught me all I knew about poultices, healing practices, and the white magic that flowed through the women of our family line. Then she got killed by a mugger on her way home from the market one evening, which I'd always thought strange because she got the Goddess Messages, too. How had she not known that was coming?

I shook my head before my mind wandered over old paths of pain and anger and grief. Despite her early death, she'd prepared me to take over the business and set up a nest egg so I'd be able to survive. Business had been going pretty well, but the building needed some renovations I'd been waiting for the new year to do. I didn't want to start over, but I had a feeling the decision was no longer in my hands.

It'll work out despite the dark clouds. My mother's voice rang in my head just as fat flakes of snow dropped onto the top of the car and the alley floor.

"I hope so, Mom."

I locked the car and went back into the shop where I found Joslyn frowning at something in her hand.

"Hey, everything okay?" I took one more look around

before I stopped beside her.

"Yeah, I think so. I was looking for those antique gift tags in the old stock cabinet and this fell out." She held up an envelope with my name written on it in elegant cursive. "It's to you."

I frowned as I took the envelope. "Where did you say you found it?"

"The old stock cabinet." She pointed at the 1970s metal monstrosity against the back wall of the stockroom. "That thing. It fell out when I got the tags."

"It looks like my mom's writing." I flipped the envelope over and found it sealed with a piece of wax. "That's weird. It looks old but I've never seen it before."

"Are you gonna open it?" She shoved the last of her gift sets in bags and peered over my shoulder.

A deep sense of foreboding crept up my back and I shook my head. "Not right now. If it waited this long for me, it can wait a few more hours until after my date." I shoved the letter into my purse and headed for the door. "Are you ready or shall I leave you to lock up?"

"No, I'm good."

She hustled out the door and I closed it behind us, turning the locks. I patted the cold brick with my gloved hand and closed my eyes, resetting the wards around the building. I'd made them strong and I reinforced them. But I had a feeling it wouldn't do any good.

"All set?" Joslyn returned to my side after depositing the items in her car.

"I think so." I shook off my worries and malaise. "You gonna call Kingston tonight?"

She rolled her eyes. "Yes, Mom. He'll be my first call."

I grinned. "Good. Now I gotta get going. Text me when he accepts your invite."

She laughed. "You're pretty damn sure of yourself, aren't you?"

"Yup."

We hugged and got into our respective vehicles. I hoped she wouldn't flake out on calling Kingston. I didn't often use my magical abilities to nudge things, but if I could make this one thing go right, it would help offset what I knew was coming.

I took a deep breath and turned on the car, letting the engine warm before I threw it in gear. *I'm gonna have fun tonight with Flint, come what may.* Big changes were coming with the New Year, I could feel it in my gut. Upheaval was rarely fun, but the ways opened to me would be worth the disarray.

I hope.

I shoved the car into reverse and backed out of my old life before heading into the unknown of my new life. A strange anxious excitement fluttered in my gut as I drove off to meet whatever the Goddess had in store for me.

CHAPTER FIVE

Flint

Nervousness wasn't something a gargoyle experienced much, but waiting for Rochelle outside the Dodgy Leprechaun took all my efforts to remain still. I hated being twitchy, but I'd waited all day to see her and 7:00 was rapidly approaching. I sat straddling my bike with my arms crossed over my chest and stared into the night, willing her to appear.

"Bloody hell, Flint. Yer scarin' me custom away. Lighten up, will ye?" Duncan Riordan, troublemaker and proprietor of the Dodgy Leprechaun slapped me on the shoulder. "Have a hot toddy or a flamin' whisky, for the Goddess's sake. Somethin' to warm yer stone-cold heart."

I shook my head and scanned the passing cars and pedestrians. "I'm waiting for someone."

Duncan narrowed his eyes. "Are ye here on Club Business?"

I shook my head again. "Personal."

"Feckin' hell, it's about bloody time." He tilted his head. "Ye haven't told Loki, have ye?"

I shook my head a third time.

"Good. Keep it to yerself until your lover is secure in yer relationship. Otherwise, he'll feck it up before ye can salvage it. Mark me words."

I eyed him a few moments, debating whether or not I wanted to learn more about the tall man with more freckles than stars in the Milky Way. On the one hand, he was a Leprechaun and prone to tell stories to shackle his listeners into one scheme or another. On the other hand, I'd known him in passing for a century or so and he'd always been a straight shooter with me.

"Did Loki burn you?" I'd never been good at friendship - it was something gargoyles rarely worked on or understood. We weren't sociable creatures. But living around humans and other Elder Races had exposed me to their interactions, and helped me recognize the paucity of mine.

He zipped up his parka and tugged his beanie tighter on his head as he nodded. "Yeah. Destroyed the one connection I'd thought I made with a lovely girl before I could make it clear to her how I felt. Hell, he'd ruined it before I'd figured out how I felt." He shook his head and snapped his fingers, a shot of Irish whisky appearing in his hand. He threw it back and snapped his fingers again, the glass disappearing.

"I'm sorry to hear that." I hoped my expression matched my signing.

"Eh." He waved me off. "'Twas a long time ago. But don't let him feck it up for ye."

I nodded. "Why are you warning me?"

He shrugged and shook his head. "I dunno. I guess because everyone deserves to be happy and this is the first time I've seen ye interested in anythin' a'tall." He rubbed his hand over his fiery red goatee. "And truth be told, you're the closest I've got to a chum around here. What kind o' friend would I be if I didn't warn ya?"

I nodded. "I've seen Loki in action with the other club members."

"Yeah, I'm sure. But have any o' them told ye about

it?"

I shook my head. "Not directly, no."

"Right, well, I'm tellin' ya. Secure her heart and understanding before you let Loki in on it." He slapped me on the shoulder with a rueful grimace. "You'll thank yerself for it."

"Thanks." I dipped my head in acknowledgment just as I caught sight of Rochelle walking around the corner of the building from the parking lot. "Here she comes."

"May the luck o' the Irish be with ye." He nodded and winked before ducking back into the bar's doors.

I didn't watch him leave. My attention riveted to Rochelle's easy stride in her tall boots with furry tops and puffy jacket over leggings. Her hips swayed with each step and my cock thickened in my jeans as I watched her come. I'd enjoyed her body the night before and I was all about enjoying it again if she was willing.

Her face lit up with a sexy smile as she spotted me on my bike and some of the anxiousness retreated from my gut. She was here, she was safe, and she was mine to enjoy. I refused to analyze why I thought she was mine already, and tried to find my own smile when she got close.

"Sorry I'm a bit late. I had to load a couple things in my car to take to storage."

Her words and presence soothed my anxiousness and I shrugged, as if I hadn't been desperate for her to arrive. "Everything okay?"

Now it was her turn to shrug. "Yeah. Just moving a few things out to clear up space. Too much clutter."

I nodded, though I sensed her words were only half truths.

"So, here I am, dressed warmly. What have you got planned?" She tilted her head and her lips curled into a delicious smile. It made my cock harden and my hands itch to touch her naked skin.

I gave her my own secret smile. "Some place very

special. Are you ready to go for a ride?"

"If I get to snuggle up against you, hell yeah."

I rumbled my laugh as she slid onto my bike behind me. If I had my way, she'd be snuggled up behind me, in front of me, beside me, and under me for the rest of her life. I mentally shook away the thoughts of forever and steered the bike back up into the icy Rockies. Part of this excursion would be to enjoy the dark snowy wilderness without light pollution. Nothing more romantic than icy stars over a frosty winter landscape. But my goal was to take Rochelle to the Cripple Creek Ice Festival they held just before the winter holidays.

Because Cripple Creek was an old mining town that depended on the tourists coming to spend money, they had to figure out a way to get folks up there in the winter. While the gambling brought a few and their miniscule ski area brought a few more, they needed more tourists to carry them through the cold season. So they'd created the Ice Festival where sculptures were made from ice. And not just little statues like at weddings. One of the best I'd seen was an alien UFO out of an old 1950's sci-fi flick with LED lights placed at regular intervals to light up. The thing had been thirty-five feet in diameter and people could sit in the icy cockpit seats.

I'd heard there would be a 19th Century coach-and-four and photos could be taken in the romantic setting. While I wasn't really interested in being photographed, I would be delighted to have a digital photo of Rochelle in the coach on my phone. I took one hand off the handlebars and grasped her arms wrapped around my middle as we sped through the night. She hugged me tighter and for a few moments, the world was perfect.

It took about an hour and a half to reach Cripple Creek but the ride had been beautiful. Rochelle had stayed plastered to my back and kept it warm, though I hadn't needed it. When we found a place to park my bike, she looked like she could use something hot to drink so I showed her over to the local coffee shop to get some tea.

"Why are we in Cripple Creek?" She held the to-go cup between her hands as she gazed at the well-lit main street. The sounds of the slot machines were muted because the cold made them shut the doors and windows, but light blazed from every opening.

"They have an Ice Festival every year." I pointed beyond the buildings to the large county fairground field at the end of the brightly lit street. "Artists come from all over the country to construct the amazing and the fanciful. I thought it would be fun to see."

She gaped at me as we walked toward the fairgrounds. "Are you serious? I've lived in Colorado all my life and I never knew about this."

I gave her a smile. "It started when a local carpenter lost his wife and wanted to do something divert his kids from their loss. So he carved animals out of ice for them. He'd show his friends and neighbors his creations. For a while it was only locals who knew about it and he'd do it every year. When enough tourists found out, the city council invited more artists and set up a charity to help the man with his bills as he got older. After a while, it became such a big thing, they made it a competition with all the proceeds going to a fund to help people with loss and bereavement, mental health and substance abuse programs, and funeral costs. It's now a big thing."

"Wow. That's amazing. I wish I'd known about it."

She sounded so wistful, I shot her a look and signed, "What?"

"Oh, my mom died a few years back. I don't have any siblings and Mom never told me who the sperm donor was, so it was just me to take everything on." She sighed and let her gaze rest on the brightly lit fairgrounds. "It would've been nice to have some help."

I bit my lip with a canine. "I'm sorry to hear this. How

did she die?"

"She was murdered, actually. That made it a lot harder."

I stopped as my anger and dismay rose, and I turned her toward me. "Murdered? Did they ever find out by whom?"

She grimaced and kept silent for a few moments, her jaw and shoulders tight. "No."

I growled. Her sorrow, anger, and frustration swirled around us like a dust devil, and I wanted to lay waste to the mudfuckers who'd caused her pain. Instead, I cupped her face until she raised her gaze to mine then I showed her my hands.

"We'll find out, Rochelle, I promise, and we'll bring them down."

She shook her head. "It doesn't matter. It won't bring her back and the police didn't find anything." She gave me a smile that didn't reach her eyes. "It's okay, Flint. It was a few years ago now. Let's just enjoy the festival. I think the cause is wonderful."

I wanted to find out more about her mother's murder, but she was determined not to talk about it and pulled me into the fairgrounds. Where she stopped with a gasp.

This year's theme had been Winter Fairytale and the artists had gone all out. There was an actual ice castle with a curtain wall and an archway with a carved portcullis. Stairs had been built up to the battlements and people could tour the battlements. Outside the castle stood a coach-and-four ice horses. The coach had room to actually sit inside and take pictures.

Farther on, there were ice statues of knights in full armor, a wizard with a pointy hat and a staff reminiscent of Lord of the Rings, and even a sleeping dragon.

I'm pretty sure Torch would have some critiques.

But Rochelle seemed enchanted with all the sculptures and I enjoyed her delight. We toured the battlements of the ice castle where they'd frozen railings and mats in the ice to keep people from slipping. Lights had been strung around the railings and the whole place sparkled. I tried to admire the icy artwork, but my gaze kept getting drawn back to Rochelle and the light glinting off her terra cotta-colored hair. I took a few photos of her on the curtain wall looking like a sorceress waiting for her lost love to return.

I want to be that lost love.

The thought took me completely by surprise and I frowned, making a young white guy and his boyfriend skitter out of the way. Rochelle raised her eyebrows and asked me what was wrong.

"Nothing."

"Are you sure? You looked like you were going to throw those guys over the wall for a minute there."

That explained their panicked looks.

"I'm good. You're beautiful." I tried to soften my expression. I meant what I'd signed. She was beautiful. The most beautiful person I'd seen in centuries.

She smiled and the beauty increased enough to stop my breath. "Thank you. Let's go down to see the carriage. This place is magical."

I couldn't argue with that, but I made sure to hold her hand as I led the way down the ice steps to the courtyard. It struck me as we stepped down that I could be the knight escorting the lady from the battlements, but the idea of me in the trappings of the aristocracy made me chuckle. Unfortunately, it came out as a deep rumble that made the patrons nearby eye us nervously. It was probably my cut with the Concrete Angels MC logo on the back and my lack of hat or gloves despite the cold.

"Come sit with me in the carriage, Flint. I want pics for my blog."

I stopped and raised my eyebrows. "You want pics *with me*?"

"Yes, with you. It'll be fun."

Still, I hesitated. "It could hurt your business. Not everyone is thrilled with the Concrete Angels MC."

She tapped her lip with a finger. "Tell you what. You take pics of me in the carriage for my blog with my phone, and then we'll have someone take a couple of us both for my personal photo album. Fair?"

I gave her a half-smile. "Yeah, fair."

I helped her climb up into the icy carriage and stepped back to get a few shots. Rochelle smiled and waved like a princess greeting her subjects, and pretty soon there was a line of people wanting to do the same, though they gave me wide berth.

"Would you take a few pics of me with my friend?" Rochelle asked a young woman standing to the side and I offered her the phone.

She hesitantly took the phone from me with a slow nod and I bounded up into the ice carriage with Rochelle. It was the weirdest thing to have my picture taken with a beautiful woman cuddled up to me and smiling. Most women found me intimidating because I didn't smile and I was big and hard. But Rochelle acted like this was a photoshoot for an event and I tried to lighten my expression enough so I didn't look like I was glowering.

The young woman took a few pics before she handed the phone back to Rochelle and we left the carriage so others could take their own shots.

"Thank you for doing that with me, Flint. Look at this one." She held up the phone.

The image captured was of me holding Rochelle's hand as she climbed down from the carriage, and for just a brief moment it appeared I was a gallant knight allowing a lady to alight from her coach. The lights around us gave the image an ethereal glow and my expression was one I'd never seen before. There was intensity and desire and something else. Something powerful that I couldn't put a name to.

Damn, that looks downright romantic.

"I'm gonna save that one as the background on my phone." She fiddled with the phone for a bit before scrolling through the rest of the images. "Wow, some of these are great. Let me post them to my social media to help promote this event. Do you know how long they do it?"

I nodded. "They do it the three weekends before the holiday. This is the last one."

"Aw darnit. Well, there's still tomorrow and Sunday too." Her fingers flew over the phone's keyboard and I tried not to be too impressed. I had to hand it to the humans when it came to technology. They perfected the art of it.

"There. All posted. Thanks for giving me the time."

She beamed and the stone around my heart cracked a little more. It was an odd feeling considering no one had ever caught my attention like Rochelle before. Her smiles and gratitude made me want to do more for her. Like treat her to supper at my place. Not that I was prepared for it that night, but maybe the next night when Loki planned to have another raucous party for the holidays. It would be a good excuse to slip away.

Satisfied with my plan, I followed Rochelle to every ice sculpture and creation, not minding the crowds or the noise of the celebration. Eventually, I caught her hiding a yawn behind her hand and suggested we head back down to Fort Collins. She admitted she was a little tired and needed to get home so we strode to my bike and mounted up.

The ride down the mountain was uneventful and I recognized when Rochelle fell asleep against my back. I made sure to grasp her arms around my belly to keep her on the bike. Satisfaction and contentment filled my chest as we rode back to The Dodgy Leprechaun. I wanted more of this. I wanted her to be around more often and I started on my plan to show her.

When we reached the bar where her car was parked,

she roused from her doze and slid off the bike, stretching enough to show me her boobs. My mouth watered remembering the night we'd shared and those firm mounds of flesh pressed against my chest.

"Thank you very much for taking me to see the Ice Festival, Flint. I really enjoyed it."

She leaned forward to kiss my cheek, but I turned my head and her lips met mine. I meant it to be a quick peck, something not entirely chaste but not a round of tonsil hockey. But Rochelle tilted her head and wrapped her arms around my shoulders with a soft moan and I was lost. Her tongue slid past mine and all I could think of was diving deep into her soft pussy folds to tease out all her hot juicy secrets.

Unfortunately, being a human witch, she had to come up for air and she smile sheepishly at me as she stepped back.

"Wow, that was a lovely ending to a perfect night." She licked her lips and my cock continued its march to hardness. "Thank you again for taking me to the Ice Festival."

I nodded. "You're welcome. Let's do it again tomorrow night. Not the Ice Festival, but going out. If you don't have any plans, that is. Or if you want to. Because I want to. Go out with you. Again."

I grimaced. I was babbling in sign language and for the first time ever, I felt the heat rise to my cheeks as my hands fluttered into silence.

She laughed and laid her hands over mine. "No, I don't have plans. Yes, I'd like to go out with you again tomorrow. What time?"

For a few moments, I just stared at her, my excitement and nervousness chasing each other around in my head like overactive puppies. *What the hell do I have to be nervous about?* Then my brain caught up with her words.

"I'll come get you about six in the evening, for supper

and more. Might be a good idea to pack a bag."

Her smile widened to a smirk. "Pack a bag, eh? Are you inviting me to a sleepover?"

I rumbled my laugh. "Sleepover. Yeah, that's one word for it."

She chortled and nodded. "Okay, I'll make sure I have my nuh-night clothes."

"You won't need those." I winked and she laughed again.

"Oh I see. Well, I might bring them anyway." Her smile softened as she dug out her keys. "Thanks again for the lovely night and I'm looking forward to seeing you again tomorrow."

I nodded and waited for her to get in her car and drive off before heading back to the Concrete Angels' compound. I had a lot to do to get my place ready for her visit tomorrow night. It was going to be unforgettable if I had my way. It was a good thing I didn't need much sleep.

CHAPTER SIX

Rochelle

I slept hard that night and woke up the next morning with a smile on my face and an unusually warm feeling in my chest. It had been a great night and I hadn't even had sex. But sharing the magic of the Ice Festival with Flint had been one of my best dates, bar none.

And I have photographic proof!

I grabbed my phone and thumbed it on to look at the images in the gallery. There were three with him and I loved all of them, but my favorite was the one where he helped me down from the ice carriage. From the outside, folks would assume he was deeply in love with me just on his expression alone. It wasn't true, of course, but he faked it so well.

I remembered that moment and the look in his eyes as he took my hand. It wasn't visible in the photograph, but he'd stolen my breath. It was something straight out of a fairytale. With his full attention on me, he'd momentarily made me believe I was his everything. Thankfully, I hadn't faltered, but the memory of his expression had stayed with me all night.

And he wants to have dinner with me tonight.

That was enough to make me roll out of bed and dump myself into the shower before I lost myself in the day's activities. I had to get the shop open for the holiday sales and set up my blog post with all the information on the Ice Festival. Between Instagram and Facebook and Twitter, I had a fairly large following, but I wanted a more permanent post and I'd make sure to include the links to the organizers of the Ice Festival Fund.

By the time I was dressed and the black tea was steeping, I had the shop open and had started on my blog post. I uploaded the pictures from my phone and wrote up my delight of the night I'd spent with Flint.

I stared at the image of us together in the carriage and marveled at how happy I looked. It took me a moment to realize I had been happy. Happier than I'd been since my mother died. I hadn't had to do anything or be anyone, I could just be. Flint had given me that and I found myself wanting more of it.

I finished my blog post just as Joslyn sauntered into the shop. I looked for signs she'd had as good a night as I, but the slope of her shoulders and her lackluster smile told me it hadn't gone that well.

"Hey lady, how are you doing? Are you okay?" I immediately handed her a square of dark chocolate as she hung up her coat and scarf and ear muffs.

"I'm fine." She popped the chocolate in her mouth, but she sounded more tired than fine.

"Uh-huh. Fine is not the word I'd use to describe you right now. What's going on?"

She poured herself some tea from the teapot and sighed as she settled onto the other stool behind the front counter.

"It was a long night last night. The city council meeting ran long."

"But you called Andre afterwards, right?" I asked the question with a hopeful lilt to my voice, but my gut sank with the expression on her face.

She shook her head and pulled her braids back into a loose ponytail tied with a plaid ribbon. "I didn't get the chance. The council meeting ran so late because of infighting that I was too exhausted at the end to call him."

"Yikes." I handed her another square of chocolate as I let my senses open to feel her energy. It definitely wasn't on the settled side. "What happened?"

Joslyn heaved another sigh. "The meeting started off well enough. They went over the minutes from the previous meeting and had a quick vote on some of the earlier issues that had been presented. Then they opened up the floor to councilmembers with new issues to present. Tyler had some new ideas about how to shift some of the city tax funds into social programs for homeless, domestic violence victims counseling, and ex-con rehabilitation, particularly cutting the surplus being sent to the cops. Though it wasn't met with a lot of favorable responses, the councilmembers said they'd consider it over the holidays because the needs of the community required a change."

"All that sounds good."

"Oh, that's where the good ended. Then the asshole Earl Creighton got up in his white suit and matching fedora hat, and starting spouting shit about our "peaceful" community being "under attack" from the "wrong element" of people being brought in because of the "occult" businesses in town."

"Sweet glory."

"Yeah, and he got worse." Joslyn cradled the tea cup in her hands. "Most of the councilmembers weren't buying his occult equals evil rant, but when he brought up taking funding from the police to give to "social programs"—he actually used air quotes—he made it sound like the world can't function without cops around to keep people in line just by the threat of their presence. Some of the councilmembers started to shift to his side and debate ensued about where money should be spent, how much of

Creighton's statements were fearmongering. Then the name-calling started, with the status quo folks spouting about "bleeding heart liberals" and "occultists" and how social programs only helping "welfare queens," while the progressive folks fired back with "fascist money-grubbers" and "stooges for the rich." Only my brother kept his temper in check, which I have to commend him for because I was about to hex someone.

"But finally the Mayor reined everyone in, reprimanding quite a few of the councilmembers with fines for the name-calling, and said they'd consider Creighton's proposal if he had the write up for it." Jos scowled and shook her head. "I think the asshole really thought they'd take his words and vote on it right then and there, so when he needed a write-up, he didn't have it. The Mayor said he could present it again in the new year, and promptly adjourned the meeting."

"Holy Mother. Did you have to smudge the council chambers?" I grimaced.

She nodded. "I did that after everyone left. But by then I was starving and exhausted and pissed off, so I didn't manage to call Andre."

"Oh, honey, I'm so sorry it was awful." I reached over and gave her a hug. "Let me make you some vanilla and chamomile tea, and we'll do some aura work later to settle things. And *then* you can call Andre."

Jos snorted. "You're not giving up on that, are you?"

"Hell no. Andre would be great for you, but you have to be in the right frame of mind not to screw it up." I'd been told before that I was a matchmaking mama in some ways, but it was only because I kept getting feelings about people.

"Thanks a lot."

I gave her a wide smile as I put the herbal tea on to boil. "You're welcome."

She straightened and tossed her ponytail over shoulder.

"So, let's talk about something fun. Tell me how your night went last night."

I shrugged, trying to keep my expression and voice nonchalant. "Oh, you know, good."

"Hah! Don't hand me that. I know you and I saw your pictures on social media. 'Fess up!" She dropped her chin and held her mug in one hand with a dry look.

"Okay, okay, it was more than fine. It was romantic and sweet and sexy and perfect. Do you know about the Ice Festival in Cripple Creek?"

She frowned. "No, what's that?"

I spent the next half hour telling her all about the Ice Festival and the reason it happened, and showed her all the pictures Flint and I had taken. When she saw the one of him helping me out of the ice carriage, she stopped and stared at it a long time.

I wanted to ask her what she was thinking about it, but a bunch of holiday customers came in and started the deluge of shoppers for the rest of the day. Joslyn eventually got her tea, but we were slammed up until closing. Most of the customers mentioned seeing my blog and the social media posts, which prompted them to come in.

The shop made record sales that day and I sold out of a lot of the holiday care packages and BOGO deals. When we locked the doors behind the last customers, we shared a look of incredulity.

"What the hell just happened?" I turned the locks on the front door and flipped over the open sign.

"I dunno, but let's thank our lucky stars and have a glass of wine and some ice cream in celebration." She headed back to the till to close it out for the night and set aside the bank deposits.

"Oh no, you don't. You're gonna call Andre Kingston and make a date with him. Right now, missy." I followed behind her and handed her the phone. "I'll take care of the till tonight."

"No, no way." She shook her head, her braids sliding over her shoulder. "I'm not missing out on my holiday bonus just because you can't count. I'm doing the till, *then* I'll call Andre."

I narrowed my eyes but I couldn't argue with her. Numbers weren't my forte and we both knew it. "Fine. But hurry it up so I can take the deposit to the bank before it closes tonight and then get to my date."

"Wait, what? You have a date tonight? Why didn't you tell me?" She scowled.

"First, we got slammed with business since this morning. Second, because I'm hoping you'll have a date tonight, too. Now get counting!" I grinned as she stuck her tongue out at me, but she set to work.

I sat down to write up orders for more product while she tallied everything up, making sure I knew what to order on the next weekday. Then I worked on paying bills for the utilities and internet. We finished about the same time and she whistled in surprised appreciation.

"Sweet glory, Rochelle. We broke ten thousand today." She gaped at me.

"What? Don't tease me. Are you serious?" I came over to where she'd done all the receipts. "Are you sure you didn't miscount?"

"No, seriously, I checked it three times." She stared at me, wide-eyed.

"Holy cow, that's better than our Black Friday sales." A smile curled my lips. "You know what this means?"

"What?"

"It means you need to call Andre and set up your date while I take the deposits to the bank."

She rolled her eyes. "Yeah, yeah, fine."

"Seriously. And here." I counted out a thousand dollars. "Take this as your bonus and have a really good time tonight. You deserve it, Jos."

"Oh my glory. Are you insane? That's a tenth of what

we made today."

"I know, and you're worth it. Thank you for all your help. Now, call Andre." I grinned as I handed her the phone again.

She threw her arms around me and wrapped me in a tight hug. "Thank you so much, Rochelle. I'll call Andre right now and I'll lock up while you go to the bank."

"How about you call him while I go pack a bag and I'll help you lock up on my way out to take the deposit to the bank." I headed for the stairs.

"Whoa, whoa, whoa back there, girl. What do you mean 'pack a bag'?" Joslyn's brows knitted. "What kind of plans you got goin' on tonight?"

I shrugged with a smirk. "I can't tell you that."

"Can't or won't? And all this after hounding me to call Andre."

"I actually can't tell you. Flint invited me out tonight and told me to pack a bag. I guess we're going somewhere far enough that we'll stay overnight."

Joslyn lost her smile. "This is the same guy from the Concrete Angels?" She bit her lip. "You be careful with him, okay? They don't have a good rep."

I dropped my smirk. "I know their rep, but my gut says he's a good guy." *And not entirely human.* "I haven't gotten any Goddess Messages about him, but I have gotten messages about this place burning down, so packing a bag serves a double purpose."

"Wait, stop. Did you just say this place, our shop, is going to burn down?"

Shit. I hadn't meant to tell her the content of the Goddess Message.

"Is that why we packed up so much of your stuff to the storage unit and you've been giving me merchandise for friends and family?" She came over to me and grasped my arms. "Sweet glory, Rochelle, is there going to be a fire here?"

I sighed and bowed my head a moment to gather my thoughts. "I don't know when or by whom, but someone is going to burn our shop down before Yule."

"Oh glory, Rochelle." She gathered me into a hug.

"That's why I want you to call Andre tonight. Go out, have fun, and stay far away from the shop." I squeezed her before I pushed her back. "Please. Promise me you won't come back here tonight. I can handle losing stuff, but not you."

"Can't you do something to stop it?"

I shook my head. "That's not how the messages work. I don't know when they'll happen. I just get a warning and have to take steps to mitigate it. It's like waiting for a phone call on a landline before we had voicemail."

"Can't you call the fire department or the cops or something?"

"And tell them what? That I have a feeling that my place is going to be a victim of arson?" I shook my head again. "They wouldn't believe me if I told them. They'd think me the crazy New Age lady who's been smoking too much weed." I sighed and gave her a tired smile. "Call Andre, have a nice time with him. Enjoy your bonus, and don't worry about it."

"But Rochelle, all our hard work." She threw her hands out.

"I know. But that's what insurance is for, and this place needs a lot of renovations. We'll start looking for a new place after Hogmanay." I tried to warm my smile up. "Don't worry. It's a blessing in disguise. Somehow. I hope. I'm gonna go pack my bag."

I didn't want to worry her and I hated that I'd probably ruined her evening after such a profitable day, but there wasn't anything we could do about it. The Goddess Message had been emphatic and we'd saved what we could. My insurance premiums were paid and I wasn't wrong about the renovations. I just hadn't planned on having to do them so soon or so completely.

Yeah, like buying an entirely new place.

I just hoped there'd be something affordable in the new year.

It didn't take me long to pack what I wanted to keep, though I threw in a few extra things. Like my good boots, a couple of my favorite skirts and sweaters, and some lingerie. I'd put my sex toys into storage. No way in hell was I going to let the arsonist take those. They'd been expensive but worth every penny and I wasn't about to lose them.

I took one last look at my bedroom. All the important things were packed up and gone, but there would be a lot I'd lose. Tears started at the thought of losing the sanctuary I'd had with my mother, but a more practical voice mentally slapped the back of my head.

It's just stuff, Rochelle. It can be replaced and a new sanctuary can be found. One where the arsonist can't find you.

That practical voice sounded a lot like my mother's and I nodded as I wiped away my tears. I straightened my shoulders and headed back down to the shop with my bag. I found Joslyn still on the phone with a silly smile on her face and some of my sorrow lifted. If I could get her together with the hot lawyer before New Year's, I'd count it in the victory column.

"Hahaha, well okay. Give me a half an hour. I gotta help my friend close the shop." Her voice squeaked a little and her smile widened before she cleared her throat. She listened to the response and nodded. "Yeah, so I'll see you around five at the Rustler's Steakhouse...Um-hm, okay. See you soon. Bye."

She ended the call and met my gaze, that goofy smile still playing around her lips. "That was Andre."

I nodded. "I'm really glad to hear that. So y'all are going out?"

"Yeah, to the Rustler's Steakhouse." She gave me a shy smile.

"That's fantastic. Have a wonderful time. Let's get out of here." I headed for the door and held it open for her as she pulled on her ear muffs and gloves, and shrugged into her coat.

She stepped through but turned to me with sorrow etching her features. "Are you gonna be okay?"

I locked the door behind me, giving me time to formulate an answer to her question. Would I be okay? *It's just stuff.* Yeah, but it was familiar stuff, a set routine I was used to. *Time to shake things up, Moenkopi.* Mom had nicknamed me for a deep, rusty red sandstone in Sedona, Arizona, because it matched my hair. And she loved the name.

I nodded sharply. "Yeah, I'm gonna be fine. The insurance is paid up, the stuff I want to keep is safe, you're off to dinner with a sexy man, and I got my own hot guy waiting for me. I'll be fine."

She shot me a half-smile. "You think Andre Kingston is sexy?"

I gave her a mock-perplexed look. "Uh, yeah. Have you seen him in his sharp suits with that black goatee framing those full lips? Holy shit, woman, that man's sexual pleasure in smoky quartz." I shivered in delight.

Joslyn laughed. "Only you'd talk about people's qualities in terms of crystals."

"Hey, I'm an earth witch. I love me some sexy crystals. Remember, a hard man is good to find." I winked and she grinned.

"Yeah, yeah, here's hoping." She hugged me one last time. "Okay, we're both going to have an awesome night and we'll deal with whatever else comes our way."

I hugged her back. "Yup. We got this."

"Okay." She straightened her shoulders. "I'm gonna go home and get ready for my date. What are you gonna do?"

"I'm gonna take this—" I held up the deposit bag. "—to the bank and then get myself a gourmet coffee at Jitters before I head out to meet Flint for our date."

"Good. I love you, Rochelle."

"I love you, too, Jos."

We parted ways to get into our cars and I let mine warm up while I watched her leave. I glanced up at my shop that I'd owned for the last twenty years, and the last three alone. The crumbling brick needed attention and so did the sagging eaves. The gutters needed repair and I'd heard birds nesting in the attic crawl space. It was sad to say goodbye, but part of me was at peace with it, too.

Shaking my head at my maudlin thoughts, I put the car in gear and headed to the bank.

****

Rochelle

I sighed in relief as I pushed my way into Jitters, the busiest coffee shop in that part of Fort Collins. The warmth eased the bite from the frigid cold snap bearing down on the city and soothed some of my continuing sorrow. I'd done all I could to protect myself and my business, and now I just had to leave it to the Goddess.

I ordered my hot peppermint tea and settled into a two-person table away from most of the other patrons. I shoved the receipt into my coat pocket and hit another harder piece of paper. *What the–?* I withdrew the letter Joslyn had handed me the day before and stared at the old stained paper with the black wax seal.

I frowned as I set down my tea and carefully opened the envelope. The wax crumbled from age and fell away in little bits under the table. I pulled the letter out and set the envelope down then hesitated. There was something other than the letter inside.

I shook it over my open palm and a micro USB drive fell into my hand. *What the hell?* I glanced at the unopened letter and swallowed hard. What did my mother have to tell me that she couldn't while she was still alive?

Taking a deep breath, I opened the sand-colored paper and read the words written in elegant cursive.

Dearest Moenkopi,

I'm sure you're wondering why I left this letter for you. I didn't want to write it or hide it, but I needed to tell you about the Goddess Message I received a few weeks ago.

I glanced up at the date she'd scrawled at the top of the page. It was dated two nights before she died. I bit my lip and kept reading.

Recently, there's been an election of the new city council for Fort Collins. Most of the candidates are pretty good people and seem to have good heads on their shoulders. They want to see the city progress toward inclusiveness, understanding, and wellness. But there's this one guy, Earl Creighton, who has some destructive energy to him. I always feel uneasy when I'm around him and he appears to be rather fanatically fundamentalist in his approach to things.

He doesn't like me or our shop at all.

I grimaced as I recalled Joslyn's remarks about Councilman Creighton's statements in the meeting. His views apparently hadn't changed in the last three years.

A few weeks ago, I received a Goddess Message. You were out with your friends doing the LGBTQ fundraiser and I'd closed the shop for lunch. The vision showed me I'm going to die, murdered by a goon trying to rob the shop. It'll be presented as a robbery and the cops will see what they want to see and let it go at that. They won't find who ordered the hit, but it's meant to look like an unfortunate result of someone desperate for money.

Don't be fooled, Rochelle. It's not that.

The Goddess told me Earl Creighton is behind it and

he will continue to erode all the good the new city council will try to build. He's poison and decay for something so plain as money and perceived power. You need to be careful of him because he'll come after you once he's gotten rid of me.

I gasped and covered my mouth with my hand as my tears flowed. Sweet Goddess, Earl Creighton had killed my mother! And she knew it was going to happen.

Why, dammit? Why didn't she do anything to stop it if she knew it would happen beforehand?

I'm sure you're sitting there reading this and demanding to know why I let the Goddess Message come true. Oh my lovely Moenkopi, there was more to this vision. The Goddess showed me several paths I could choose to take, but in all the versions where I lived, his poison would continue unabated and the community of witches, Elder Races, and progressive people would have slowly rotted away until there was nothing left to fight for.

And you, Moenkopi, you wouldn't find the love of your life, the one who will set your heart ablaze, and will help you defeat this vile creature infecting our sanctuary. You also wouldn't be given the opportunity to find your true strength and passion if I'm still there. I never meant to stifle you, but the person I am, the one whom the community knows, would hide you in my shadow too long to be healthy.

"No, no, Mom, it's not true. I needed you." I whispered the words as tears streamed down my face.

I know you don't believe these words and it will take you a long time to see the truth of them, but the Goddess doesn't make mistakes. She knows what She's doing, and you're the warrior She's looking for to defeat this monster. Earl Creighton hired goons to kill me, and he'll try to do the same to you. But you've got so many people who love you and will protect you. Don't fear the ones who look scary on the outside. Look beyond their outer layers to see the real allies underneath. That's how Creighton hides. His surface looks benign, but he's the worst kind of monster.

So now you know why I'm not going to do anything to stop my murder. It has to be. I'm in your way. But the Goddess also told me I'd be able to help a little here and there along the way. Look for the signs and don't give up. You're the one who's meant for this challenge.

I love you, Moenkopi, and I'm so proud of you.

Blessed be.

Love, Mom

P.S. the enclosed micro USB drive holds images of Mr. Creighton and the men he meets with regularly. I don't know all their names, but the one he's always shaking hands with goes by Mr. Butler and his favorite goon is named Bosworth. I only managed to get a few pictures of them after council meetings, but it was enough to tell me there's something strange going on. I'm sorry to leave this with you, Moenkopi, but you're the right woman for the job.

I closed the letter and let the tears fall unheeded down my cheeks as I gripped the USB in my hand. Mom knew she was going to die and she knew who'd do it. *Fucking Creighton.* Rage and loss fought for dominance in my chest and I couldn't keep it in anymore. So I let it flow down my cheeks as I carefully slid the letter back into its envelope and shoved it into my pocket along with the USB drive.

My hands shook as I grasped my tea but the heat soothed some of my tremors. There were too many things to feel to pinpoint any one of them so I just sat there and cried. A few people shot me worried looks, but I must have been wearing enough of a "fuck off" vibe that no one bothered me.

Thunder rattled the windows of the coffee shop and I looked up. Snow fell hard outside, decorating the cars and parking lot with a swift, thick blanket of white. It reflected the flashing lights of the fire engines and trucks hauling ass past the coffee shop, headed back in the direction of my shop.

Another flash of lightning and the rumble of thunder sparked my awareness of what the flashing lights meant. *Oh shit, my shop!*

I tossed my cold tea and headed for my car, the sirens of the emergency vehicles echoing in the oddly muffled air. I threw my door open and slid behind the wheel in time for it to slam closed on its own. I cranked the engine and backed out of the parking spot, careful not to hit any other vehicles. The last thing I needed was to get involved in an accident right then.

I trailed after the fire department, my gut sinking deeper the closer I got to where my shop should have been. But there wasn't much left beyond a large white man's fire engulfing my cute home. I pulled over to the curb a few stores down and got out, staring in resigned disappointment.

My phone pinged with a text and I pulled it out of my coat to look at it.

I'm on my way. Are you at your place?

I grimaced and shook my head as I typed my response. No, a few doors down. I don't want to get in the way of the fire dept's attempt to put out the fire.

Flint's response didn't take that long. WTF? ARE YOU ALL RIGHT?

Yes, I'm fine. I was at a coffee shop when it started. I sent the text to him, then started a new one to Joslyn.

Hey Jos, it looks like the shop is a total loss. The fire dept is trying to save it right now, but I'm pretty sure it's done. Don't worry about anything for the next 48 hours. I'll handle the cops and fire dept. We'll figure something out after the Christmas holiday. Love you.

I sent that off and shoved the phone into my pocket as

thunder rumbled overhead. Snow dumped from the sky, but it didn't seem to touch the flames rising from my shop. I leaned against my car and watched it burn with the other local bystanders, grateful I'd moved all the important items into storage. All the hard work and effort I'd put into my professional life flickered into oblivion as lightning flashed through the leaden sky.

I tilted my head back and grimaced. *Thunder snow.* It seemed appropriate.

I had my mother's words in my pocket and I'd gotten the Goddess Message, but it still felt like a double gut punch. Earl Creighton had targeted my mother and now me.

Welp, I knew it was coming. The question was why. Why would he come after a relatively small business? I looked at my home and wondered if there was something valuable about the land it was on. All was lost despite the valiant efforts of the firefighters. I'd put up wards and barriers, but whoever had destroyed my shop either knew enough magic to combat them or was a complete brick to magical energy.

My tears cleared up and my mind turned to strategy and calculation. I was done playing games. Creighton had killed my mother and then his goons had come after me. Now they'd torched my home. My current history had been wiped off the map.

Did that mean I could be anyone I wanted to be? Could I play the Phoenix and rise again, different, and yet the same?

The rumble of a Harley motorcycle swelled over the thunder in the sky as Flint pulled up behind my vehicle. He swung off his bike and charged up to me, his gaze assessing my physical form. He scanned my body before stopping in front of me.

"Are you all right?" He watched my face and body language as much as he listened.

I nodded. "I'm okay. I got most of the important things out."

He frowned and tilted his head. "How?"

I sighed and glanced around before I leaned closer. "I knew this was coming. I was given a warning." I wasn't quite ready to tell him about the Goddess Messages.

He turned and let his gaze rest on the rising inferno of my home. Anger tightened his features.

"What the hell happened?" His sign language was short and angry.

I grimaced. "Arsonist took out my shop and home because I'm a witch."

"Arsonist." He repeated the word and his eyes narrowed. "Do you know who?"

I shrugged. "Can't be sure until I check the magical archives saved to the cloud, but I'm pretty sure it was Earl Creighton's goons."

"Who's Earl Creighton?"

I grimaced. "Local city councilman. The bastards who were trying to throw me off the cliff mentioned him."

He nodded and a small smile quirked the corner of his mouth. "You can save magic to an archival cloud?"

I couldn't help the smirk. "Yup. One of my many talents."

"That's fuckin' cool." Flint turned his head to watch the firefighters battling the blaze consuming my home. "So this Creighton tried to take you out?"

I shrugged. "Yup. Twice now."

His expression turned to granite. "Then he'll pay."

I nodded, but I was too tired to do anything about it that night. "It's getting close to Yule."

He blinked. "Yule?" He spelled the word out in letters.

"Yeah, you know, 'deck the halls with boughs of holly, fa-la-la-la-la'?" I gave him a sardonic smirk. "Any of that ringin' a bell?"

To my surprise, he shrugged.

"You don't celebrate Yule?"

He shrugged again. "Not for a long time."

His response totally derailed my misery and sorrow.

"Well, we gotta change that. But first we have to find a place that's warm, dry, and has good food."

He smiled and nodded to his bike. "I know a place like that."

"Oh yeah?" I let my own smile curl my lips. "Is it okay if I take my car and follow you? It's pretty much all I have left and I don't want to expose it for another fire."

He lost some of the wattage of his grin. "Yeah, that's a good idea. Just follow me."

He returned to his bike as I settled back behind the wheel of my car. I sighed and wished I could ride with him, arms wrapped around his waist, leaning against his back. But better to wait to do that when we arrived at whatever destination he hand in mind. We left my burning shop behind and headed into the snowy night.

I'm not sure how long we drove, but the visibility sucked and I had no idea how he could see where he was going. We arrived at a small stone cabin built from the hard rock of the Colorado Rockies. The cabin seemed to grow out of the hillside and overlooked what appeared to be one of those road-side no-tell motels. Strangely, the motel was cleaned up and glowed with holiday lights.

Who in the Goddess's name would decorate a road-side motel at this time of year?

I shook my head as Flint parked the bike under a wide lean-to attached to the side of the cabin. He directed me to park beside him and waited for me to secure the car for the night. He waited for me to grab my bag from the trunk and took my hand as I let the silence of the winter night fill my awareness. Where had the thunder gone? Maybe it was cold enough up there in the mountains that it killed the electrical storm.

"Come on. Let's get you inside." Flint's signs were

short and emphatic as if he was impatient with the cold.

I can't blame him. He's the one running around with nothing but jeans and shirt with the arms cut off.

He let me in through a side door under the lean-to and flipped on a light switch. I expected fluorescent light, but what I got was starlight and magic. He'd strung up white holiday lights all over the inside of the cabin, creating a fairytale boudoir if rustic furniture and cozy fleece blankets. I stood gobsmacked in awe.

"Wow. It's beautiful in here, Flint."

He paused in what he was doing to raise his eyebrows, but instead of asking any questions, he gestured to the bag in my hands.

"Let me show you where we're going to sleep."

We. He said we. I couldn't help the thrill of delight that shot up my spine at the thought of snuggling with Flint again. Hopefully he'd be there when I woke up in the morning. *Duh, it's his house. Of course he'll be there.* Not that he couldn't leave, but at least there'd be less of a likelihood.

The bedroom was a lot like the rest of the cabin. Rustic chic, I thought the designers called it. Three of the walls were constructed of stained and lacquered logs that gleamed in the soft tract lighting. The bed stood against the back wall of polished rose-colored granite with large creamy white feldspar inclusions against the tiny black speckles of amphibole and biotite. The stone felt alive, warm, and comforting in ways the brick of my shop had not.

"Oh, Flint, this room is lovely."

He turned from where he'd dropped my bag on a large, rough-hewn chair with matching rose-colored upholstery on the seat and back.

"You like it?"

"Oh yes." I took a deep breath in and closed my eyes as I tipped my head back. "It feels safe, warm, comforting, protective." I opened my eyes to find him staring at me with rapt attention. "What?"

"You can sense the stone." It wasn't a question, but amazement showed in his widened eyes and dropped jaw.

"Yes. The stone is happy you're here within its embrace. It likes to protect you."

He rested a hand against the rock wall before turning to me. "It likes to protect you, too. You'll always be safe here, Rochelle."

I nodded. "Thank you."

"Come out to the table. We'll eat and talk about what happened to your place." He gestured for me to lead the way.

We returned to the main room of the cabin and he pulled out one of the hefty rustic chairs at the thick ax-hewn table. I sat down and watched as he brought out a feast and set it on the table under the twinkling lights. He'd even lit candles and set out cloth napkins.

"Wow, this is really spectacular. It definitely offsets the shitty day I've been having." I rested my elbows on the table and smiled at him. "Thank you."

He gave me his beautiful crooked smile as he served me a plate full of food. "I wanted a special night with you tonight. I was hoping you'd spend the night. Now I insist on it."

I snorted. "Yeah, I'm definitely not going to turn you down since my place went up in flames."

He sat down in the other chair and grimaced. "Let's eat before you tell me why this guy Creighton is coming after you and how you knew it would happen."

I nodded, grateful for the reprieve. "Sounds perfect."

I just hoped the cops and Joslyn would give me enough time to enjoy tonight before I had to deal with the repercussions of my property loss. *One step at a time completes the journey.* Mom was right, but the world didn't always follow suit.

CHAPTER SEVEN

Flint

Some of my unease faded as Rochelle relaxed in my home and tucked into her supper. When she texted me about the fire at her place, I damn near shifted into my natural form and crashed my bike on the side of the road. The idea that she was hurt inserted enough fear and rage in me to start my shift and fill my mouth with jagged teeth. But when she texted that she was all right, only her place burned, I was able to settle a bit.

I had a lot of questions, but I didn't want to start in on them until Rochelle had gotten something to eat and a chance to unwind. She was calmer than I expected, but tension sang in her shoulders and tightened her mouth. I wished I could erase all her concerns, but I couldn't do that until I learned more about who had targeted her.

It had been a century since I'd celebrated the Solstice or Yule, and I'd rarely been interested in making an effort to celebrate it for myself. What was the point? But today, I'd taken our time apart to make my home a place where she'd like to stay.

And by "stay", I mean forever.

I'd cleaned every surface and fabric. I'd bought and

prepared food I thought she might like. I'd even made sure I had tea and coffee in the cupboards, and eggnog in the fridge. All of this effort mirrored my thoughts about her staying for longer than just a weekend, but none of it made sense. I'd known her a handful of days and made love with her once. How was it rational to be even considering long-term?

"Thank you so much for this meal. I wasn't looking forward to cooking." She grimaced and shook her head. "Guess I wasn't going to do that anyway now that my kitchen is a smoking ruin."

I nodded and freed up my hands. "You're welcome. Let's talk about the fire. You said it was arson. And you think it was from someone named Creighton."

She wiped her lips with a napkin and nodded. "I won't know for sure until I check the Cloud, as I said, but I'm pretty sure it was him. As I mentioned, Earl Creighton is a city councilman for Fort Collins, but he has an overwhelming hatred of witches and he's targeted my family before."

"What?" I blinked. "When? How?"

"I told you my mother was murdered a few years ago. It turns out she knew it would happen, and she knew who'd do it." Rochelle rose and went into the bedroom. I almost got up to follow her, but she came back quickly with something in her hand. "I didn't find this until yesterday. Well, my best friend Joslyn found it and gave it to me. I just read it today." She sat down and tapped the edge of the envelope against the table as she considered me.

"What?" I tilted my head as her eyes narrowed.

"I'm going to tell you something about my family that most people don't know, and I need you not to freak out."

I raised my eyebrows but nodded. "Okay."

She eyed me for a few more moments before she nodded. "Okay. So my family are witches, real witches with real connection to the elements. My mother's line was of the earth witches, connected to the stones, the mountains, crystals, farming and gardens. But one of the extra talents my mother passed on was what she called the Goddess Messages."

"Goddess Messages? Like actual messages from the Goddess?" I beat back my envy. I'd always wanted to hear directly from the Goddess.

"Yeah, kinda. They aren't like emails or notes left where we can find them. They're more like visions or snippets of future actions that come as warnings to allow us to decide how we're going to deal with them."

I nodded slowly. "And they always come true?"

She nodded as well. "Yeah, in one way or another, unless we take steps to mitigate them."

She stopped and swallowed hard, and I realized she was trying to compose herself against something emotional. The emotions washed through me, stronger than I'd ever felt anything. Anger, frustration, indignation, betrayal, and overwhelming sorrow. How the hell was I feeling her emotions? I shifted uncomfortably as she took a deep breath and settled, pulling the emotions back to normal levels.

Sweet glory, what the hell was that?

"So I found this letter from my mother. It was written just before her death and it explains what happened and why she allowed it to. She knew she was going to be murdered, and she knew who would perpetuate it. She wrote it all down here in her letter." Tears beaded at the edges of Rochelle's eyes and my gut cramped with the need to cradle her, but I held still. "Earl Creighton was a new councilman back when my mom was alive and he hated her and our shop from the moment he showed up. More than likely, he hated us before and that's why he ran for city council.

"The Goddess sent my mom a message that he'd send goons after her to take her out, try to make it look like a robbery gone bad, and that the cops would see what they wanted to see. It would go down as an unsolved murder, but Mom knew who paid the killers." Rochelle choked a moment and looked away, her frustration and angry sorrow surging. She cleared her throat. "She...she said the Goddess showed her several paths...you know, like Dr. Strange in that last movie about those comic book heroes?"

I nodded, wishing I could sign something that would help, but I kept my hands still.

"She said that in all of the ones where she lived, I'd be stifled and unable to reach my full potential. She said she had to die so I could grow and be a warrior and hero...But I don't feel like either of those things without her."

The tears overflowed her eyes and I couldn't stand it anymore. I rose and came around the table, tugging her into my arms. I steered her to the little couch I had brought in and settled her on it, her back against my chest.

"I'm sorry, I'm not usually this emotional."

I growled a dismissive sound and hugged her gently, allowing her to feel my empathy and comfort, if a gargoyle could even offer emotions so soft. I broadcasted all the kindness and love I could muster at her, hoping she'd feel my emotions as much as I could feel hers.

Her sniffles settled a little. "Apparently, the Goddess told her I was the one meant to take on this monster and I couldn't do that, I couldn't grow into this warrior, unless I was out of her shadow." She twisted to look at me, her glorious eyes full of tears. "I didn't want this honor, you know? I didn't ask for it or pine for it. I just wanted my mom to be around so I could learn everything from her. But she said the Goddess doesn't make mistakes and I was born for this."

I didn't have anything useful to say to explain the Goddess's actions or her mother's, so I just held her, offering my support and love.

And damn, son, it is full blown love. Holy shit.

She sniffled a bit more and wiped her eyes, gathering up her composure once more. "Anyway, so yeah, I know Creighton had my mother killed and I suspect those goons who tried to throw me off that cliff were from him, too."

"And your house tonight?" I signed with one hand.

She nodded. "Yeah. I got my own Goddess Message about it a few days ago, so I moved out all the sentimental items and the important things I wouldn't be able to replace. I knew it was coming and I know who had it done."

"Creighton." I spelled out the name.

"Yes. I'll need to check my digital records to verify, but yeah."

I tilted her head up to look at me again. "You really have digital records?"

A small smile curled her lips and I counted it a victory. "Yeah. Do you want to see them?"

I did, but not that night so I should my head. "Later. Right now I want to make sure you've eaten enough."

She frowned a little and tilted her head. "Yeah, I'm fed. Why?"

I pulled her to her feet. "Because I have a gift to give you."

"What?" She shot me an owlish look. "What kind of gift?"

I laughed. "A Yuletide gift."

Rochelle narrowed her eyes. "I thought you didn't celebrate Yule."

"No, I said I hadn't celebrated in a long time. But the last few days have put me in the spirit so I'm counting this as my Yuletide gift to you. Ready?" I handed her coat and scarf to her as I led her to the side door of the cabin.

"Uh, okay." She shrugged into her coat and zipped it up as I led her outside.

I'd never really given anyone a gift at this time of year. Not in the traditional sense and not in a long time.

That evening's gifts hadn't been traditional either or even planned as representing Yule. But Rochelle was worth all the effort I'd gone to and she seemed more curious than disappointed.

"Where are we going?"

"You'll see. Trust me."

I tugged her out the door and led her up a snowy path that led into the rocks behind the cabin. The storm had cleared, leaving the world decorated in white lace, and the moon sprinkled the world with ethereal light. The granite stones I'd used for steps up to my personal overlook glowed pink in the moonlight, a function of the red feldspar crystals among the quartz.

"Oh glory, this is so beautiful." Rochelle stood at the foot of the stairs and gazed upwards. "Did you build this yourself?"

I nodded and gestured for her to climb the steps. Beauty filled the staircase, but the greatest gift sat at the top. She grinned and started up, her breath pluming in front of her. Snowflakes sparkled in the air as the breeze shook them from the trees.

This gift might have been for her, but she was the only gift I wanted. Over the last few days, I'd started to understand that she might be more important to me than just a lovely tryst for sex and recreation. I couldn't stop thinking about her and wishing I could come home to see her face when she woke up in the morning. Gargoyles didn't sleep much, but being there to share tea with her when she opened her eyes had become a driving desire.

We reached the overlook and I turned her to face east. The winter world spread out below, city lights sparkling like the stars had fallen to decorate the earth in Yuletide glory. We stood together and let the silence deepen, and even the breeze settled into whispers instead of a soughing torrent.

I'd learned centuries earlier that magic sometimes

happened when we grew silent and experienced the world
instead of trying to shape it. In that moment with Rochelle,
the magic returned and wove a deep spell around us both. I
kept my gaze on her, watching as she took in the beauty
and silence, and my heart cracked the stone shell I'd kept it
in beyond repair.

"Sweet glory, it's beautiful."

Damn right, you are.

When I didn't say anything, she turned her gaze to me
and I finally nodded. "Yes, you are."

She smiled without discomfort and signed, "Thank
you."

I matched her smile as she turned back to the view,
letting out a deep breath. She seemed to be gathering her
thoughts on something and I was content to wait for her to
find the words she wanted to say. I was damn good at
waiting.

"Flint, would you be okay with me staying here for a
while?" She swung back to me, her expression hesitant. "I
mean at your place, not here in this beautiful overlook."

I nodded. "Yes."

"It won't be forever. Just until I can find a new place
for my shop and home. Just temporary."

I shrugged and nodded again. "It doesn't have to be
temporary."

"What?" She blinked before her eyebrows lifted.

"It doesn't have to be temporary. I like having you
here. You are welcome to stay."

Whoa, that was fast. I'd never let anyone visit much
less stay in my personal retreat. I used it to get away from
people. But I couldn't picture it without Rochelle anymore,
and she'd only been there a little over an hour. *I'm in deep
with this woman.* Maybe it had something to do with my
biting her during sex. She was the only woman I'd ever
bitten, the only one that sparked the desire to bite in a
sexual way. I was experienced with sex, but the desire for

biting was new.

"I—thank you. I think right now, I'm going to think of it as temporary so I don't freak out and ruin this thing between us that feels so crazy right." She gave me a goofy smile. "I'm sure I sound like I'm being too cautious for someone who just met you a few days ago, but I don't want to take advantage and sabotage something I'm really enjoying. Does that make any sense?"

She'd put into words exactly what I was feeling so I simply rocked my fist, "Yes."

She blew out a little breath of relief. "Good. Can we go back to your cabin? I'm cold and I'd like some tea."

I wanted more than that if I could convince her, but I nodded and helped her back down to my retreat with my heart more full than it had ever been in my life.

****

Rochelle

By the time we got back to Flint's cabin, I was ready to drop. Between the letter, the fire, and the cold, my energy had hit the skids. Flint moved past me to start the kettle on the stove while I took off my shoes and coat. I dug out my phone just in case the insurance company called. I didn't really feel like talking to them that night, but it wasn't like I could ignore the events of the day. Flint helped me onto the couch and wrapped me in a blanket.

"Aren't you going to sit down?" I set my phone on my knee.

He nodded. "After the tea is ready. Chamomile for you?"

"Yes, please."

He gave me a thumbs up and returned to the kitchen just as my phone vibrated with an incoming call. I glanced at the ID before I put it to my ear.

"Hey, Jos."

"Oh my glory, Rochelle. Are you all right? I just drove by the shop and it's gone. There's damn near nothing left. Where are you?"

I closed my eyes and took a few steadying breaths, the anger and sorrow surging through my chest. *It's going to be okay. Phoenix, remember?*

"Yeah, I'm fine. I got there just after the fire department did and watched it burn. I wasn't hurt or anywhere near it when it started."

"Oh thank the Goddess. Where are you now? Do you need a place to stay?"

"No, no, I'm with Flint. He's putting me up for the night, so I'm good." The man in question appeared beside the couch and handed me a mug of tea. I mouthed my thanks.

"Oh?" Surprise and cautious pleasure echoed in her voice. "That's good, I think. It's good, right?"

Despite our rough day, I laughed. "Yeah, definitely good. He at least made me some tea. That's a point in his favor."

"Damn skippy." Joslyn sounded relieved. "Okay, well, I just wanted to be sure you were all right. And I called the insurance company to let them know about the fire. I suspect they'll call you tomorrow to get the details."

"Okay, I'll be expecting their call. But before you go, tell me how your evening went." I paused and narrowed my eyes. "You had an evening, right? With a hot guy of your own? The guy with that smooth, dark skin, fathomless eyes, and hot body?"

Flint shot me a look with a raised eyebrow and I winked.

"Shut up!" Joslyn laughed. "Yeah, we were at dinner when a friend called to let me know the shop was on fire. Why didn't *you* call me?"

"I didn't want to disturb your date, but I did text you

the moment I found out. Didn't you read the text?"

"Oh, uh, no. I guess I didn't see it."

"Um-hm, you were too deep into your dinner companion, huh? I see where I stand now."

"Shut up, you know no one could replace you." She laughed but quickly sobered. "Seriously, Rochelle, are you gonna be okay? Do you need me to come by or anything?"

"Nah, not tonight. You have fun. I'm okay and Flint's watching out for me. I'll call you tomorrow and we'll start to figure shit out then, okay?"

"Yeah, okay. Take care of you, sis."

"You too. Have fun tonight and don't worry. It'll all work out." I sounded more positive than I felt, but my mom had insisted so I was going off of that.

"Okay. Love you."

"Love you, too." I ended the call and dropped my head back against the couch, closing my eyes. "Glory, I hope it'll all work out."

I went back over all the things I'd learned about my mom, Creighton, and the Goddess until they jumbled up in my head and made me exhausted. Apparently, it was too much because the next thing I knew, Flint lifted me from the couch and carried me into the bedroom. I tried to protest but my eyes refused to cooperate and when he settled me on the bed, I didn't want to open them anyway. The bed and pillows cradled me in addictive softness and it wasn't long before I'd lost the fight with sleep.

CHAPTER EIGHT

Flint

I watched Rochelle succumb to her exhaustion and wished there was more I could do to help her. Who the hell was this Creighton asshole anyway? I slid off the bed and headed for the main room, closing the bedroom door most of the way. I didn't want her to wake up closed in a strange place. That had happened to me enough to times not to wish it on someone else.

I grabbed my phone and settled on the couch, bringing up the search apps to run Creighton's name. I didn't have the sophistication of Neo's skills, but I could find a decent amount of information when I set my mind to it.

The search engines brought up a lot of information, some about a thriller writer, some about a character in an old sci-fi TV show, but finally I found the links to stories about the local Creighton in Fort Collins. There were articles from when he'd been elected to the city council, pointing out his efforts to bring a more conservative view to the progressive city. Other articles addressed his stances on commerce, water quality, and school funding. All of it looked ordinary until I started digging deeper.

Someone had looked into his background and found

he'd started out as a small-time thug working for the salt barons in Louisiana as muscle to keep the workers in line. He'd moved up through the organization until the Feds cracked down on it in the early 2000s, then he disappeared for ten years.

I narrowed my eyes. *What the hell was he doing until 2013?*

I kept digging. Creighton reappeared in 2013 as a businessman in Colorado, with a small business in manufacturing communication equipment for the police. Earpieces and radios of military quality. All the records appeared to be clean, without connection to his former bosses or their mafia ties, but Creighton had effectively disappeared until that point. I wasn't the internet sleuth Neo was and after a couple of hours, I had to concede defeat. Instead, I checked the time and texted our Dark Web master.

Neo, I need you to look up the background of Fort Collins councilman Earl M. Creighton. He's threatening my woman and needs a closer look. I don't know who he's connected to, but he disappeared from 2003 to 2013 and I want to know where he went and with whom. Text me when you have some news.

I glanced at the clock. 02:31 glowed back at me from the stove and I sighed. I wanted to crawl into the bed with Rochelle, wake her with soft kisses, and make love with her until she forgot her problems. But the more logical side of my brain reminded me she needed rest more than I did and I'd tire her out more with sex.

Dammit.

I growled and rubbed my hands over my face as I let my mind relax from puzzling out who Creighton was and how we could dismantle his unhealthy fixation to Rochelle.

"You think too hard and smoke will come out of your ears, dearie."

I jerked my head up to find a woman seated in one of the chairs of my living room. She had white hair with silver highlights woven into a complex braid system and pointed ears much like mine. Her skin reminded me of polished andesite with little flecks of ruby and olivine that caught the light when she smiled. Her eyes were solid black but filled with stars, and I immediately recognized who'd come to visit me.

"My Lady." I slid off the couch and knelt, bowing my head.

She snorted as She leaned on a gnarled and polished walking stick. "I hope you don't expect me to bow back to you. These old bones don't move like that anymore."

I almost barked a laugh but thought it bad manners to laugh at the Goddess when She graced me with Her visit. Instead, I smiled and rose, gesturing to the kitchen.

"Can I make you some tea?"

She shook Her head and leaned forward to pat the couch. "Come sit with me a bit, Flint. I understand you have some questions for me."

I raised my eyebrows as I sat down. "Questions?"

"Um-hm, something about not understanding why you bit Rochelle, perhaps?"

I didn't blush often. Not much embarrassed me. But having the Goddess of All remark upon one of the most intimate moments in my life caught me off-guard.

"Uhhh..." Not my most eloquent response.

"It's okay, Flint." She patted my knee. "I've seen all sorts of things in my day and your connection to Rochelle isn't even the most astounding."

I frowned. "Thanks, I think."

She laughed. "The point is, nothing to be freaked out about. But it is important to talk about. How much do you know about gargoyle mating?"

My jaw hit the floor and I sat there, gaping at the Goddess as if She'd asked me to pierce my cock. I wanted to sputter, but that would've made me look like a prude, and I was anything but. So I swallowed hard and tried to take Her question seriously.

"I didn't know there was anything special about it. Is it more than just sex?" That sounded reasonable, didn't it?

She patted my thigh again. "Maybe I will take that tea."

I gulped and put the kettle on before returning to the couch. "So, um, what did it mean when I bit Rochelle?"

"No pussyfooting around. Excellent. It'll make this easier." The Goddess set Her staff aside and wove Her fingers together as She clasped one knee. "I'm a big fan of having no guessing games and there's enough guessing at stuff in the human race, so I made things easier for the Elder Races."

I damn near barked my disbelief. "Easier? How are things easier?"

She dropped Her chin and raised Her eyebrows. "The urge to bite your partner while having sex is an indication that the person is the right one for you. One with whom you can learn and grow and maximize your potential. And once you bite that person, they're your one-and-only, your perfect partner, your happily-ever-after. I was always a huge fan of romance."

I blinked. "So when I bit Rochelle…"

"She became your mate, the one other being who fits you best and will not only bring out the best in you, but you'll bring out the best in her."

The Goddess's words sent a shaft of panic through me. "Became, as in it's already a done deal? Is it reversible?"

She paused and tilted Her head, one eyebrow slowly rising. "Reversible?"

I nodded quickly. "Yeah, can it be undone?"

Her pause was longer this time and unease sank in. *Oh shit. Not only have I screwed up with Rochelle, now I've pissed off the Goddess.*

"Let me see if I'm hearing you correctly." The Goddess lifted Her chin and fixed me with Her starry gaze. "It sounds to me like you're trying to get out of this connection, one that will bring out the best in you and in Rochelle. That seems completely daft to me. So why don't you explain your thought processes to me and we'll go from there."

I took a moment to gather my thoughts into some semblance of order before I met Her gaze again. "I didn't mean to make this connection so soon. And I didn't do it on purpose."

Her brows lowered and I scrambled to make my concerns clear, though it appeared I was digging myself deeper with every ill-chosen phrase.

"I didn't know that biting her meant she'd be my mate. Had I known, I wouldn't have done it. Yet."

"Why not, Flint?"

I swallowed hard. "Because, if it's not reversible, that means I gave Rochelle no choice. She didn't get to make this decision. I took it from her, even unintentionally, and she's already had so much taken from her." I sighed and looked away. "I wish I'd known so I could've held back until I talked to her about it."

The Goddess's expression softened. "Ah, I see now."

"Maybe you could talk to her."

"Me?"

I nodded. "Yeah. Maybe you could give her one of those Goddess Messages to let her know your plan for her, so she understands we're the perfect partners?"

"Hmm." The Goddess sat back and tapped Her chin with Her fingers. "That's a possibility, but it doesn't get you out of talking to her about it."

Yeah, I'd been afraid of that. Afraid that Rochelle would be angry with me for having taken away her choice. Of course, I could sit back and wait for her to realize that we were meant for each other and then let her know I'd known for however long it took her to get it. But that smacked of arrogance and smugness.

"Yeah, I know. I'll talk to her about it over Yule."

The Goddess narrowed Her eyes at me as if checking the truthfulness of my words. But I meant it. I'd have to tell Rochelle at some point, and maybe if I presented it as a surprise on my end, too, she'd take it better than if I just said, "We're mates. Surprise!"

"Very well. Yule it is. But if you haven't told her by Hogmanay, it'll be much harder for you."

I didn't like the sound of that. "Yes, ma'am."

"Good. Now that that's settled, what are you going to do when Loki finds out?" She tilted Her head and a sly smile curled Her lips. "Because you know he lives for making people's love lives weather more storms than necessary."

I groaned. "I know. I've seen. We don't have to tell him, do we?"

She laughed. "He's going to notice, and that's why you have until Hogmanay to make sure you secure Rochelle's agreement. Because after that, Loki will be all over it like buzzards on carrion, and he'll make it harder."

"I know, I know. We have to keep him distracted with something else." I rubbed the back of my head with one hand, wracking my brain to find something that could keep the Prez out of my love life.

"I'm sure something will come along to grab his attention." The Goddess smiled mysteriously and I ached to know what that meant, but She waved Her hands and fixed me with an intense look. "You're already aware of Earl Creighton, but you need to keep an eye on him. He means to do harm to Rochelle and she'll need your help to nip that in the bud."

I nodded and I gritted my teeth. "Is he going to try to kill her again?"

The Goddess's expression closed into stoicism. "What

do you think?"

Anger kindled in my chest. "I think he will do anything to harm her and he's already tried. But I also think it's not gonna happen. Rochelle is my mate and I'll do everything I can to defend her."

The Goddess smiled. "Then you're going to be fine." She rose to Her feet and wrapped Her shawl more tightly around Her shoulders. "Well, I must be off. Thank you for the tea, Flint. Remember, time's up on Hogmanay, but if you talk with her before then, the benefits will outweigh the discomfort. Merry Yule to you."

She opened the front door and stepped out into the snowy night, giving me a warm smile before closing it behind Her. The click of the latch had me startling awake and looking around. Had it all been a dream? I thought back to the conversation with the Goddess and realized I hadn't been using sign language. She'd talked to me as if I'd spoken aloud. I shook my head. *I should've known She wasn't really here.*

But then my gaze fell on the tea mug on the coffee table in front of the couch and steam still rose from the hot contents. My eyes widened and I shot a look out the front windows. *Holy shit, She really was here.*

The only response I got was laughter in the winter wind.

****

Rochelle

Morning showed up on soft little kitten feet, pitter-pattering across my awareness gently before sinking its claws into me with pinpricks of my memories.

Fire, complete destruction, and Mom's murderer.

Nothing like unhappy events to start my day off right. I groaned and sat up, still dressed in the clothes I'd worn the day before. Then I remembered the call with Jos and some pleasure returned. I hoped her night had been better than awesome and maybe she'd get a Happily-Ever-After with Andre. She definitely deserved it.

I checked my phone on the bedside table, but there were no missed calls or texts. I would have to call the insurance company and submit a claim, then I'd have to start looking for a new place to set up shop.

"And find a new apartment." I muttered the words under my breath, but apparently they were loud enough to reach Flint's ears.

He growled to get my attention and I glanced up to see him holding a tray with breakfast and tea.

"Wow, are you on the ball or what? How did you know I was awake?"

He shrugged as he set the tray down to free his hands. "I just had a feeling. Are you okay?"

I nodded. "Yeah, I'm just remembering all the things I need to do. Adulting sucks."

He barked a laugh. "Yeah, it does, but I can help, starting with restating my offer of a place to stay."

I blinked. "Are you sure you want me here?"

He nodded. "Would that be okay for you? I have fiber optic WiFi and plenty of space. It's quiet, no one will bother you, and it'll be safe from assholes like Creighton."

I bit my bottom lip. "I don't want to intrude. You seem like a guy who likes his privacy, and I can take up a lot of space." I grimaced and ran a hand through my unruly hair. "And it's kinda way out here in the mountains. Not very conducive to running a shop."

He sat down on the bed beside the tray and tilted his head. "But it's great because creeps like Creighton won't be able to find you—your home, your sanctuary, will be safe from his influence and reach if he doesn't know where you live."

I narrowed my eyes. "Flint, are you saying you want

me to move in?"

He had the grace to shrug uncomfortably. "Yeah, I am. I know it's fast and we haven't known each other long, but my gut tells me this is right."

I couldn't ignore how my heart leapt with excitement at the prospect of moving into this mountain retreat where I could literally commune with the stone of the Rockies, but I didn't want to seem too eager. And I needed to think it through because while it sounded good, what about my own needs for privacy? Would he be able to handle the rituals I performed regularly?

Although you gotta admit the High Beltane rituals will be a lot more fun with him.

"I want to accept your offer, but I have some questions before I do."

He swallowed hard and nodded, rearranging the plate and mug a little. "Okay."

"First, this is gonna seem like an impertinent and personal question, but I kinda need to know before I move in." I straightened my shoulders and met his gaze straight on. "Which one of the Elder Races are you?"

His eyebrows went up and he blinked a couple times before he swallowed. "You knew I wasn't human?"

I gave him a self-conscious shrug. "Yeah. I mean, I didn't know what you were, but I knew you were more than you seemed. So help a witch out."

He chuckled at my joke and took a deep breath as he rose. He shoved his jeans to the floor and shrugged out of his cut. Then he shifted. It wasn't immediately obvious, just little changes here and there. His mouth widened and his brows became more pronounced, overshadowing his golden-blue eyes. But when his ears became pointed and short horns sprouted from his skull, I got a good look at my boyfriend.

Gargoyle.

His fingers grew talons much like an eagle's and wings

sprouted from his back. But instead of leathery webbing between his wing-fingers, the flesh appeared ragged and damaged from an old injury. A long muscular tail sprouted from his ass and his feet grew until he stood digitigrade on his toes while his shins shrank and his feet extended to look like a dog's.

"Sweet Goddess of all." My words came out breathy with excitement and arousal. He'd been sexy before in his human disguise, but his true form made my nipples harden and my pussy grow wet. I could imagine what it would be like to fuck that rock hard cock hanging between his thighs and it made me shiver.

He growled and I glanced up at his hands. He signed with his talons.

"I know. It's a lot, which is why I don't show it very often."

My eyes widened. "No, no no! No, I think you're fuckin' sexy. Holy Goddess, you're so beautiful it makes me tremble."

He blinked. "You think so?"

"Oh glory, yes." I slid out of the bed and approached him carefully. "May I touch?"

He nodded, still wearing suspicion in his body language.

I ran my hands over his shoulder and arm, enjoying the smooth warm skin. It didn't feel like regular skin of mammals, with the tiny pores and hairs, but it had more texture than smooth stone.

"You're so warm." I continued my examination down to his waist and slid one hand along his muscular tail. "This is very cool and beautiful. I really like the subtle stripes on the dorsal surface."

He tilted his head to eye me with one eyebrow up. "Stripes?"

"You haven't noticed?" I grasped his tail and brought it around to his front so he could see it. "See here and here and here? If you tilt it in the light a little, there are slightly darker marks on your skin to give the impression of stripes."

He looked at his own tail for a while before meeting my gaze. "I've never seen those before. They're new."

"Well, they're sexy. Let me look you over to see if you have other ones."

He snorted. "You just want to look at my naked body."

I grinned and winked. "Busted."

He rumbled a chuckle as I trailed my hands over the warm skin of his thighs. His flanks had their own set of subtle stripes and so did his arms. I found some on his back as well, and the fingers of his wings had grown darker than the webbing between them. But the best part were the stripes on his cock. Sweet glory, I was looking forward to sucking on that in his true form.

"I'll say it again. You're beautiful." I stood between his legs. Even crouched as he was, we stood eye-to-eye, making me realize just how big he was in his natural form. "What happened to your wings?"

His lips tightened around his long canines. "I was in a bad fire. My wings never recovered."

"Is that why the Concrete Angels' emblem has torn wings?"

He nodded. "I was the mascot for a long time. I think Loki wanted to make me feel valued after he fished me out from under the debris of the building he'd burned."

I gaped. "Wait. *He* burned the building that ruined your wings?"

Flint nodded. "Yup. He hadn't realized it was a gargoyles' day roost. I was the only one there at the time, thank the Goddess, but when he realized he'd harmed me, he offered me a place with him in his new venture of a motorcycle club."

"And you joined him, just like that?"

Flint shook his head. "No, it took me a couple of

months, but it's hard to say no to the Norse God of Mischief."

I nodded, then stopped and swallowed hard. "Wait, stop. Did you say, Norse God of Mischief? As in *the* Loki of legend?"

Flint tilted his head. "Yeah, *the* Loki."

"Sweet glory." I backed up and sat down on the bed. "I knew the Elder Races were real, but it never occurred to me that the gods would actually be here, in Fort Collins, Colorado."

He shrugged. "There weren't any other clubs based here at the time, so the niche was open."

"And he needed a mascot."

He nodded. "Yes."

"Do your damaged wings cause you any pain?"

Flint frowned and grimaced. "Not physical pain, no." He shrugged again. "But they're why I ride a motorcycle. It almost feels like flying."

"Can you feel this?"

I ran my fingers over the tattered skin, stroking carefully. He shivered and rocked his fist forward, signing *yes*. A smug smile curled my lips and I moved behind him, stroking those wings with the tips of my fingers. He groaned and closed his eyes, tipping his head back as his tail shook with pleasure.

"Does it feel good?"

He shook his fist again.

"Does it turn you on?"

Instead of answering, he growled and spun around to show me his rock hard shaft. I dropped my gaze and licked my lips, aching for the chance to suck him off in his natural form, those stripes making my pussy wet. I even dropped to my knees with that intention when my cellphone started ringing. My gaze shifted away from the delicious treat toward the bedside table. I didn't recognize the ringtone.

"Dammit. I gotta get that." I scrambled away from him

to grab the phone. "Hello?"

"Ms. Stone?"

"Yes, who's calling?" I straightened my shoulders and turned around.

Flint had returned to his human disguise and was tucking his unruly cock back into his jeans with a grimace. I grimaced along with him as I'd rather he let me give him a blowjob than talk to a stranger.

"This is Alan with your homeowners insurance. I understand there was a fire?"

I sighed. "Yes. There's no official word until the fire department finishes their investigation, but we suspect it was arson."

"Arson? Are you sure?"

"Yes, I have digital security footage that shows someone setting up the fire." I hadn't looked at them yet, but I knew they were there. I'd check them as soon as I got off the phone.

"Wow, okay, that will help. But let's get the claim filed and go from there."

I sighed and nodded. "Okay." This wasn't going to be a fun conversation, but maybe it would turn out for the best and I could start hunting for a new place to set up shop by Hogmanay.

CHAPTER NINE

Flint

I bit back a groan and tried to think about something other than the fantasy of Rochelle's lips stretched around my throbbing shaft as she continued her phone call with the insurance company. *Son of a friable schist!* I stuffed my natural form back in my human disguise and headed for the main room of the cabin to get away from her sultry scent.

I pulled out my phone to check for anything to distract me and found a series of texts from Neo about his research on Creighton.

Man, did you pick a winner. This guy's a creep with a capital C. Hell, he makes the Concrete Angels look like real angels. If he's threatening your woman, we need to move on him soon. I got the missing decade for you. It goes something like this:

In 2003, Creepy Creighton manages to escape the heavy hand of the law and strikes off on his own until he lands in Dodge City, Kansas. Despite its history of being a lawless town, it's pretty quiet in Dodge and Creepy Creighton decides to try his hand at running an organization. Racketeering and small time drug running.

For a couple of years, he does okay and the organization grows, but while he was always good at threats and intimidation, he sucks at leadership and delegation and pretty soon there are far more capable people muscling in on his operation. Not to mention the FBI and the local PDs have gotten wind of his shit and they start taking down the members.

It was all headed for the shitter in 2009 and the FBI were closing in when Creighton gets "killed" and his organization goes to complete crap. Half the guys working for him get thrown in prison and the other half end up working for the real drug runners who'd been muscling in.

Nothing much else comes up for Creighton until 2010 when he starts showing up in Colorado doing odd jobs for various people. Nothing bold or in the spotlight, just working for random companies as a driver or warehouse worker. While that wouldn't be news, some of the companies are those we've pinpointed to belonging to Backlog fronts.

In 2013, he started his company in Fort Collins with a generous and anonymous donation from a wealthy benefactor. He had a cleaned up record, cleaned up façade, and a successful business right off the bat.

Looks like Creepy Creighton got himself set up with the help of Backlog and then he started his campaign for City Council. But he's just a glorified thug with Backlog backing.

And now he's coming after Rochelle.

I frowned. Other than her being a witch, why the hell would Creighton target her mother's business? Was it simply Wiccaphobia? Or did she have something that Backlog needed to control?

Thanks, Neo. Creighton seems to have a hardon for my woman and her mother. They had a shop called The Herb Cabinette. Last night, Creighton had it burned down. It could be a case of Wiccaphobia – Creighton suffers from that, which we might be able to use to our advantage – or maybe Backlog wants something only the Stone family had, either in location or possession. Can you dig around and find out?

I set the phone down just as Rochelle came out of the bedroom with a resigned look on her face and the tray of breakfast half eaten in her hands. She brought it to the kitchen counter and set it down.

"Everything okay?"

She sighed. "Yeah, overall, I think so. The shop and apartment are a total loss, but I told him my electronics and my car are safe. Still, since I owned the building, I will be getting a decent chunk of change to find a new place."

"Isn't that a good thing?" I didn't understand her resignation.

"No, no, it's good. It's definitely good." She sat down near the table. "It's just that the shop and apartment was the last little bit of my mom that I had left. It's a loss I can't get back and no amount of money can replace the sentimental cost." She scrubbed her face. "Anyway, because of the age of the building, it being paid off, the size, and the zoning, they're actually cutting me a check for about three quarters of a million dollars."

I coughed, shooting her a surprised look. "$750,000?"

She snorted and some of her amusement came back. "Yeah, sounds like a lot, doesn't it?"

"Hell yeah, it's a lot. That'll give you a damn good head start on finding a new shop location." An idea sparked in my mind as I leaned against the kitchen island. "If you want some help finding a prime location, I could ask Attila if he'd be willing to help. He's our Realty Acquisitions Manager, and knows all the prime places in Fort Collins."

"I—really? That would be very helpful, actually." Her expression lightened and made me feel like a frickin' hero.

I pulled out my phone. "I could text him right now and let him think about it. How much time do I have before you need a new place?"

"I was thinking I'd start looking around the beginning of the year. January is usually pretty slow when it comes to retail. February is when it picks up again for Valentine's Day."

I brought up Attila's number in my contacts and opened a chat window.

I'm in the market for a new place, zoned retail, herbs and crystals and shit. Price tag: half a million or less. Closing mid to late January. Want to go shopping?

I sent it off and set the phone down. "Done. Now what other questions do you have?"

She blinked. "Huh? Questions?"

I nodded. "Yeah. You said you had a few questions before you'd accept my offer of moving in with me."

"Oh." She barked a laugh and reached for the tea cup. "The main ones were what kind of Elder Race you were and what I would do about finding a new shop. Both of those have been answered."

"So you'll move in? Today? Right now?"

She laughed and held up her hands. "Wait, wait. Are you sure you want me in your space? Just like that?"

I nodded vigorously. "Just like that."

Rochelle sat back and let her gaze slide around the room, her brow wrinkling. "Is there enough room for my stuff?"

I shrugged. "How much stuff a we talking here? Furniture?"

She shook her head. "No, I didn't have the ability to take any of the furniture other than a few of the decorative tables and standing lamps. But there are books and bags of linens and clothes, and I'll need a reading and writing nook." She grimaced. "Maybe this isn't a good idea. I'm already setting terms."

"No, no, it's a good idea. And I think I can accommodate your terms." I pulled her to her feet. "Go get your coat and boots."

"What? Why?"

"Because there's something outside I have to show you and you can't go out there barefoot."

She gave me a funny look, but she went to get dressed for the cold while I headed outside to shovel a path.

Years ago when I first found this piece of land for sale, the previous owner had left one of those old shipping containers behind. He'd offered it to me as part of the sale if I wanted it. I'd kept it and fixed it up inside, figuring I'd use it as a workshop. It had electricity for lights and tools, a concrete floor for easy cleaning, and retracting sides that exposed huge windows when the weather was nice. A woodstove sat in the far end and heated the whole container in the winter so equipment and vehicles wouldn't freeze. When the walls were up, they created overhangs where I could sit on a small wooden deck outside. But when they came down, they protected the windows from the harsh mountain weather.

I hadn't done anything more than insulate and finish the inside with a small bathroom and pegboard walls so I could easily hang my tools. But since I spent most of my time at the compound, I used the Barn for working on my bike. Now I saw a great use for the space.

"What's this? It looks like an old shipping container." Rochelle followed after me as we tromped through the cleared snow to the workshop.

"Yes, that's exactly what it is. But not just that. Watch." I opened the door and flipped on the lights in the container.

"Wow." She stepped in beside me and gazed at all the work I'd put in. "Did you do all this?"

I nodded, enjoying her wonder.

"Wow." She took in the improvements of the walls with shelves and cupboards. "This is amazing. It would make a perfect workshop for poultices and medicinal herbs."

I waited for her to look back at me. "That's what I was thinking. Do you think you could use it?"

"Hell yes, I could use it. I've always wanted a space like this. Before I'd been using my kitchen." She stopped and bit her bottom lip. "Are you sure you don't need this for your bike?"

I shook my head. "I haven't used it before now, so I don't think I'll need it after."

"Oh, thank you!" She took a few running steps and threw herself into my arms, which surprised and pleased me all at the same time. "This is the best Yule gift ever."

I hadn't even considered it a Yuletide gift, but I was more than happy to make it one if I got that response.

I would've liked to enjoy her attention more if my phone hadn't buzzed with a series of incoming texts. I reluctantly set her back on her feet and pulled out the cell.

Fuck yeah, I wanna go shopping. Whose money are we spending?

Did you get a wee lassie at last? About fucking time.

By the way, Loki is having another holiday party tonight. You should bring your bonny lass with you.

I blew out a long sigh and shook my head.

"What is it?" Rochelle craned her neck to look at the screen.

I shoved it away and signed. "Party tonight at the clubhouse. Attila suggested I bring you with me."

"Okay...Don't you want to go?"

I shook my head as I turned off the lights in the workshop and closed the door, locking the padlock on the latch.

"Why not?" She caught up with me and we headed

back to the main house side-by-side.

I gave her a one-shouldered shrug. "They're loud and full of drunk people." I grimaced at her raised eyebrows as I let her back into the cabin. "I'm usually the one helping them to bed after they party too hard. Plus, this is how the president and the 1% members scope out my prospective old lady. They don't really care if I show up or not. They just want to know about you."

"I can tell you right off the bat I'm not a fan of that term. I'd rather be your matron rather than your old lady."

I immediately recognized one of the principal forms of the Goddess in her answer and thought it fit her better than old lady as well. When I told her about our mating, a prospect that still made me nervous, I'd call her my matron and insist my fellow club members do the same.

"Fair enough. We'll tell them that's what you need to be referred as, Flint's Matron."

"So you're going to go?" Rochelle took off her coat and hung it on the coat tree beside the door.

"Yes, I have to as a member."

She nodded. "Okay. We'll go. But let's look at my digital records of the arsonist. I want to know who it is and they're associated with Creighton. I really want to nail this guy."

She strode over to the chair where she'd left her bag and pulled out her laptop before bringing it back to the table. She powered it up and asked me for the WiFi password so she could connect to the internet. I stood behind her as she logged into her Cloud archive and brought up what appeared to be video files from inside her shop.

"Wow, there are a lot more of these than I expected." Rochelle shook her head. "They must have been trying to break through the wards for a while."

Some of the videos showed the outside of her building, mostly of the alley behind it. A few showed the same vehicle visiting the side street entrance with someone in a dark hoodie and sunglasses trying to get close to the door. In all of those, the intruders were rebuffed.

But in the last two videos, the intruder not only made it through the door but also all the way up into Rochelle's apartment, as if he was looking for something.

"What the hell is he doing?" Rochelle frowned at the screen.

I shook my head as we watched the guy looking through bookshelves and in drawers in her home. He even went through her bedroom bureau, which infuriated me. No one got to enjoy Rochelle's underwear but her and me. Apparently he didn't find what he was looking for because he tossed her place, throwing down everything he could before dousing it with what looked like gasoline.

The guy glanced up a few times, letting the camera catch his face clear enough to identify him with good enough software. Neo would have his name, birth date, shoe size, and coffee preference within minutes of getting his face.

The last thing the guy did was toss a match into the flammable liquid covering the floor and the whole place went up. The video turned into white light and cut off. Neither of us said anything as Rochelle cued up the next video. This one showed the same guy dumping accelerant over the shop. The only thing different on this video from the first was the sleeve of his hoodie rode up and exposed his wrist.

"Wait." I grabbed the mouse and clicked pause. "Can you rewind it a bit and stop when he shows his wrist?"

"Okay." Rochelle moved the progress bar back a bit and hit play again. She narrowed her eyes as the video moved forward. "You mean, right...here?"

I rocked my fist forward. "Look at that closely. It looks like a tattoo on his wrist, doesn't it?"

She leaned forward and right-clicked on the image. A

menu came up that allowed her to zoom in to the point where she clicked the mouse. The man's wrist filled the screen and when the pixels resolved, a small Ace of Spades stretched across the skin of his wrist.

"Deadman's hand." Rochelle clicked a still of his wrist then zoomed back out to get a good one of the guy's face. "Let's get his pre-mug shot, shall we?"

I nodded. "Text me both those images, please."

She raised her eyebrows. "Why?"

"I want to make sure Neo has them so he can find out who that guy is. If we know who he is, we can find out who he works for and go after the mudfucker."

She grinned. "Mudfucker? I like it. Let me send you the images."

My phone pinged with the incoming text and I immediately forwarded it on to Neo with a note.

And just in case you don't have anything else to do, here's the guy who burned down my woman's place last night. Can you find out who he works for?

I sent the text and didn't have to wait long for Neo's reply.

You don't want much, do you, Flint? What do I look like, your personal Google?

I smirked at the screen. Uh, yeah. And you love it. Don't try to tell me you don't.

I shot a look at Rochelle, but she was back to frowning at the screen as she replayed the video of the guy going through her house.

"He looks like he's searching for something, doesn't he?" She replayed it again as I rocked my fist forward. "What does he think I have—"

She sat up straight before she rose and headed for the coat tree near the door. I watched her dig around in her pockets until she withdrew something and returned to the computer.

"What do you bet he was looking for this?"

My gaze dropped to where she held a micro USB drive no bigger than the size of pea gravel. I raised my eyebrows and gestured my question at her hand.

"This was in my mother's letter. She said it had images on it of Creighton with some men named Butler and Bosworth respectively. She didn't know who they were, but she said there was something off with their association."

"You should make a copy of it and put it somewhere safe." I frowned. "The name Butler sounds familiar but I can't place it. Do you mind giving me a copy of the images? Maybe the Club can figure out who he is."

She bit her bottom lip as her hand closed around the USB drive and she eyed me for a long time. I could almost read her thoughts, but she didn't speak as she thought things through.

"I haven't seen what's on it yet." She plugged it into her computer. "Let's look at it first and I can make a copy of it." She opened the directory and highlighted all the files before saving it both to an innocuous folder called Matriarchal History. Then she copied that to her Cloud service.

"Okay. Let's look at this thing."

Rochelle opened a series of images of the same three men. The shorter one with the smarmy smile had to be Creighton. He had an oily look to him, like he could squirm out of the tightest spots. The other two were more average, though one looked like he had a stick shoved up his ass, all prim and proper in perpetual three piece suits. The third man appeared to be muscle. He had shoulders twice the width of the other two and a good six inches of height on them. He tended to wear turtlenecked sweaters and a sport jacket or trench coat, depending on the weather. He also looked fit, like he could bench press a crossover SUV.

I was about the dismiss him when Rochelle clicked on the pics after the meetings with Creighton. Prim dude conferred with the muscle, but his body language suggested that he deferred to the muscled goon. *Holy shit, is the goon the man in charge?*

Before I could share my thoughts, my phone chirped with a text from Neo.

Your arsonist is the right-hand man and local muscle for your pal Earl Creighton. Has the name Keith Grover. He's been arrested a few times, but the charges never stuck. Seems like your boy Keith has someone in law enforcement watching his back.

Now why did that sound familiar? I tapped Rochelle on the shoulder and showed her the text. She read it then frowned.

"Do you think that's why Creighton has gotten away with so much is because he has an in with the cops?"

I nodded. "Not just an in." I bit my lip then took a chance. "There's a shadow group within law enforcement. They're called Backlog and they make most biker clubs look like tricycle rallies with all the shit they're into. And they can get away with it because they're made up of cops, FBI, national law enforcement, judges, and politicians. Looks like Creighton got his start in Fort Collins because of Backlog's help."

She glanced back at the images on the screen. "Do you think Butler and Bosworth are part of Backlog?"

I nodded. "I don't know for sure, but I'd bet my sack of rocks they are."

She snorted. "I've played with your sack of rocks. No bet."

I barked a laugh as she closed the files and ejected the USB.

"But why would Creighton come after my mom? She didn't get these images until after he was elected to the city council. She didn't actively campaign against him, yet he targeted her. Why?"

"What was the date on the image files?"

She clicked on the images she'd saved. "A few weeks

before she was killed."

"Grover obviously was looking for something. I'd bet it was that USB with the images she'd captured."

"But why now? My mom was killed years ago. Why wait until now?"

I shrugged. "Maybe they wanted enough distance between your mother's murder and this new break in. Didn't you say she was murdered just outside the shop?" She nodded. "Maybe they didn't want to come under suspicion by anyone who cared to look. Plus it was another way to make Creighton look like he was right. The proprietor died just outside her shop and now the shop burns down. The shop itself must be bad luck."

She growled and it was the sexiest thing I'd heard from her other than her moans of pleasure. "There's nothing bad luck about my shop other than someone else's hatred."

"It depends on who's talking about it. If the only ones around are Creighton and his goons, people will believe what they say." We'd had that happen to the club, but it had worked in our favor. The rumors were actually started by Loki to create our reputation as a badass biker club and they only grew in the retellings.

"Well, he's not, but it didn't stop him from torching my place." She scowled. "There has to be a way to make him back off or leave me alone. And I want consequences for his murder of my mother."

I nodded. "We're working on that. We'll start with Grover and work up to Creighton."

"But Neo said they probably have someone in law enforcement watching their backs."

I smirked. "I didn't say we'd use law enforcement to take them down."

CHAPTER TEN

Rochelle

Flint's wicked grin gave me the chills as we backed up the images on the flash drive and shut down the computer.

"If I'm going to stay here, I'd like a few of my things, maybe even set up the workshop to start making product again." I reluctantly gave him the flash drive so he could pass it on to his friend Neo. "I'll need to run to the grocery store and my storage unit if you're serious about me being here longer than a couple of weeks."

Flint made sure I was looking at him as he signed his response. "I want you here forever, Rochelle."

It seemed a little soon for that, but I nodded. "Okay, then. Let me get my keys and we can head out."

"Let's stop at the Concrete Angels compound to get a van and we can move some of your larger items, or more of the smaller." He grabbed his phone and boots before heading for the door.

We stepped outside and the cold smacked into me like a frigid sledgehammer. I pretty much gasped and reminded myself to get my favorite scarf from my storage unit. I hated when my face got cold.

I hurried to my car and cranked the engine, hoping it

would heat up faster than it usually did. Flint wasn't bothered by the cold at all, and I had to admit I was jealous of his species' immunity. I got out to clear the snow off the windows and he helped as the engine warmed.

Once my car warmed enough to move, I slid behind the wheel and threw the heater fan on full blast, hoping it would make it to my frozen core. My teeth were still chattering as I pulled out after Flint, but at least my fingers had defrosted.

It was a pretty drive though I had to keep my focus because the tires slipped more than once. *Note to self – get snow tires.* I snorted. *Or an SUV.* We made it down to the main road safely and he turned us toward the massive front gates of the Concrete Angels MC compound. They actually resembled the fancy wrought iron gates I'd seen on the ultra-wealthy homes around Fort Collins, only with twice the height and thicker tines holding sharp arrow points.

It had been painted that primer gray I'd seen on old junker cars waiting to be painted their luminous colors and in the faded winter light, it blended right in with the shadows on the rocks and snow. But someone must have been manning the gate because it opened as Flint approached. He slowed up and waited for me to pull alongside.

"Wait out here. I'll bring the van and we can go to your storage unit."

I blinked. "You want me to wait for you out here?"

He nodded. "Trust me this once, Rochelle. Let's wait for the evening to face the firing squad of questions with my club."

"It's going to be like facing a firing squad?" I swallowed hard and bit my lip. "You know, I can get my own stuff and meet you back at your place. We don't have to use the van."

He shook his head. "It will go faster to use the van. Just wait out here. We'll save the drama for later tonight."

"There's going to be drama?"

He winked and waved as he drove his bike through the open gates past some of the guards. No one watched him, but there were plenty of curious gazes directed my way. The saucy side of me wanted to smile and wave at them, but the wiser part of me tried to decide if I wanted to deal with more drama after having ended up homeless because of arson. I also needed to decide if I wanted to be permanently involved with a biker from the Concrete Angels MC.

I'd heard that once a woman became a biker's old lady, she got the biker, but his first priority was always to the club. I'd also heard that women became property of their men and it was meant to protect them. It irritated me that the other men of the club didn't seem to see women as full people, just possessions that were either claimed or unclaimed. I was no one's unclaimed property.

My initial reaction was anger and disappointment, but the saner side of my mind insisted that I talk to Flint about it rather than fly off the handle and refuse to be anywhere near him for that reason. But I swore I'd lay a hex on anyone treating me as less than a full person.

To keep my mind away from the frustrating thoughts, I opened up my social media accounts to check on how the world was going and found it blown up with prayers and blessings and good thoughts.

What the?

Joslyn had posted about the fire, complete with images of the burnt building and the hot firefighters trying to beat back the flames. Some of them where Life Magazine-worthy. But people had come out of the woodwork to wish us well and offer their good energy. Someone else had even set up a GoFundMe drive to help us get back on our feet with supplies and incidentals.

The kindness of the community blew me away and I wiped away tears when Flint pulled up with the van. He shot a worried look my way and asked if everything was okay through the windows.

I nodded as I cleared my eyes and put down my phone, giving him the thumbs-up. He didn't look completely convinced but gestured for me to start driving down the mountain. I threw my car into gear and headed to my storage unit. I tried to get my emotions under control as we drove into town, but the sweetness overwhelmed me. When we arrived at the self-storage place, I texted Joslyn to check out the posts and to thank everyone for their generosity.

"Are you okay? I saw you crying." Flint scanned my face with worried eyes when he helped me out of my car.

"Yeah, I'm good. Great, actually. Sometimes this world can surprise me with the level of kindness and generosity." I wiped my face for the thousandth time and unlocked the padlock on the storage unit.

"What happened?" He stepped to look in the storage unit and grunted in surprise. "Sweet Goddess, are you taking all of this?"

I laughed at his look of dismay. "No, just the clothes, the brewing and cooking equipment, and the oil, cream, and soap supplies I stashed. And maybe my favorite reading chair. But be careful. That bitch is heavy. I'm impressed Joslyn and I could carry it."

"It won't be a problem." He waved my concerns off and given his gargoyle heritage, I supposed it would be easy for him. "Why were you crying, though?"

I shrugged as I grabbed the boxes into which I'd stuffed most of my closet. "Someone set up a GoFundMe account so we could start over in the New Year. It was very kind. Most of the time, we only hear about the shitty things people do to each other. But every now and again, people surprise me."

Flint nodded as he helped me load up my car with the personal items I wanted to take. Then we worked on loading the van with the chair and the equipment for the shop. It didn't take us too long, but Flint insisted on helping me reorganize the storage unit to make it easier to get to important items later. I didn't expect to get back into it until the New Year, but I couldn't argue with his logic.

By the time we'd finished the reorganization, it was late afternoon and the snow had started to fall again. Flint said he wanted to get the stuff up to his place before the snow got too thick, but my stomach growled and I realized I hadn't eaten since breakfast. I urged him to head on up the mountain while I stopped at the local grocery store to pick up some of my favorite teas and non-perishable foods.

He wasn't keen on leaving me, but I'd lived alone without him up until last night and I was perfectly capable of going shopping on my own. He snorted at my remarks and told me he'd empty the van at his place before he took it back to the club's compound. Then he'd meet me at his place unless I was still in town.

We parted ways and I headed to the closest grocery store as Flint continued on to the road leading up the hill. He waved as he passed me and I let his attention warm me down to my toes. It wasn't as cold in town as it was up on the mountain, but I still bundled up as I took my reusable bags in with me.

I tried to think of all my favorite meals that I might want to eat if we got snowed in, but I kept getting distracted by thoughts of being snowed in with Flint. *I definitely won't be getting much sleep.* That might not be true. Maybe I could convince him to do mid-day fucks so we could get plenty of sleep each night.

I laughed at myself as the cashier rang me up and then carried my groceries out to the car. I'd bought a couple of things that needed to be refrigerated but I figured they'd stay cool in the trunk if I got held up.

It was strange to think about this time of year and not being alone. This was the fourth Yule that my mother had been gone, but now I got to spend it with someone else, someone special and downright hawt. Mom would've approved. My holiday tree and ornaments had burned with the apartment, but it occurred to me we could actually put up a real tree this year.

And I'll need to get Flint a Yule gift.

The snow continued at a steady rate, but it wasn't bad enough to stop me from walking down the road to the boutique shops along the way. I locked my car and headed out, not sure what I could find that a gargoyle would like but hoping inspiration would strike me.

I'd found a couple little things that I hoped would make him smile when I walked past The Black Swan, a swanky place that had the reputation of serving the most exclusive clientele. The Who's Who of Fort Collins and Denver often ate there and it wasn't uncommon for celebrities who'd come to town to drop by for a bite.

I glanced in the windows as I passed and stopped dead. There, as if he'd never done anything wrong and couldn't be touched, sat Earl Creighton. He looked like he'd just been seated and was waiting for his party to join him.

Oh, I got your party right here, asshole.

I pulled open the elegant wood doors carved with two swan frescoes and stepped into the well-appointed foyer.

"Good evening. How many in your party?" The hostess picked up her pen as I stepped between the other diners waiting to be seated.

"Oh, I'm meeting someone here." I craned my neck to get a look around the fancy carved wooden partition. "And I see him now. No need to seat me. I can find my way."

She looked rather non-plussed at my assertiveness, but she didn't follow me as I headed straight for Creighton's table. His creepy right-hand man sat a few tables away but his gaze landed on me and he flinched in surprise. *Ah-ha, recognize me, do you, asshole?* The goon started to rise to his feet as I sashayed over to Creighton's table and plopped down in the chair across from him.

Earl Creighton was scum of the earth. That he existed at all said a lot for how much the human race had messed with nature, theirs or the usual kind. I'd seen a lot of disgusting things in my almost-forty short years, but he reminded me of the tar monster from Scooby Doo. On the outside, he looked rather put together, as rich people can, but on the inside he oozed rot and decay like the Bog of Eternal Stench.

"Good evening, Mr. Creighton. Might I have a word?"

He blinked in surprise and a little fear before his slimy smile curled his lips and he waved his personal thug back into his chair.

"Ah, Ms. Stone, how nice to see you. To what do I owe this honor?"

Glory, could he be any more frickin' pretentious?

I didn't bother to smile. "It's all to your own merits. You had me abducted in an attempt to kill me and now you've burned down my home. I'd like reparations."

His eyes widened in mock-astonishment. "My goodness, that's quite a list you have. And of course you have proof."

He said it like there was no way on the Goddess's green earth that I had dirt on him. I gave him a long, slow smile, and he swallowed hard. For once, his lack of understanding about witches and earth magic gave me an edge. The wards I'd placed kept a complete record of violations.

"Yup." I held up my phone and waved it at him. "Got it all digitally. Enhanced and in full color, too. Wanna see it?"

His smile vaporized and his eyes glittered with malice. "You nasty… bitch."

"I think the word you're looking for is 'witch'." Now I smiled sweetly. "The images got your boy back there, too. The malignant tumor with the ace of spades on his wrist. Looks like he's the one who torched my home. I'll make sure to inform the cops when I report you. Think of it this way. At least you won't be alone when arrested."

His malevolent smile returned. "You be sure to tell the Fort Collins police hello for me, and ask them if they got their Christmas donations. I'm sure they'll be thrilled to hear your fanciful tales."

I sat back in my chair, wondering how much I could goad him into saying. He already admitted he had the police wrapped around his little finger. I narrowed my eyes as he reached for his water glass and sipped. It would've been a stronger statement if he'd had some sort of alcohol, but the sentiment was there nonetheless. My anger ramped up and I fought to keep it off my face while I plotted my rejoinder.

"Maybe they'd change their minds if I showed them the images my mother captured of you and your chummy cohorts." I shrugged. "Ah well, we'll just have to see how they react. Nothing ventured, nothing gained, right?"

"Your mother. Didn't she get herself killed a few years ago?" Malice dripped from his falsely honeyed words. "Such a shame, that. I always liked her."

I barked a derisive laugh. "Cut the crap, Creighton. I know you had a hand in her murder."

He scoffed. "There's no proof of that. As I heard it, it was an unfortunate accident. A mugging gone wrong. So sad."

My anger spiked again. "You think there's no proof?" I snorted. "Then what was your creepy sidekick looking for in my house before he torched it, hmm? He went through a lot of my drawers and cabinets looking for something. Too bad he didn't find it. He was working so hard." I spread my hands as if there was nothing I could do about incompetence.

Anger glittered in his eyes, though his malicious smile remained. "Why are you here, Ms. Stone?"

"As I said, reparations for the damage you've done."

"And as I said, there's no proof, and even if you had some, no one would believe I had anything to do with it. Now if that's all, I have a meeting soon. Leave now, and I'll forget this ever happened." He sipped his water again.

I laughed. "Does that line actually work for you? Like I'm gonna believe you'll forget anything. And guess what, I won't either."

Earl looked like he wanted to throw a punch at me. Or at least his fork, but in the middle of a swanky restaurant in Fort Collins, he didn't have the pull to be allowed back.

"So now that I have your attention, Mr. Creighton, I think there's a deal to be made. What do you say?" I sat back in my chair as I stuffed my phone into my purse. I had no illusions about him getting a hold of it. We'd secured the images in various places, but if he got the phone, he'd be able to reach those places too. At least the Concrete Angels had copies and I doubted Creighton could get to their servers.

"I don't truck with witches." He crossed himself.

I laughed at his old fashioned phrasing. "Oh, buddy, you already set yourself up for "trucking" with witches when you came after me and burned my home to the ground. Now, if you don't want the magic to rebound on your ass, you're gonna make a deal with me." I shrugged one shoulder. "Do you want to hear my terms or are you gonna just sit there with that sour look on your mug like a petulant child?"

"I'm gonna get you for this." He snarled the words but I rolled my eyes and shook my head.

"You're not off to a great start, Mr. Creighton. The thing is, the more energy you put into trying to take me down, the faster the rebound of magic will be." I spread my hands again. "Now is your only chance to make this right. So do you want to hear my conditions or not?"

"Fuck you, bitch."

I almost spat out one of my curses. It wasn't deadly,

just extremely uncomfortable and uncurable if one didn't make efforts to take care of it. But someone walked by our table and dropped a folded napkin in front of me. I blinked, the intensity of the moment broken by the action, and a familiar scent accosted my nose. *Petrichor.* The scent of dry stone after the first rainstorm. One of my most favorite and treasured scents, and belonging to the one man who'd recently asked me to move in.

I glanced down at the napkin and realized there was a note tucked between the folds. I shot a look at Creighton, but he was whispering to his henchmen Keith over his shoulder. I used his distraction to slide the note below the table's edge and unfold it in my hands.

"Shit's gonna hit the fan. Time to go."

Unease slithered through me and I wondered how much time I had. Taking a deep breath, I shoved the note in my purse and grabbed my shopping bags as I straightened my shoulders.

"I'll give you some time to think about it, Mr. Creighton. I'm just gonna run to the ladies' room while you mull it over. Mmkay?" I rose and rapped my knuckles on the table as I shot him a mocking smile.

He scowled back at me but I wasn't waiting around to see what was coming. I threw my purse strap over my head and headed for the bathrooms near the front door. As soon as I was out of sight of the table, I zipped up my jacket and sailed out the door, scanning the road outside for my favorite Concrete Angel. I didn't know what was coming, but if Flint had walked through the restaurant, I knew it would be exciting. I was just surprised he hadn't beat Creighton to a pulp right there.

Would've been hell on the furniture. And bloodstains rarely came out of clothing.

I found Flint sitting on his bike down the block a bit and he nodded to me.

"Get on. We need to get you away from here. Now."

His sign language was emphatic and fast.

I didn't hesitate. I swung my leg over the back of his Harley and clamped my arms around his waist just as he drove us into the evening traffic. I had no idea what was about to befall Creighton, but it seemed better not to be present for it.

If for no other reason than to establish an alibi.

I tapped him on the shoulder and shouted into his ear. "My car's still in the grocery store parking lot. Take me there and we can drive the last of my stuff up to your place."

He nodded and pointed the motorcycle in the direction of the store as I held on tight. It didn't take too long and he pulled up beside my car as if he already knew where it was parked. I dismounted and threw my bags into the trunk before I headed for the driver's side door. Flint stayed on his bike and kept an eye out for anyone suspicious.

"Why did we need to leave so fast? What's going on?"

Flint fixed me with a smug smirk. "Neo hacked Creighton's accounts and reported all his credit cards stolen. He won't be able to pay for that fancy dinner he's planning to have."

I choked a laugh. "Oh my glory, you froze his accounts?"

Flint grinned but shook his head. "No, only canceled the cards. He'll get new ones in the mail in a few days."

I laughed again. "Damn, that's awesome. Let's go home and unpack the groceries to celebrate."

He nodded as he pushed his bike into motion, and I started my car. The grin stretching my lips wouldn't quit as we headed into the mountains and the thickening snowstorm.

CHAPTER ELEVEN

Flint

I didn't like Rochelle spending any time alone with Earl Creighton, but I really didn't want her around him when Neo's little prank came to pass. More than likely he'd blame Rochelle for the problems with his cards, and in some respects, he'd be right. Oh, Creighton would receive new cards in the mail eventually, but he'd have a tough time paying for supper tonight. Rochelle didn't need any more of his rage than she'd already received.

In addition, I'd given Karma a couple of Life Years™ to make sure this would be a very frustrating and scary Yule for Earl M. Creighton, and we were just getting started. But I didn't want Rochelle to get caught in the crossfire.

Though I usually dreaded when Loki demanded yet another holiday party in celebration of the Solstice, tonight I felt fairly festive. As long as Rochelle was with me. This would be the first time I introduced her to the rest of the club. And she'd know right away who was human and who was Elder Races.

The snow had let up and the night sat at a warm 28 degrees by the time we made it back to my place. Not bad with the cloud cover. It also meant the roads were pretty clear from what little sun had come through during the day. I'd unloaded most of her stuff into the workshop so it was out of the way, but her favorite reading chair I'd placed in the main room of the cabin. I would've done more but the spikes in her emotions had sent me flying down the mountain to get to her as quickly as possible. And I'd texted Neo to make sure the mudfucker Creighton had a rougher night than hers.

Rochelle pulled up under the overhang and we unpacked her car. She took the groceries and put them away while I brought in all her non-edible things. I didn't know where she'd want them so I took them to the bedroom and set them to the side. I figured she could put them away later.

When I came back out to the main room, I found her standing in the middle of it, holding up a small brightly colored gift bag. I tilted my head and frowned.

"What's this?"

"It's for you, for Yule Eve." She gently shook the bag. "Open it."

I took the dainty gift bag, surprised at its weight. I wanted to ask what it was, but that seemed a stupid question when I held the bag in my hands. I pulled out the dove gray tissue paper and looked inside…to find more tissue paper wrapped around something else. I mentally rolled my eyes at myself and pulled out the bundle, unrolling it in my hands.

Sweet goddess!

A long black velvet box fell into my palm. I discarded the tissue paper and pried open the lid. Nestled in golden satin lay a thick steel linked chain with a large polished labradorite pendant strung from it. Electric gold, green, and blue fire flashed across the stone as I balanced the pendant in my hand.

I raised my gaze to meet Rochelle's in wonder.

"I saw it in a local shop and immediately thought of you." She stepped forward and took the chain from my hands. "The pendant will look so sexy resting at the hollow of your throat."

She stepped behind me and fastened the chain around my neck. The stone settled on my chest right where she said it would and for the first time in centuries I felt grounded in the present. This was where and with whom I was supposed to be. Rochelle fit me better than anyone I'd ever met.

So now you just gotta tell her that she's bound to you for life. No biggie.

The snarky voice killed some of my joy and reminded me I had one week left before the consequences of not telling her spiraled out of control.

"Flint?" Rochelle stood in front of me with a worried frown. "Are you okay? Don't you like it?"

I wrangled my unease and gave her my best smile. "I like it a lot. It's perfect for me. Thank you."

"Are you sure? You looked like you were disappointed there for a moment."

"Not disappointed at all." I cupped her face and brought her lips to mine.

She tasted of rich mineral water and smelled of sun-warmed stone even in the dead of winter. The flavor and scent made me think of home, a place I was most welcome. I deepened the kiss, the slide of her tongue over mine making me entertain the thought of missing the holiday party completely. When she moaned, my cock hardened to solid basalt and I ground it against her softer mound.

All I wanted was to take her into the bedroom and fuck her until neither of us could remember our names. We'd renew the bond that entwined our lives and everything would be perfect.

Except you still haven't told her, numbnuts.

Yeah, that was a mood dampener, for sure.

I pulled back and rested my forehead against hers as we caught our breaths.

"We should probably go." Even my signing was half-hearted.

"Do we have to?"

I rocked my fist. "Yes."

"All right. But when we get back here, I want to ride your cock like a wild pony." She licked her lips and grinned, and I growled. My hot witchy woman knew just what to say to make me crave her more.

"We'll only stay as long as we need to." I let her go reluctantly.

"Good plan." She headed back over to the coat tree to grab her things. "The sooner we get there, the sooner we can leave. I have plans for you for Yule."

I liked the sound of that. I adjusted my dick into compliance and followed her out into the cold, locking the door behind us. I figured we'd take my bike since it wasn't far and it would fit in better than a car, and no one would stop us at the gate.

We made great time to the club's compound and Rochelle gasped as we came down the hill to the entrance.

"Good glory, that's a lot of lights."

The compound blazed like a fireworks display without all the explosions, though no lack of sound. Every cabin had been festooned with lights along the rooflines and even the barracks and the Barn had been decked out. More light ropes had been wound along the tops of the chain-link fence around the perimeter and the clubhouse had a glowing ropes around each window.

Damn, the grounds crew's been busy.

When we pulled through the gates under the stoic gaze of Quan-Yin, my security partner and Foo-Dog shifter, she gave us a nod and a hand signal to be careful.

What does she mean with that?

I found out soon enough as the yard was full of people

in various states of inebriation and dress. I hissed as I damn near ran over one of my brothers wearing a Rudolph the Red-nosed Reindeer costume with a honey riding his back. I jerked the handlebars to miss them, barely, and picked my way through the partygoers to the Barn. Music filled the yard from the clubhouse playing *Grandma Got Run Over by a Reindeer.*

We parked and Rochelle dismounted, but didn't venture far. Instead, she took in the festivities with a sexy half-smile on her face. I secured my bike in the Barn and stopped beside her.

"You okay?" I signed with one hand as I touched her shoulder.

She nodded. "Yeah. This is one helluva Yule celebration. Is it always like this?"

I shrugged and kept my hands in the light. "Pretty much, though this year we have more to celebrate. A couple of our members found their..." I stumbled over the word to accurately describe Numbers and Marshal. "Significant Other" sounded so impersonal, but Numbers wasn't Scott Free's mate—I'd learned humans didn't mate like the Elder Races.

"Long-term Lovers?"

That was as good a description as any so I nodded.

"That's a great reason to celebrate." She sounded wistful and I wanted to tell her she was *my* long-term lover, but it didn't seem the right time.

And timing is everything.

"Let's go get something to drink." I waved at the clubhouse and we wove our way through the melee of drunk bikers and honeys around burning barrels to keep them warm. Some were already canoodling and making their own fires.

The party was really rocking inside the clubhouse, though, and Rochelle stopped to take it in as we stepped through the door. Samurai stood like a sentry and stopped us, wearing a wizard's hat with golden stars and the tip folded over. Usually he was the most stoic member of our crew, but tonight a spark of amusement glinted in his eyes.

"None shall pass...without trying my Shochu and Bailey's White Christmas." He thrust a pint glass into Rochelle's hands with a white concoction that smelled like sugar, cream, and misadventures.

"Uh, okay." She gave Sam a half smile and sipped the drink, her eyes widening as it hit her tongue.

"Oh, that's very good." She offered the glass to me. "Have some, Flint."

I shook my head. "I'm working."

Sam's gaze fastened on me with a challenge. "None shall pass without a taste."

I narrowed my eyes and he cracked a rare smile.

"It's the price of entry."

I shook my head but sipped the frou-frou drink. It was surprisingly good with just enough kick to make anyone happy quick, particularly humans. Sam bowed with amused reverence and nodded.

"Thank you, Flint. You've made my night. You may pass."

We entered without more trouble, but I found out later that Viper, Torch, and Attila had bet Sam I wouldn't try his drink. The loser of the bet got a full week of snow shoveling the yard.

"What was that about?" Rochelle followed me over to the real bar.

I shook my head and shrugged. "No idea. He's usually not in the thick of things when it comes to parties. But he's in rare form tonight." We stopped at the bar. "What do you want to drink?"

Rochelle let her gaze rest on the rowdy partiers behind her and narrowed her eyes. "Any chance I can get a virgin hot apple cider? I recognize it's a party, but I'm not much of a drinker and that white Christmas thingie had enough alcohol in it to knock me on my ass."

I nodded and waved to Chem behind the bar. Our resident bartender moved in my direction, her dark eyes taking in me and Rochelle with her typical watchful expression.

"Tell her what you'd like." I signed to Rochelle but mouthed the words so Chem could read my lips.

"Virgin hot apple cider, please."

Chem raised her eyebrows. "Who's this, Flint? You got yourself a honey tonight?"

I shook my head and gestured for the pen she had stuck between her boobs in the corset she wore. Chem raised one eyebrow and handed me the pen. I wrote "NOT HONEY, ROCHELLE" on one of the paper napkins and showed it to her.

"Woops, sorry. Didn't recognize you so I thought you were one of the hangers-on. You said you want virgin apple cider?"

Rochelle nodded. "Yes, please."

"Comin' up." Chem turned away with a small derisive smirk on her face.

Rochelle noted it as well because she raised her eyebrows at me. "Something wrong with my drink choice?"

I shook my head. "Not at all. It might be she has to make some fresh because we usually spike it."

"Oh. I didn't mean to ask for something extra. Although." She turned and looked behind her at the various people drinking unusual concoctions. "Seems like there's plenty of other extra going on around here."

"Here's your cider." Chem held out another oddly shaped mug. It looked more like a beer stein and steam rolled off the top.

"Thanks." Rochelle took it and sniffed. "Smells delicious."

Chem nodded. "Should be. Grub made it fresh for

you."

Rochelle sipped. "Tell him thanks. It's very good."

Chem waved and moved away down the bar to help someone else. I followed her with my gaze, wondering what that had been about. No one usually cared who I brought to the clubhouse. Of course, it was rare that I brought anyone at all. *Maybe that's it.*

"What is all this, then?"

Rochelle and I turned to see Attila standing with Dollhouse and Loki, all of them fixated on Rochelle. I swallowed a groan and tried to find my patented stoic expression. Things rarely went well when Loki showed up. The Goddess had warned me I had until New Year's to tell Rochelle about our relationship, but Loki rarely did anything expected.

Neither of us said anything and waited them out. It became a weird staring contest of wills, as if anyone could outstare a gargoyle. And apparently, Rochelle felt no need to chime in. I didn't know what she was waiting for, but she said nothing at all, and after a few unspoken seconds, Attila and Dollhouse began to fidget.

Rochelle took a sip of her cider and looked up expectantly, as if surprised at their attention. She didn't say anything, though, and I found myself amused at their discomfort.

"So who is this, Flint?" Dollhouse broke the silence first, her gaze fixed on Rochelle.

"Rochelle Stone." I spelled out her name.

"Och, is this your wee lassie you were tellin' me about?" Attila's gaze became assessing as he looked Rochelle up and down. "Ye dinna tell me she was a ginger temptress."

I raised an eyebrow. Was he really trying to hit on my woman?

Rochelle destroyed Attila's appraisal when she turned to me and grinned. "Ginger temptress? Sounds like a good

Samhain drink. I should add that to my recipe grimoire."

"You have a recipe grimoire?" Dollhouse's voice lightened with curiosity.

Rochelle nodded. "Yes. I use it to keep track of all the mixtures for the salves and creams and treats I make in my store."

Dollhouse's eyes lit up. "You have a store? What do you sell?"

"I sell crystals and healing items for anyone who wants to take a more balanced and natural approach to skin and beauty regimes. I even write a blog about it called The Better Bitter Brew."

"Oh my glory, I know that blog and your shop, The Herb Cabinette. Didn't it burn down recently?"

Rochelle nodded.

Dollhouse leveled her gaze at me with a scowl. "Why didn't you tell me you were going out with the owner of The Herb Cabinette? It's like my favorite shop."

I shrugged and spread my hands in helpless surprise.

"Is this why yer lookin' for a new place, Flint? The lassie needs a new shop?" Attila smiled broadly.

I nodded but Rochelle answered for me. "He was hoping you could help me find a good place, but I understand if it's too much to ask."

"Och, it's nothin', lass. As long as we're usin' yer money, I'll find you the best place for your needs." He winked.

Rochelle smiled, unaffected by his charm. "That would great, thank you. It seemed like it was going to be a dark Yule with the loss."

"Weel, no need to worry yer pretty head. We'll find ye the right spot after Hogmanay." Attila raised his glass of beer and sauntered away to join the mob around the pinball machine where Trigger was holding court.

"I've always wanted to learn more about herblore. Can we talk about it some time?" Dollhouse had become more animated than usual and it was good to see. Even I'd noticed her withdrawing a bit over the last year.

Apparently, Rochelle sensed something because she shot me a look and then smiled wider at Dollhouse. "How about now? I have time, don't I, Flint?"

I rocked my fist. "Yes. Take your time. I need to talk to Loki."

"Great." She leaned in and kissed me on the lips, momentarily distracting me from the president still waiting. "I'll come find you when I'm done."

I squeezed her in response as she pulled away and followed Dollhouse to a somewhat quieter part of the clubhouse. She passed Numbers ruling the pool tables again and schooling someone at pool while Scott looked on. Torch was actually drunk, something I'd never seen in the dragon shifter, and plucked at a guitar as he stared with moon-eyes at Quan-Yin who stood with Karma. She didn't seem to notice Torch's attention as they both watched the ensuing party far more stoically than the rest of our brethren.

"Flint, a word, ja?" Loki had made his move and I tilted my head to consider. "It'll be short, I promise. I know you want to get back to your woman."

The latter was true, but I wasn't certain about the former. Loki had a habit of making mountains out of cairns for his own amusement, especially when it came to the hearts of others.

"Yeah, okay."

I followed Loki through the partying crowd to his office and closed the door behind us to keep the noise down to a dull roar. He settled behind his desk with one leg hanging over the arm of the chair.

"So, this is the woman who is taking all your time, ja?" A smile curled his lips when I didn't respond. "You are lucky, brother. It has been a long time coming, ja?"

I nodded carefully.

"Does she know you're not human?"

I nodded again, wondering where he was going with this line of questioning.

"Det er bra." His smile lost some of his wattage.

Score one point for me. Now he couldn't fuck with our relationship because she wouldn't be surprised that I was a gargoyle.

"I understand from Neo you have him looking into this Earl M. Creighton, ja?"

I nodded. "We have video of his henchman burning down Rochelle's place, and we suspect he was the same guy who murdered her mother three years ago. And from the digging he's done, it looks like Creighton has been bankrolled or supported by Backlog. Neo has all the footage."

Loki's smile disappeared completely. "Who is this Creighton person?"

I gave Loki the rundown of everything we'd learned and why we'd messed with Creighton that night. Loki's expression grew more and more amused as I mentioned hacking his credit cards.

"That is a good trick. I think he will have a rough night, ja?"

I rocked my fist. "Yeah, but I also think he'll blame Rochelle. He seems to have Wiccaphobia and with Backlog's help, he has local power. I don't want any of it to come back to her."

Loki nodded and tapped his lower lip with one finger. "I understand this. Is she your woman, Flint? Is she going to become part of the club?"

The question was trickier than the words suggested. The easy answer was yes, but with Loki, that could mean one of his contracts, and those rarely benefited anyone other than Loki. *Though, Numbers, Eric, and Haley have made out pretty well.*

Yeah, Michael and Scott's old ladies weren't suffering

at all, though they had initially, and Karma's old man had definitely found peace in his life being her sub. Yeah, I knew all about Karma's proclivities, and I was glad she found happiness. I also knew about Loki's, but I wasn't about to say anything to him. I just kept it as an ace up my sleeve should I need to move him in the right direction.

"She is my woman, and that means she'll be part of the club. But she won't be living here on the compound and she'll have her own business in town."

Loki's eyes narrowed. "Where she has her business is immaterial, ja? She's your woman so she's a member and must abide by our rules. This isn't up for debate, my old friend. We have these rules for a reason, and even I must abide by them in my own way. Contracts must be signed."

My gut sank. I didn't want to deal with contracts. What if that ruined what I'd finally managed to find with Rochelle? But no one got out of signing a contract with Loki, not even me.

"All right." I rocked my fist. "But not until after Hogmanay. And we will defend her against Creighton and Backlog, even before she signs a contract."

"Agreed." He rolled to his feet and spit into his palm before offering it to me.

I licked my own palm and clasped his hand, sealing our bargain in the old way. The magic of our deal rippled through the room and fluffed the golden rutile-colored strands of his long hair away from his face. His blue fluorite eyes sparkled in the light and I hoped I hadn't stepped into something I couldn't control. With Loki, anything was possible.

CHAPTER TWELVE

Rochelle

"Oh my glory, I'm going stir-crazy here. There's nothing for me to do now that I've designed most of our public holdings." Dollhouse rolled her eyes as she took a gulp of Sam's magical white drink that he'd tried hand to me more than once since we'd arrived. "It's not enough, y'know? I'm bored out of my skull!"

She'd shouted the last line but with the party noise going on in the clubhouse, it went unnoticed.

"I mean, I got my architectural degree and I've used it plenty of times, but I need something else to do." She rolled her eyes to me and gave me a pout that was probably supposed to be cute if she wasn't drunk. "It's the end of another year and I'm nowhere different than I was...I am, whatever. That's why I want to learn herb lore. I love plants. Why do you think we have all those planters around the compound? I made sure because the energy of plants is so good for everyone."

I couldn't do anything but agree since Dollhouse seemed to be on a tear and I was just along for the ride. We'd discussed herb lore a little and it seemed like she'd be great at it, but Sam's drink had eroded her sobriety and with it, her inhibitions of talking to a complete stranger about her personal feelings.

"Tell you what, after Hogmanay—"

"Hog mah what?"

"Hogmanay, New Year's, we'll talk more about herb lore and your interest in learning it." I patted her arm as she swung a brilliant smile to me.

"Okay! That would be wonderful." Her face crumpled into a grateful smile. "You're good people, Rochelle. Really. Flint's a lucky guy to have found you. You're gonna be his old lady, right? That'll be so awesome."

I just smiled as she slurped down the last of her drink.

"Welp, I better go get another drink." Her smile turned goofy. "Can't be at a party without a drink. Can I get you anything?"

I shook my head. "Nope. I'm good. You go ahead." I hoped she'd get water or maybe some tea as she tottered off toward the bar.

I took a deep breath and let it out slow before sipping the last of my cider. Thank the Goddess I'd chosen to go with non-alcoholic drinks tonight. I didn't need to figure out how to negotiate this biker club while intoxicated. *And Flint intoxicates me enough as it is.*

Speaking of my hot biker, I glanced around the festivities from where I stood near the offices in the back. I hadn't seen where Flint had gone but between the guy plucking the guitar over by the bar and the raucous pool competition at the tables, there was plenty to watch while I waited.

Despite my intention to keep focused in a strange place, the world blurred a bit and the sound faded to be background noise as a Goddess Message filled my awareness. The picture in my mind showed me standing with Flint beneath a large tree with the bare branches of winter. He held my hands and gazed at me with intense hunger and desire. My nipples hardened beneath shirt and I

146

was grateful I still wore my coat.

As we stood there holding hands, new buds and leaves sprouted on the branches above our heads and the snow beneath our feet melted to reveal the new grass. Warmth touched our cheeks but Flint's hunger and desire never waned. In fact, it only intensified like a bonfire at Ostera.

Then the leaves on the tree filled out into full growth and the grass rose to our knees, carpeting the world around us. The tree shaded us from the summer heat and the air cradled us with the love and fertility of Lithia while Flint held my hands.

Again, change came in the form of the leaves of the great tree turning wondrous colors of gold, orange, red, and brown as the temperatures cooled. But Flint's attention never wavered and his hunger and desire heated me up and down until I felt consumed with the need to harvest the fruits of his love at Samhain before the year swung back to the cold of Yule.

The vision broke and brought me back to the light and sound of the party around me, but my mind remained on the vision of the changing tree, and Flint's unwavering presence beneath it. What was the Goddess trying to tell me? I rubbed my chin and pushed the festivities away as I puzzled it out. Was She telling me Flint was the perfect man for me, the perfect partner to weather all the seasons?

I let those questions tumble about in my mind as I caught a few people giving me curious looks, but none of them approached me. I definitely felt like the outsider until a pair of arms slid around my waist from behind and the scent of petrichor filled my nose. A rough growl made my heart flutter as the man kissed my neck under my ear. I shivered with delight and closed my eyes as I leaned into his warm, hard chest.

I felt safe and protected in Flint's embrace and for just a moment I fully relaxed into his arms. This was where I wanted to be, nestled close to him with his scent and his body surrounding me. Or over me or between my legs. I wasn't picky.

He let go and turned me in his arms so I could see his hands. Glancing down at my empty mug, he pointed. "Do you need more cider?"

I shook my head. "No, I'm good. I don't really need to go through that argument again. But if there's any tea, I'd take that."

He nodded. "Let's go out to the pool deck. It'll be cold, but quieter there. I want to talk to you about something."

I tilted my head. "Is everything okay?"

He tipped his flat hand from side to side. "Mostly. Don't want any confusion between you and me. Wait here. I'll get your tea."

He ducked off toward the bar as I contemplated his words. What confusion was he talking about? I shot a look toward the offices and found Loki observing me with quiet calculation in his gaze. What the hell had happened in that office? If Loki was truly the Norse God of Mischief, it would definitely be exciting no matter what happened.

And not always in good ways.

Fortunately, Flint returned with a cup of tea in a regular-sized mug and ushered me down the hallway past the offices with a nod at Loki. The prez of the club nodded back and his lips curled into a smug smile that gave me the creeps.

Yikes, that guy makes me nervous.

Flint pushed open the door to the pool deck and the silence of the wintery night closed around us. The sound and overwhelming heat of the party disappeared, and we were left with the almost sacred quiet that only happens around that time of year. There was peace, and promise, and patience in the air, and I took a few moments to bask in it before it was disturbed by whatever Flint had to say.

"It's beautiful out here."

He nodded as he guided me over to some benches with thick blankets waiting on them. "I made sure we had something to keep us warm."

I raised my eyebrows. "So you've been planning this for a while?"

He shrugged as he swept the snow off the bench and handed me a thick wool blanket. "It was the only place I could think would be quiet enough to talk and I don't want there to be any room for confusion. I'm too old for that shit."

I laughed as I settled onto the bench with the tea steaming in my hands. "That makes two of us. So what do you want to talk about?"

He sat beside me with the other blanket over his lap and kept his gaze on me. "I need to talk to you about the club and what it means to be my woman."

Unease skittered across my awareness. Was he saying he'd have to break up with me? That would make a shitty Yule for sure. But I'd meant what I said when I'd told him I was too old for confusion, so I told my conclusions to jump somewhere else until I had all the information.

"Does this have to do with being your property? Like wearing a leather jacket that says "Property of Flint" on my back?"

He nodded and shrugged. "Kind of. The Property banners protect you from others who might not see you as an old lady."

"Like Chem tonight?"

"Right. She thought you were a honey, one of the women who come here to get some biker dick or pussy, and have no say in what happens in the club."

"I didn't see a property tag on Dollhouse tonight."

"No, she's a full member. If she ever gets a long-term partner, that partner will get the property tag on their jacket."

I frowned a moment as I let my fingers smudge the

condensation on my mug. "Is that what I am to you, Flint? A long-term partner?"

He rocked his fist. "Yes. You'll always be my partner."

I bit my lip as hope surged in my chest. I so wanted to be his, but stuff like this faded all the time and bikers weren't necessarily known for monogamy.

"How do you know that's true?"

He sighed and glanced up at the icicles hanging from the edges of the eaves. Each one caught the light around the pool deck and reflected it back like jewels against the night.

"The Goddess visited me last night."

I blinked in surprise. Why did his face look so grim? "Okay."

"She congratulated me on finding my perfect partner. The mate who would make my world seem complete and balance me in every way."

That sounded like good news, but he still looked uncomfortable.

"Isn't this a good thing?"

He nodded. "Yes, yes, very good news."

"Then why do you look like someone just gave you a death sentence?"

He rubbed the back of his neck and looked away, and some of my unease came back. Why was he acting so fidgety? I sipped my tea and waited him out, trying to loosen the knot in my chest that tightened with every breath. *It's going to be okay. It can't be that bad...can it?*

"I'm sorry."

I blinked. Had I read his signs right? "Did you just apologize?" He nodded, contrition all over his face. "Why?"

"I didn't know. Had I known, I would've made a different decision."

"Know what? What decision?" The knot tightened more and I rubbed my breastbone to make it loosen up.

"To have sex with you."

Well this was turning out to be a shitty Yule after all. He wouldn't have chosen to have sex with me? I couldn't look at him anymore and tried to hold onto my composure. The man I'd had the best sex of my life with was telling me he was sorry we'd done it. I grunted when the pain stabbed me in the chest and I rubbed my breastbone again to relieve it.

"You're going to have to explain that because right now it sounds like you're breaking up with me, even after you said the Goddess congratulated you on finding your perfect partner." I was amazed my voice sounded so steady.

"What? No, no, not breaking up with you." His eyes grew wide and he got off the bench before kneeling in the snow in front of me. "Oh, glory, I'm fucking this up. I should've just told you and let the gravel land where it would."

"Tell me what?" I held back tears and hoped he didn't say he was already married or mated.

Oh sweet Goddess. Did he find someone else who was his perfect mate? The spike of pain drove impossibly deeper.

"Just don't hate me when I tell you." He searched my face but my fear rose too high to contain.

"Just spit it out, Flint!"

He swallowed hard. "Okay. We're mated for life and bound by that mating. When I bit you. It bound us together as perfect mates." He hunched his shoulders and turned his head to look at me out of the corner of his eye as if he expected me to hit him.

"What?" All my fear morphed into surprise.

"When I bit you during sex, I accidentally bound us together as mates." He gave me a guilty grin that looked painful.

I narrowed my eyes. "Why would you apologize for that? Didn't you tell me you enjoyed the sex?"

"I'm not apologizing for the sex, I'm apologizing for biting you." He grimaced.

"I'm still not getting this. Why are you sorry?"

"Because I didn't know it would bind us together permanently and I didn't give you the choice beforehand. It was never my intention to force you into anything before talking to you about it. So I'm sorry for taking the choice from you."

Oh. "So it's a done deal?"

He nodded, the edges of his mouth turned down.

"But the Goddess said I'm your perfect mate?"

He nodded again.

I took a sip of tea to organize how I felt. On the one hand, I understood his concern. He'd never struck me as a man who made any spontaneous decisions or those he hadn't carefully considered. It was a momentous decision, one that affected me as well as him, and I appreciated his reluctance to make a unilateral decision without me.

But on the other, I would've been cheering with joy to know the Goddess approved of our match and had taken all the guesswork out of the start to our relationship. We were perfect mates in the eyes of the Goddess and She knew a helluva lot more about love than most of us. Plus, She'd sent her Goddess Message just before we came outside to talk.

"Is that the only reason you're not happy with our connection?" I met his gaze and tried to gauge his reaction, which wasn't easy given his species.

"Not happy?" His brow wrinkled in puzzlement. "Why would you think I'm not happy?"

I barked a disbelieving laugh. "Uh, let me think. You're twitchy. You're apologetic. You're sorry we had sex."

Flint snarled something incoherent before he settled and met my gaze with the same hunger and desire I'd seen in the Goddess Message.

"I want you, Rochelle. I want only you. I didn't do this right. I should've asked you if you wanted to be the mate of a gargoyle, but I didn't know the urge to bite you during sex was the clue that we were meant to be mates. Now that I have bitten you, I can't get you off my mind and all I want to do is love and protect you, no matter where you are or what you're doing. You are my perfect mate, like the Goddess said, and I want you in my life forever more." He tilted his head and the corner of his mouth quirked upward. "Is that better?"

I laughed again, this time with amusement. "Much better. It wasn't fun to think you felt like you'd made a mistake having sex with me."

"I'm sorry. I hadn't thought out how I wanted to tell you and when Loki showed up tonight, I knew I'd run out of time. So I was flustered and rushed, and that made me fuck it up." He grabbed a hand and kissed my knuckles before releasing me and holding up the pendant. "You gave me this because it made you think of me. But the moment you put it on me, I was exactly where I needed to be. You're my perfect mate, Rochelle, and nothing anyone does will change that."

I looked at the pendant resting against the hollow of his throat, just as sexy has I thought it would be, and smiled.

"It just suited you so well. But I still have one question."

He inclined his head to let me ask.

"Do I still have to wear something that says "Property of Flint" on it?"

He shrugged. "It might just be easier than fending off the advances of every single guy in the club or anyone who visits with the club."

"Would it mean a lot to you if I wore it?" As much as I hated being someone's property, I'd do it to make Flint happy. Because in my mind it went both ways. No one had better touch my gargoyle.

He shrugged again and rocked his fist. "Yes."

I nodded sharply. "Okay."

"Okay?" He raised his eyebrows.

"Okay, I'll wear a jacket or vest or whatever that shows I belong with you." I narrowed my eyes. "But I need to be sure it goes both ways. I better not find you riding any of the honeys around here or there will be hell to pay."

Flint growled and leaned into my space. His intense gaze locked with mine. "Neevvvrrrrr."

The sound from his growly voice rumbled inside my chest and down into my soul. He meant what he said and I felt it deep. Then he brushed his lips across mine and slid his tongue into my mouth when I opened to him.

He tasted of petrichor and hot desire, and I suddenly wanted to skip out of the Yule's Eve party to go home. I wanted to seal the deal when we both understood the ramifications.

"Take me home, Flint."

He pulled back and grinned. "To the cabin?"

"Yeah, to the cabin where I want to ride your cock like a wild pony, remember?"

He grinned as he helped me up. "I remember you saying something like that, yeah. Let me say our goodbyes and we'll scratch gravel."

I grinned as we draped the blankets over the bench and headed back inside. The party hit us with a wall of sound and light, but it didn't matter to me. I floated on excitement and desire as if I'd received a proposal for happily-ever-after. Considering a madman had burnt down my shop and still threatened to come after me, I'd never expected to feel this way, ever. But I was going to ride it all the way to the end.

And Flint's cock, too.

We just had to get out of the party to do it.

****

Flint

Despite the rocky start, I'd managed to tell Rochelle everything about our mating before Loki stuck his nose into it. The only thing I hadn't mentioned was the contract that was no doubt in the future of our relationship. But that could wait. I was determined to get out of the party and back to my home as quickly as possible.

Our home.

The thought sparked pleasure in my chest and I grinned, which made a few of the brothers and the honeys take a step back. I rumbled a laugh. Not many people could handle a grinning gargoyle and most of my Elder Races brethren had never seen me grin.

"Holy fuck, are you okay, Flint?" Torch eyed me suspiciously. "What the hell are you grinning at?" He swayed a little as he faced me and I hoped he wouldn't keel over, taking those near him down.

"I'm gonna get laid tonight."

Torch's eyes narrowed and smoke rose from his nose as his shifter's disguise failed a bit. "What did you say?"

"He said he's going to get laid tonight." Rochelle stepped up beside me and grabbed my ass through my jeans. "And boy, is he ever."

"Fuuuuccckkk." Torch's jaw dropped and he staggered a bit as he waved a wine goblet. "I wanna get in on that."

I growled but Rochelle just laughed. "You need to find your own partner to celebrate with, this one's mine."

"Aww." Torch gave a good impression of a drunk puppy dog but Rochelle wasn't swayed.

Her amusement was the only thing keeping me from reminding him she was my mate. I stalked through the partiers until I got closer to the doors where Karma still stood with Quan-Yin and Viper. A half smile curled Quan-

Yin's lips as she watched Torch's antics, a noteworthy occurrence for my stoic security partner.

"Everything good?" I signed at Quan-Yin and she nodded.

"Yes, everything's fine. Are you heading out for the night?"

I rocked my fist. "Yeah. Gonna spend some quality time with my woman."

"Good choice. Just remember, you're on duty for New Year's."

It was unusual for Quan-Yin to ask for any time off, but then it was strange for me to do so, and I'd asked for tonight. She hadn't said what she was going to do with her time, but I admit I was curious.

I nodded sharply as Rochelle tugged me out the door into the relative silence of the yard. Michael stood outside under the eaves with his woman tucked against his side, watching the snow fall. He didn't say anything as his gaze took in Rochelle, but he nodded with an approving smile. I never thought I'd want the approval of an Archangel on my actions, but it was a nice addition to my already good evening.

Settling Rochelle on the back of my bike felt perfect, like she was meant to be there, and the Goddess had said she was. I fired up the engine and let it warm a bit as we watched the snow fall outside of the barn. She snuggled up to my back and it was the most magical Yule I'd ever experienced.

We rode home in the snow, a gentle curtain of white in the cold night. Home. It hadn't really felt like that before I met Rochelle. It was a place I crashed when I was sick of company. A spot for a little bit of peace in the humans' overly hectic world. But with Rochelle's presence, suddenly my quiet spot became a peaceful sanctuary.

I parked the bike under the overhang and helped Rochelle dismount in the relative warmth of the carport.

She smiled at me before hurrying to the cabin door. I let her in and hung up my jacket just in time to see her carry a tuning fork and a small silver hammer.

"I'll be back."

Before I could say anything, she ducked back out the door. I followed, curiosity igniting in my chest, and watched her withdraw a candle and a lighter from her pocket. I wanted to ask what she was doing but her back was to me and she couldn't see my hands.

"I'm setting up the wards." She glanced over her shoulder with a smile. "I don't want us disturbed tonight if I can help it."

She lit the candle and stood it in the snow at her feet. Then she closed her eyes and struck the tuning fork with the hammer. The sound echoing through the night silence resonated with me and all the rocks around us until the whole mountainside hummed with untapped energy.

The humming intensified as she raised her hands and gathered the energy between them like a woven tapestry. I couldn't actually see the strands she wove together, but I could feel them chime each time she grasped one and pulled it taut against the others. She worked methodically, tugging, weaving, and releasing until a virtual net of earth energy stood in a dome over our home.

She hit the tuning fork again and whispered words as old as the earth, asking for the rocks and stones to protect us and warn us of impending intruders. She asked for protection against malicious and toxic energy that would erode our peace, and she thanked the mountain for the strength of its embrace and foundation. She hit the tuning fork a third time and bowed her head in thanks before snuffing the candle at her feet and turning around.

"There, that should do it."

Hell yeah, it should. I'd never run across another earth witch with that much power or connection to her environment. I probably shouldn't have been surprised given how the stone in my cabin had resonated for her, but she still drew my admiration and adoration.

"Let's go inside. It's freezing out here and I want to ride your hot cock."

And that was why I loved her. She went from reverent to sexually insistent in seconds.

"Fuck yeah."

We retreated into the cabin and she locked the door behind us before shucking her coat and boots beside the door. I hadn't bothered to put my coat back on but I removed my boots before following her into the bedroom where candles dropped pools of soft light into the darkened corners.

Rochelle hadn't turned on the lights, but the candlelight was enough to show off her sensual curves and the softness of her hair. My cock rose hard and insistent against my fly. I growled and her enticing smile widened while her eyes flashed. She sauntered closer and rested a hand on my chest as she met my gaze.

"Let me help you get undressed." Her hand slid across my chest and over my shoulder as she stopped behind me. "Starting with your vest."

"Cut." I spelled out the word as she watched over my shoulder.

She pulled the leather off my shoulders and laid kisses along the muscles, making me shiver.

"Why do you call it that?" She set the cut on a chair and returned to my side, trailing her fingers around the waist band of my jeans.

I whimpered just a little as her finger tips sent sparks of erotic sensation straight to my dick. My hands trembled as I tried to sign an explanation.

"It came from back when bikers wore cut-off denim jackets—leather used to be too expensive…" My hands faltered when she unbuttoned my jeans and slid the zipper down my sensitive shaft. I moaned and closed my eyes before continuing. "When bikers started forming clubs, they needed a place to…"

I hissed as she pushed my jeans off my hips and stroked the skin there. Every seductive touch set my body on fire and I could barely keep a coherent thought in my head, much less sign what she wanted to know.

"They needed a place to what?" Rochelle crouched at my feet and I jerked my eyes open to take in every fuckin' sexy inch of her lush body. "What did they need a place for?"

I shot her a blank look.

"You said the bikers needed a place for something when they joined clubs." She helped me step out of my jeans as my mind finally reconnected to our conversation.

"They needed a place to put their patches and colors. Leather worked better than denim at protecting the biker if they ate asphalt. Some bikers insist the name "cut" came from the German word *kutte*, which means "battle coat" where you display your colors and affiliations, but I don't care as long as you keep doing that."

She'd started to stroke my cock with her hands, sliding one along the stiff veined shaft while the other caressed my balls, and I was done with explanations. I just wanted to watch and feel and enjoy.

"Don't stop talking on my account." She grinned up at me before she wrapped her lips around my dick and licked the head.

I couldn't have answered her if I tried. All that came out was a groan as the wet heat closed around my cockhead and pulled me into an erotic stupor. She hummed against my stiff flesh and it reverberated throughout my body, making my cock flex and my balls tighten up.

Holy fuck, her sweet mouth.

She took me deep, caressing the shaft with her tongue. She followed the veins with the tip while she massaged my scrotum with her fingers and I had to brace my knees to keep from collapsing in delicious pleasure.

So much for the famed gargoyle strength.

Yeah, it wasn't working well for me if this one lovely witch could literally bring me to my knees. Rochelle pulled back and dragged her teeth over the edges of the head. Stars exploded behind my eyes as ecstasy zapped my balls, threatening my release. How the hell had she done that so fast? Like the stone I was connected to, my orgasms usually built slowly, like a magma diapir rising closer to the surface of the earth. But Rochelle had accelerated my need and desire, until I was holding on to my release by my claws.

I must have stiffened enough for her to notice because her humming increased along with the strokes to my balls. I glanced down to find her hazel eyes trained on me, watching with rapt attention to my reactions. That was even hotter than her sucking me off and I pulled my lips back from my elongating teeth as my human disguise slipped a little.

That just encouraged her and when she encircled my cock with her hand and squeezed, I was done for. I threw back my head and roared as my release shot from my tightened balls. Rochelle's humming stopped as she swallowed down my load, but she kept stroking my balls and squeezing my cock like a cock ring, and I rolled with the momentum of her erotic massage.

I want more.

Fuck yeah, I wanted more. I wanted to sink my cock deep into Rochelle's folds and stay there forever, settling in as her protector, partner, and lover. I needed her to make my world bright and beautiful. I'd been living in a fog of existence, but she lit me up like lightning and molten gold.

With one last swipe of her tongue, Rochelle let my cock free and rose to her feet wearing a satisfied grin.

"How was that?"

I didn't bother to answer as I growled and wrapped my

arms around her waist, taking her straight to my bed. She shrieked with delighted laughter and relaxed against the bed as I settled my body on top of hers. The full softness cradled my harder frame and I nestled into her, enjoying the sensations and scents. Sun-warmed stone with the tang of hot gold hit my nose and I inhaled deeply. Those smells grounded me in feelings of safety, warmth, and peace.

Rochelle connected me back to the Earth Mother, the Goddess of All, and I realized she was the treasure I'd been looking for. I was a guardian, and like the Concrete Angels Motorcycle Club, she was mine to protect.

She grinned down at me with hooded eyes. "Do you like what you see?"

I nodded and wrapped my hands around her breasts as I braced my weight on my elbows. I strummed her nipples to harden them to delicious peaks. She gasped and squirmed a little, making her full mounds jiggle in my hands. I loved the softness pressed against my palms and I took one turgid nub into my mouth.

"Oh glory, yes, suck on my tits, Flint."

I didn't need more encouragement than that. I rolled my tongue over her hot peak and tugged on it before biting down gently. She whimpered and rocked her hips, rubbing her soft mound against my belly. The perfume of her woman's scent, that sun-warmed stone with molten gold, surrounded us and I damn near lost my mind. I'd never found a better aphrodisiac.

I shifted to suck on her other breast, enjoying the stiff tip against my tongue as I rasped it over the areola. When I closed my teeth over it, she yipped and whined, thrusting her chest up higher to get closer to my mouth. I closed my lips around her nipple and sucked hard, enjoying the sensation of her mound rubbing me harder.

"Sweet Goddess, Flint. You make me so hot."

I growled. *You're not even close to hot yet.* My hands were busy so I let her nipple pop out of my mouth and peppered kisses down her belly until I could nuzzle her mound. The soft curls around her pussy lay soaked with her cream and my mouth watered with the need to taste her. It had been too long since my last taste and I wasn't about to waste this opportunity to dig in.

I met her gaze as I dipped my head and swiped my tongue through her wet curls. She threw her head back and moaned deep in her throat as her molten gold tang filled my mouth. Damn, she tasted better than she smelled. I couldn't get enough and inserted my tongue between her folds. Hot warm stone settled on my tastebuds and spurred me to lick some more. I used my thumbs to peel apart her outer labia and swiped my tongue straight into her delicious pink center.

"Oh glory!"

Yes, ma'am. I hope it's glorious.

I settled in to feast, licking and sucking on her delicate tissues. I held her pussy open to me and fucked it with my tongue, driving as far up her channel as I could with the tip. She rocked her hips against my face, trying to pull me deeper with little spasms of her inner muscles. I gave her every inch, curling the end to stroke the walls as I rubbed my teeth against her hot little clit.

Her hands grasped the bedding beneath her and tightened into fists as she spread her legs wider and rocked harder. A gush of new cream filled my mouth as she whimpered in time with her thrusts. I rumbled a growl against her sensitive flesh as I pulled my tongue back, lightly caressing her hot folds.

"Sweet glory, please, Flint."

She sounded desperate and I went back to tongue-fucking her pussy as I strummed her clit with a thumb. She whined and rocked, her inner muscles squeezing my tongue rhythmically until I pressed her clit between my thumb and forefinger.

"Oh, oh, oooohhhhhhh!"

Another flood of cream filled my mouth as she came and I swallowed it down, taking her offering with joy and delight. This was what I wanted. Her pleasure, her release, and her indulgence of her Goddess-given delight. I loved that she wasn't afraid or embarrassed to take her pleasure, and a new form of satisfaction filled my chest as I watched her relax bonelessly onto the bed after her passion settled.

I raised up on my knees. "How was that?" My signed question got a breathless laugh.

"Yeah, that might be okay."

"Okay?" I widened my eyes and scowled in mock-indignation. "That just means I'll have to try harder." I lowered my hips and rubbed my stone-hard cock against her soaking mound. "Care to take a ride?"

"Ride?" She gave me a dazed smile.

I nodded and pointed to my cock, rising like a rhyolite stalagmite between my legs. "It needs a little more attention from you."

A wide grin split her lips. "Oh hell yeah. Like a wild pony. Give me that cock."

I flipped over onto my back and settled my shoulders just as she rolled to her knees. Her breasts swung beneath her body and I wanted to gather them to my mouth again, but she dropped her face to my groin and licked her way from my balls to the tip of my cock. The slick heat made my shaft jerk with anticipation and I grabbed her shoulders to pull her closer.

"Rrrhhide." That was as close as I could make my voice say the word, but she grinned and wiggled her body into position.

"You want me to ride this?" She grabbed my cock and ran her thumb over the head dripping pre-cum from the slit.

I nodded, my gaze fastened on her hand.

"And you want your cock in my pussy?" She pushed my shaft until the head brushed the wet curls of her labia and dragged the tip through the hairs.

I moaned as the tickling heat sent sparks of pleasure through me and I grabbed her hips, urging her closer.

"Rrrhhide."

Rochelle laughed and sank down on me, enveloping just the cockhead with her slick warmth.

"Like this?"

I growled. "Rrrhhide!"

She widened her grin as she pressed down slowly on my shaft and I saw stars the more her pussy enveloped my cock. When she'd seated herself completely, she moaned right along with me. Then she squeezed those inner muscles and the stars returned to the back of my eyes.

"Fuuuuuccccccckkkkk!"

"Oh yeah, I couldn't agree more."

She rose off my straining shaft until only the head remained inside, then she dropped back until her ass hit my thighs. The pleasure sparking from the friction between us tightened my balls and warned me I wasn't going to last long despite the orgasm she'd given me before. But I gritted my teeth and held back. I wanted Rochelle to get her pleasure first. I wanted her to come apart on my cock so I could reaffirm our connection.

She stared at me, her eyes brilliant with hot desire and need as she rocked harder and faster on my cock. The muscles of her pussy squeezed me tight and the friction built my release up higher. I tried to focus on the smoothness of her skin beneath my hands or the way her tits bounced as she rode me, but everything kept coming back to the pleasure she gave me with each thrust.

"Rrrroocchhheellle, cooommmingg!" I couldn't stop the rush of pleasure straight from my balls.

"Oh glory, Flint. Fill me up. Fill me up so hard. Oh yes!"

She rode me as our mixed releases perfumed the air with the scents of sex and pleasure. She cried out as her pussy tightened on my shaft and sweet cream soaked my groin. I pumped my own load into her and pulled her down on top of me, sinking my canines into her shoulder once more.

She cried out as her pussy spasmed again with a second, sudden orgasm, and we both rocketed out into the blissful void. It was a new experience for me and I floated there, lost in the peace of my mate, anchored to Mother Earth for the first time in my life.

Rochelle collapsed on my chest as I emptied the last of my cum into her. This was where I wanted to be, held by my mate, warm and safe in the home we made together. I was bound to my beautiful witchy woman and I didn't regret any of it.

"Oh glory, that was amazing." Rochelle raised her head enough to look at me with a satisfied smile. "You're amazing."

I chuckled, both flattered and pleased.

"I'm going to clean up." I eased her back to the bed, all languid and soft, and rolled to my feet. "Be right back."

"Okay." She sighed as she snuggled down into the pillows.

Despite the full workout she'd given me, I felt rejuvenated and energized. I grabbed a washcloth in the bathroom and ran hot water over it to clean our collective releases from my cock and balls.

Rochelle made me feel alive in ways I never had before. She connected me, grounded me in the energy of the earth Goddess, and it recharged my well-being. She was my connection to the divine, and the source of my life's energy. I gaped at my reflection in the mirror as the true meaning of our binding became clear.

Holy sweet Goddess.

A laugh rippled through the rocks around me and I blushed to my eyebrows. Damn, She was still watching us take pleasure in each other.

Shaking my head, I rinsed out the washcloth and made

sure it was still warm to bring out to Rochelle. She lay in the bed, her hair in sweet disarray, and her chest rose and fell in slumberous inhalations. I knelt beside her and carefully cleaned away the evidence of our loving, though my gaze strayed to the renewed mark on her shoulder, and my cock twitched with approval.

Settle down you.

I tossed the cloth into the laundry pile and crawled back into the bed beside my beautiful mate. I gathered her into my arms and she sighed with contentment, wrapping her body around me with her head on my chest. My own satisfaction filled my chest and I settled down to rest in the folds of the Earth Mother's bliss.

CHAPTER THIRTEEN

Rochelle

I woke up in a state of complete contentment and peace, something I hadn't felt since before my mother had been murdered. I'd been relaxed before, but not this bone-deep, full-blown "I'm happy" feeling. And the reason behind it apparently banged around in the kitchen on the other side of the cabin, humming tonelessly.

It made me smile to know Flint sounded as happy as I was after last night. The sex had been phenomenal and the connection transcendent, and I weirdly felt like I'd married and celebrated it the night before.

Wait, what?

I settled back against the pillows and let the thought rest in my mind for a few moments. Had I gotten married? Not according to any human agency, but the Goddess connected people all the time whether there was a piece of paper to signify the agreement or not. Most traditions around the world agreed that the deal was done when it was consummated.

And we definitely consummated it.

I'd be up for consummating it again tonight, and as many more times as he cared to let me.

The thought made me laugh and I rolled from the bed to pad naked into the main room. Flint hadn't bothered to get dressed either, if I didn't count the white with red polka dots apron he wore to keep whatever was cooking on the stove from burning his sensitive bits. Still, the view of his ass with the apron ties above it was delightful first thing in the morning.

"Happy Yule." I had the pleasure of watching him turn around with a tray of some sweet roll-looking thing on a tray in one hand. "Are those for me?"

He shook his head with a smirk and gestured with his free hand. "All mine."

"What?" I put my hands on my hips and pushed out my chest. "What about me?"

His smirk morphed into a grin. "Dunno, but keep standing there like that so I can think it over." His gaze slid over the exposed parts of my body as he waggled his eyebrows.

I laughed and sauntered over to see what he was cooking. "What did you make?"

"Cinnamon rolls." He set the tray down and grabbed me around the waist. "But I want this right here. Best dessert ever." He cupped my face and pulled me close so he could take my lips and give me another toe-curling kiss.

I grasped his cock under the apron and squeezed gently. "I so agree."

He rumbled a laugh and let me go. "Coffee?"

"Oh yeah."

I moved to sit down at the table and he brought me a mug of steaming hot goodness along with a cinnamon roll. He settled across from me with his own mug and roll and dug in, and it was the most domestic moment I'd had with him so far.

"Do you feel like we've gotten married?"

Flint blinked and stopped mid chew. His hand fluttered. "What?"

"Does it feel like we got married last night?" I held my coffee mug in both hands. "Because it does to me. It feels like we're connected in a way that's permanent. And no, I haven't forgotten what you said about biting me during sex. But this feels more than it did the first time. Maybe it's because I know about it now. But it feels official somehow."

He finished chewing and swallowed, then took a sip of his coffee before he raised is gaze back to me and freed his hands to speak.

"Are you okay with that?"

At least he hadn't tried to talk me out of the idea.

"Yeah. It was a really good feeling first thing this morning."

He nodded and a smile curled his lips. "Good. I'm happy to hear that. I didn't know if you'd feel that way and didn't want to push. There wasn't a ceremony or a party to celebrate. Do you want one?"

I shrugged one shoulder. "I don't need one, but it might be nice to have a celebration with your friends and mine in attendance. And I'd like a cake."

He grinned. "Not a dress or a ring?"

I shook my head. "I have your mark on my shoulder. I don't need a ring to tell me you're mine." I winked.

He laughed. "I think a cake can be arranged." Then he sobered. "But I need to talk to you about something else." He took a deep breath. "Loki is going to hit you with a contract."

"I'm sorry, a what?" I blinked and set down my cinnamon roll.

"A contract. We all have to sign one to be part of the club. And it's as much to protect you as to protect the club."

I frowned. "What if I don't want to sign a contract? I'm not really part of the club."

"You are if you want to stay with me."

I straightened. "Are you saying I can't be with you without a contract? That you'd forsake the bond we just made?" The cinnamon roll in my stomach sank like a weighted balloon.

He shot out of his chair and knelt beside me, his expression as intense as I'd ever seen it.

"No, Rochelle, I can't forsake the bond we have. It would destroy who I am. But the club is important to me and it is family. I need you both, and I can't have both unless you sign a contract that says you'll protect it, too." He swallowed hard and looked at me full of entreaty. "Please, Rochelle, understand why we do this. It protects our secrets from humans and corrupt organizations like Backlog from harming us. But it also extends that protection to our loved ones who might operate outside the club's purview. And you can set the terms to benefit you and keep your business safe. Do you understand?"

I didn't, not entirely. I'd never been in a position where I had to choose between the person I loved most and the life I wanted to live. Would I have signed a contract to keep my mother from being murdered? In a heartbeat, but that had never been a choice. Now I was faced with choosing to live my life by my own rules or keeping Flint in it.

And if Flint's not in it, how is that living by my own rules? How is that living at all?

I pushed my chair back and rose. "I need to think about this."

I didn't like the sorrow and dread I read in his face, but he nodded and let me go. I wanted to run into his arms and let him hold me, to take away the fears that suddenly assailed me. But he was the source of those fears and I needed to find my balance in the newly shifting landscape of my life.

I retreated to the bedroom and closed the door behind me. I didn't know what to do. I usually was pretty good at going with the flow, but this was an obstacle I hadn't considered. Granted, I didn't know what this contract would entail or what the terms were, but it sounded like they'd be an "accept all or get nothing" sort of deal, and I'd never been good at stark choices.

I sighed and looked around the room. *Flint's room, in Flint's house.* Aw hell, I didn't even have my own space anymore. I'd moved in with him when I had nowhere else to go. I strode to my bag to grab some clothes; a warm sweater, a turtleneck to keep the sweater from itching, and jeans. I tidied up the room and packed all my dirty clothes back into my bag, not wanting to take up any extra space. I even made the bed and tucked my bag off to the side out of the way.

When I finished, I stared at the door to the bedroom. I couldn't stay in there forever – it was Flint's room and he'd need access eventually. But I couldn't face him right now. Neither of us had any answers to the problem of the club and their contract. We didn't even know the terms, but if we were dealing with Loki, Goddess knew the terms would be tricky at least.

And what if I choose not to sign it?

I'd have to break up with Flint, find a new place to live, start over alone without the man, the being, who now held my heart. Crushing sorrow and fear slammed into me and made me want to run somewhere safe.

And where is that, Goddess? Where is my sacred and safe place? More panic rose as the answer came back as my workshop. That had burned to the ground yesterday. Sweet glory, I really had nowhere to go. Tears sprang to my eyes and ran down my cheeks. I had to get out of there, but where could I go?

Then I remembered the workshop Flint had said I could use. It wasn't technically mine, but it would provide me a place to get away and think before I made any hard and fast decisions. I yanked some socks onto my feet and stepped into the front room. Flint stood in the kitchen, a wary look on his face as I headed for the front door.

"I'm going out." I shoved my feet into my boots and grabbed my coat. "May I please have the key to the workshop padlock? I'm going to take a look at the space again to get a sense of it."

"Give me a moment and I'll join you." He signed as he moved toward the bedroom.

"No, Flint. Right now, I need to be alone. I need to think this through on my own terms and decide what's right for me. I just need the key." I shoved my hat on my head and held out my hand.

He looked so defeated in nothing but that polka dot apron and I had to firm my heart against giving in. I didn't want to hurt him, but what he asked of me was a lot to think about. And I couldn't do it in the presence of his naked beauty. I wanted him and my heart needed him to grow and blossom, but there were real consequences of signing a contract with the Concrete Angels, and I needed to know what I was getting into.

And I don't even have the contract yet.

It was a fucking mess and only my herbs and tinctures made me feel calm in times of crisis.

"Please, Flint."

He nodded, his face gone back to the stoicism he'd shown when I first met him. "Let me get dressed and start a fire in the stove out there. It'll be freezing without it."

I wanted to protest, but I didn't really like being cold when doing my thinking. The only warm place on the property was the cabin and I couldn't stay there, so I nodded. He disappeared into the bedroom to get dressed and I wrapped my scarf around my neck, wondering how the day would end. So much for a happy Yule.

He came back in a flannel shirt, his cut, and jeans, and I envied his easy ability to deal with the cold. He shoved his feet into his boots without looking at me and headed out the door, leaving me to follow on my own time. The sun had risen and painted the world with bright white snow and blue shadows from the surrounding trees. It was beautiful and brought tears to my eyes. The world was happy and serene, uncaring of my heart and the tribulations affecting it.

As it was when Mom died.

Yeah, the world moved on and I was left to make my own way through it again. I watched Flint stalk across the open space between the cabin and the container, and my heart ached some more. There was anger and frustration in his movements, but he never said a word as he unlocked the workshop and disappeared toward the back to start the stove.

My breath fogged in the frozen air as I swallowed my tears and followed him in. He'd brought my things and stacked them carefully on one side of the container, giving us room to move around and set things up when we were ready.

Not sure we'll ever be ready now.

It all depended on what I decided to do. Flint closed the stove door with a harsh clang and rose to his feet. He strode past me to the front door without a word, but he paused at the entrance and faced me so I could see his hands.

"I'm sorry I didn't tell you about the contract before. I knew it was something Loki required of all of us, but I didn't think it would affect anything. I didn't mean to spring it on you." He huffed a sigh and scrubbed his face before meeting my gaze again. "I will abide by whatever you decide. You are my heart, Rochelle, and that will never change. But I've made promises and to be true to myself, I must uphold them."

"What about your promises to me?" My voice was small but held all my hurt.

He grimaced. "They aren't mutually exclusive and

they can coincide, but that depends on you. You have all the power and choices here, Rochelle. I will follow your lead." He raised his chin and firmed his expression but the pain leaked through. "I'll leave you to think."

Then he slipped out the door and closed it behind him. I half expected him to lock the padlock and secure me inside, but all I heard were his footsteps walking away and my tears refused to stay inside.

Anguish erupted in sound and water as I hurried to the wall closest to the stove and slid down it onto my ass. I wrapped my arms around my knees and wept for all I could potentially lose.

****

Flint

Pain and overwhelming sorrow stabbed through my chest as I heard Rochelle's sobs and I damn near ran back into the workshop to gather her into my arms. But I was the source of her pain and I had to grit my teeth and head back to the cabin, leaving her to her grief.

It damn near killed me.

Anger and frustration welled up and I wanted to hit something, pummel the stone of the mountain around me to gravel, but that would only damage the gracious rocks of my home and my own hands. Still, pain in my hands might distract me from the agony in my heart. I shifted direction toward the back of the cabin to pound out my anger and fear, but found the ax and the wood waiting to be chopped into firewood, and growled with satisfaction. Pounding on old stumps would take the edge off my anger and might wear me out enough not to roar.

I hefted the ax, positioned a piece of stump, and let fly. The impact of the blade in the wood shot up my arms into my shoulders and jarred some of my emotion loose. I set up another chunk of stump, and slammed the ax into it. The crack of the wood splitting made me grin with maniacal glee.

Again! Hit it again!

Rather than ruin a perfectly good piece of firewood, I turned my attention to this year's downed tree that had fallen with the first heavy snows. It still had bark that needed to be stripped to make a good clean fire and pieces too large to fit into the stove. I snarled at it and picked a spot, then attacked with the ax. The blade bit into the wood with a satisfying blow, but it wasn't enough. I pulled the ax back and went at the log again, over and over, until the insistent buzzing in my pants made me stop, breathing hard, and drop the ax.

I sat down on the log and fished out my phone as I tried to rein in my emotions. It had felt good to hack at the wood and for the moment I was tired enough to be calm. I swiped the phone's face and brought up a series of texts from Neo. He'd been tracking Creighton's movements since we'd pissed him off and had hacked the councilman's private email.

Looks like Creepy Creighton has been blaming your woman for his misfortunes. He sent a couple of emails off to someone named Butler, asking for more help in, and I quote, "Destroying the wickedness that has infested our fair city." Who the hell talks like that these days?

Butler replied that Creepy Creighton needed more patience, that any more moves had to be done in the new year when the "bigger plan" would be set into motion. I checked earlier emails, but this bigger plan was never specified so we'll just have to wait and see what that means.

Haley reminded me that Butler was one of the head honchos of Backlog she caught talking with ADA Mitchell last summer, but she didn't think he was the top guy. I suspect this Butler and that one are the same person.

Creepy Creighton was pissed and tried to get more out of Butler, but he only sent a one line email back, reiterating patience. I bet Creepy Creighton beat the living shit outta his computer, LOL.

I snorted. It didn't surprise me that Creighton was pissed. Neo messing with his credit cards would've put him in a foul mood and Rochelle was his number one culprit. We'd have to do something about that and soon, it sounded like.

Creepy Creighton doesn't have anything on his schedule for the weekend. The only thing I could find was a holiday fundraiser party on Tuesday evening for the Fort Collins Senior Center. Creepy Creighton is their honored guest and he'll be making an appearance there since they made a generous donation to his campaign for re-election this past year.

I narrowed my eyes. If we wanted to take care of Creighton, Tuesday would be the day to do it. And regardless of what Rochelle decided about the club, I wouldn't leave her unprotected. Even if I had to do it from a distance. She was my bound mate, and no matter what I'd promised Loki, Rochelle was now one of my priorities. Creighton would never touch her again.

Thanks, Neo. Where is the fundraiser taking place?

I hit enter on the text and rose to stack the chopped firewood out of the way. I'd calmed down and now could prepare the wood without destroying it or the ax. I set up the new piece and split it with one strike. I grabbed the next piece and did it again, getting into a rhythm while I waited for Neo to answer.

By the time the phone buzzed, I had a cord of wood ready to be stacked in the overhang where we parked the vehicles.

It'll be at the Willow Universalist Church on the corner of E Horsetooth and Ziegler Roads at 1800.

I sent a thumbs up emoji and closed the phone. We owned a little bit of property across E Horsetooth Road from the Willow Universalist Church. It was an old homestead that had gone under auction and we'd acquired it for a song. But it was dark, remote, and quiet enough for anything we wanted to impress upon Earl Creighton, and just the prospect of it made me smile.

Looking forward to seeing you on Tuesday, Creighton.

I gathered up the firewood and headed around the front of the cabin to stack it in the overhang. I shot a look at the container where Rochelle worked, but the door remained closed and smoke rose from the chimney in the corner. It took everything in me not to deviate from my path to check on her. Fortunately, another phone text claimed my attention.

Blessed Yule to you and yours, Flint. May it be grand.

I stared at the text for a long time before I could think of anything to answer. I set the wood down on the stack then retreated into the cabin to gather my thoughts and come up with a response.

Thanks.

It was all I could think to say as I stared at the remnants of the disastrous holiday breakfast. All the food had been put away but the dishes still mocked me from the sink. I'd been hoping for food and sex this morning, but I'd barely gotten the food.

Thanks? What kind of bawbag says 'thanks' to a blessing?

I growled and typed my response back. Bless you and fuck off.

I expected him to text me immediately, but when the phone rang with a video call, I blinked in surprise. Attila wasn't fucking around this time. I let the phone ring a few times before I decided to answer it. Maybe taking my frustration out on my friend would help.

I set the phone on my handy-dandy little stand and answered with, "What the fuck do you want?"

"Who pissed in yer Cheerios this morn?"

"What do you want, Attila?"

He narrowed his eyes at my emphatic signs and tilted his head. "All right, brother, start at the beginning. What the hell happened between last night and this morning?"

I tried to act nonchalant. "Nothing."

"Don't hand me that wee bit o' shite. I can read it in yer face and body. What did ye do, ye numpty?"

I snarled. "Why do you assume I did anything?"

"Because if ye dinna do anything, ye'd be less riled up. What happened?"

Just thinking about it made me want to hit something again, but there was nothing convenient that wouldn't require repair later. "Loki. Loki happened." Well, sort of. Close enough to warrant my anger.

"Bloody hell." Attila sighed and ran his hand through his long, dark curly hair. "What the fuck did he do?"

"He hasn't done it yet, but he will. I had to tell Rochelle about the contract. Loki told me she'd have to sign one and I warned her this morning. She didn't take it well."

"Why the hell did ye tell her *this* mornin'? Why didn't ye enjoy the weekend before springin' it on her?"

I rolled my eyes. "Because I already surprised her with the fact that we're bound mates without asking her first. I didn't want her to get ambushed by Loki after I spent the weekend loving her up. What kind of a son of a friable schist does that shit?"

Attila opened his mouth to refute me, but blew it out with a defeated sigh. "Aye, that makes sense. What did she say after?"

I moaned like I'd been stabbed, which was how I felt. "She said she needed time and space to think about it and retreated to the workshop about an hour ago."

"Bloody hell."

"Yeah." I agreed with him. I didn't know how to fix the problem, but I hoped the time apart would give Rochelle the answers because I sure as hell didn't have them. "What if I lose her, Attila? What if she won't sign the contract?"

"Now ye listen to me, Flint. From what I've seen, Rochelle is a smart one, and she doesna let bumps in the road derail her. Ye give her time, all the time she needs, and she'll come around. Ye told her yer bound mates, aye?"

I nodded.

"Did ye also tell her yer a gargoyle?"

I nodded again. "I even showed her so she wouldn't run away screaming."

He snorted. "Aye, that's a wise move, all right. Ye doona need panic when she kens yer true form."

I wasn't sure I would've preferred that to the silence and distance she'd presented me with this morning.

"She'll come around, Flint."

"But what if she doesn't sign? We're bound mates. I can't stay away from her, but I've promised to guard the club. What then?"

"Och, doona borrow trouble when there is none, brother." He shook his head. "Ye canna ken what the Goddess has in store for ye. This might be just the first of many tests and ye havenae pissed off Karma recently, have ye?"

I blinked and thought back. "I don't think so. Karma and I are on pretty good terms."

"Weel then, doona fash yerself, laddie. Let it bide a bit. Rochelle will find her footin' and it'll all work out right, ye'll see."

I hated being unsure of things. My world had made

sense before Rochelle. But her withdrawal had thrown everything into disarray. "How do you know?"

A compassionate smile curled Attila's bearded lips. "Because I know the Goddess, brother. She never leaves ye hurtin' long. Ye just have to trust She's got a brilliant plan for ye, even if ye canna see it. Right?"

My shoulders dropped as I sighed. "Yeah."

"Right. So, recharge that famous gargoyle patience and wait Rochelle out. She'll come around. Text me later when she does, yeah?"

I nodded and rocked my fist. "Yes."

He nodded sharply and ended the video call. A growl sounded in the still air of the cabin and I wasn't sure if it was me or my stomach protesting the meager breakfast I'd eaten. I grimaced and scrubbed my face with my hands, rubbing my eyes. Attila was right. The Goddess tested us and let us dangle in the web of our own making for a while, but She always showed us the way out of things if we gave it enough time.

And pay attention.

I could hear Her laughing as I went to make something useful to eat.

CHAPTER FOURTEEN

Rochelle

I tried to find something to do after I cried myself out,
but the idea of unpacking into a space I didn't even know if
I'd keep killed all my motivation. I was still turning around
in a circle, trying to decide which box to start with when
my phone rang with Joslyn's ring tone.

"Oh thank the Goddess, Jos."

"Uh, good morning to you, too. That's not the greeting
I expected on Yule. You wanna help a girl out and tell me
what's going on?"

"I have to break up with Flint!" I wailed the last bit as
tears started again and I sank back down on the stool he'd
left in the workshop.

"Whoa, whoa, whoa. Back up. What are you talking
about? I thought things were going great."

"They are—were. But now they aren't, and I don't
know what to do."

"Slow up, girl. I wasn't there when whatever this is
went down. Start at the beginning and take me through step
by step." Her measured voice calmed me down better than
a bath and a glass of wine, and I took a deep breath to clear
my thoughts enough to be coherent.

"Last night, Flint and I agreed to a commitment, kinda like a handfasting ceremony before the Goddess." It was a mating that bound us together, but close enough.

"Sweet glory, woman, you had a handfasting without me?" Joslyn shrieked into the phone and I winced.

"No, it's not like that. It was spur of the moment, like Vegas, but not. There's nothing official. No one was there but me and Flint and the Goddess."

"Hmm, all right then. So what happened between then and now?"

"This morning everything was perfect, y'know? I woke up feeling magical, like all the planets had aligned and the world was right." I sniffled and wiped my eyes. "And then...then he said the president of the club was gonna hand me a contract I had to sign if I wanted to stay with Flint. He said it was for protection not only of the club but of me and my business by the club. But if I didn't sign it, I couldn't be with him. I asked him if he was going to break up with me and he said he didn't want to, but he'd made promises to his club, and it was his f-family."

The tears overwhelmed me again and I sobbed into the phone.

"Oh, honey, I warned you bikers are trouble with a capital T. Has he at least shown you the contract?" A murmured voice sounded on the other end of the phone, and I hiccupped to a stop.

"Who's there with you? You're not alone?"

"Andre. I was calling to tell you about my night."

My shoulders slumped and I wanted to crawl into a hole in the floor. "Oh glory, Jos. I'm so sorry. I should've asked you how things were going with him. I'm so happy for you." The last statement came out in a wail, and I had to admit even I didn't think I sounded happy.

"Don't worry about it. We'll get to that as soon as we sort out what's goin' on with you." She kept her voice firm. "Now, has he shown you the contract?"

I shook my head. "No, not yet. Apparently, it hasn't been written yet and I can name my own terms. But Joslyn, what am I giving up? Will the club run everything the way they want to now? Do I have to give up my business to them?"

"Hell no, girl. You listen to me. He said you could make your own terms, right?"

I sniffled. "Yeah."

"Okay then. You and I will come up with terms to make sure you're safe, the club's safe, and you get to be with your man. You still want Flint, don't you?"

"Yes, and I know what you're going to say, it's too fast. But I know in my heart he's the one. Hell, even the Goddess approves of him."

"Well then, we'll just have to make sure this contract benefits you more than it does them."

"Do you think we can do that? The president's really crafty, Joslyn. Sly like a fox times ten. He's like Loki, the Norse God of Mischief." He was *actually* the Norse God of Mischief, but I didn't need to tell her that. Not yet at least.

"Please, girl. Two women are smarter than a sly man any day of the week and twice on Sunday. And I'm the queen of contracts, you know that."

I laughed. "Hell yeah, I do know that." I didn't sign anything until Joslyn looked it over. "But I don't think you'll get to see it before I sign it."

"When are they handing it to you?"

I shrugged. "I don't know. I told Flint I needed to think things over before I agreed to anything and I've been out here in the workshop sobbing my brains out."

"I'm so sorry, honey. Give me a moment to get some coffee into me and we'll come up with some terms so they can't run roughshod over you, okay?"

I sniffed again. "Okay, but first, you gotta tell me what you're doing with Andre at your place. Or are you at his place? Come on, I want details to make my Yule better."

"Girl, I still need that coffee. So give me two shakes."

I nodded and stood, looking around for a bandana or a tissue to wipe my nose. There was nothing sad about Joslyn getting together with Andre. They were perfect for each other and I wanted to enjoy every moment of her story.

"Okay, I got my coffee. You still there?" Jos sounded determined.

"Yes, I'm still here. Now spill. I want to know everything."

She laughed. "Everything everything? Or almost everything?"

"As much as you're willing to share everything." I grinned.

"Well, after we found out the shop had burned to the ground, Andre said he didn't want me alone just in case it was a targeted attack. So he asked me to stay over."

"Oh ho, so you're movin' quick, I see." I laughed.

"No, it wasn't like that. He gave me his bed and he slept on the couch." I never expected Joslyn to sound so prim, but she pulled it off flawlessly. "But then we got to talking the next morning and since he doesn't have any family in town, I offered to share the holiday with him. We had a great day together. We decorated his tree and had lunch at a cute bistro down on Timberline and Prospect, and then we drank mulled wine over dinner at his place to celebrate."

"And I assume you celebrated Yule in the old-fashioned way that night?"

"Girl, you know I won't turn down some good hard man." She grunted her approval. "Um-um, so fine."

"So will you be moving this relationship forward into the New Year?" I held my breath, hoping she would. She deserved the best this world could offer, and my gut said Andre was one of the best.

"I don't see any reason not to. There's so much about him I like, and I feel I need to explore all his options." She sounded pleased and I couldn't help but laugh along with her.

"I'm so very happy for you, Jos. You deserve this."

"Damn right, I do. Now let's work on you, and get you everything you deserve and want, starting with a beneficial contract and that hot man you've been riding like wild pony."

I threw my head back and laughed. "That's what I told him last night."

"See? Great minds, girl. Great minds. Ready to use yours?"

"Hell yeah, I am." I straightened my shoulders. "Let's do this."

****

Flint

Rochelle didn't come back to the cabin until early afternoon. By that point, I was ready to rip the doors off the container and beg for her forgiveness. But the only thing that kept me from doing so was the knowledge that she needed to make this decision without interference from me. If I pushed her to decide to stay, I'd never know if it was because she wanted to stay or because I'd cajoled her to do so. And I needed her to want to stay.

When she did step inside the door, she was quick to turn her back to the room to remove her coat and boots so I couldn't read her expression. My gut sank a little deeper than it had that morning and I hadn't thought I could feel dread so strongly. I was losing Rochelle one breath at a time and there was nothing I could do to stop it.

I desperately needed her to turn around so I could demand what she had decided; to beg her to stay; to plead my case one more time. But the problem with being mute was I had to be patient, usually a skill I excelled in. Not that day. I could barely hold still while I waited.

She finally turned around, but she wouldn't look at me directly. I had to wait for her to square her shoulders and take a deep breath before she raised her gaze.

"Is there any tea?"

I shook my head. "Not yet. What kind would you like?"

"Something soothing. Lemon balm or chamomile, if you have it." She settled at the table as I put the kettle on to boil. "You should have some too, Flint. You're wound tighter than a watch spring."

I didn't want tea, I wanted to fix this problem. I wanted to change her mind. I wanted her to stay. But I ground my teeth together and told myself to be patient as I pulled out the chamomile tea and threw bags into two mugs. She didn't say anything as I worked and it set my teeth on edge. Usually, humans were too damn loud all the time, but Rochelle's silence killed me slowly, bleeding my joy away one drop at a time.

At last the kettle whistled and I took it off the stove, trying to keep my motions fluid and easy. But I ended up pouring hot water over one hand and damn near dropped the kettle.

"Here, let me do that. Get some ice for your hand."

"I don't need any." I waved her away. "I'm fine."

"You're not fine, but ice will help." She dug around in the freezer for ice, grabbed a paper towel, and held it against my skin. "Hold this there for five minutes. I'll be back in a second."

She disappeared into the bedroom, leaving me standing in the kitchen with ice on my hand. I didn't really need it. My skin was tough and I'd heal in a matter of hours, but the ice felt good and so did her concern for me.

After a few moments, she came back to the kitchen with a little frosted glass jar. She unscrewed the top and dipped her finger into the stuff inside. It smelled like lavender and oil, but when she smeared it on my burn, the pain lifted away like it had never been.

"There, that should help." She replaced the lid and grabbed her mug to take it to the table.

"Thank you." I picked up my own mug and followed her, sitting across from her to give her all the space she needed. "That really helps. What is it?"

She shrugged. "It's a burn salve of my own recipe. Lavender oil, calendula, and olive oil. I've used it for years. Minimizes scarring and removes the pain."

"It's remarkable. Do you sell this in your shop?"

She nodded. "It's a best seller." She sighed and sipped her tea. "So I've made my decision."

I swallowed hard and burned my tongue on the tea. I kept my expression stoic but my gut tightened so much I swear I was rock hard from the waist down, and not in a good way. It was a good thing I couldn't speak anyway because I would've squeaked.

Rochelle raised her gaze and met mine. "I'm going to stay and I'll sign the contract Loki requires."

I blew out the breath I hadn't realized I was holding. Relief ricocheted through me, loosening my gut and all the muscles in my chest. Hell, even tears threatened in my eyes. I surged to my feet and grabbed her out of the chair, hugging her tight.

She laughed a little uncertainly and wrapped her arms around me. "So I had you a little worried, huh?"

I growled and pushed her back so she could see my hands. "You've been locked in the workshop for hours without a word. It was just a little unsettling."

She laughed. "Damn, even in sign language sarcasm comes through."

I snorted and let her go back to her chair, but this time I sat close to her rather than across the wood surface of the table.

"I'm sorry I worried you for so long. I was talking to

Joslyn and the time got away from me." She sat back down and wrapped her hands around her mug. "We worked out the terms I'm going to offer in my contract. Jos is the contract queen and I won't sign one without her looking at it."

That made sense and anyone who signed a contract with Loki should have someone knowledgeable look it over. Loki was the master of sneaky clauses. Many an intelligent human had signed contracts with him and ended up locked into something they didn't expect despite careful wording and reading.

"Good plan. Loki is conniving and he gets you on word choices, too. He caught Numbers by using the word "can," as in physically able." I shook my head. "He's a bastard."

Rochelle tilted her head and narrowed her eyes. "Why are you telling me this? I thought you'd made promises to protect the club first?"

I nodded slowly, a half-smile curling my lips. "I am protecting the club. I don't want them to be in danger if my witchy woman is pissed off at them."

"*Your* witchy woman?"

I rocked my fist. "Yes, mine." I leaned over and kissed her, licking the seam of her lips. "Property of Flint."

She grimaced but nodded. "It's going to take a while for me to get used to that term. I don't like thinking of myself as property."

"It's to protect you."

She held up a hand. "I recognize that. But the protection is that anyone hitting on me is more afraid of what you'll do than they are of what I'll do to them if they don't take no for an answer."

I bit my lip and nodded. "It's an antiquated system, but it works."

"It works for the men. Have you asked the women what they think?"

I hadn't. There hadn't been a need. Rochelle was mine and I wasn't sharing. Hell, I wasn't interested in having sex with anyone other than her, so I belonged to her just as much as she belonged to me. But now I wanted to order her a jacket to show everyone who she belonged with.

Hogmanay gift.

"It was never important to me to find out until now." I shrugged. "If it helps, I belong to you as much as you belong to me. There will never be anyone else I'm interested in. We're bound mates and you're the only one I want."

She shook her head. "I'm glad to know that. Of all the concerns I had, your interest in me wasn't one of them. But that doesn't change the problems of men taking what they want unless other men stop them and women are only seen as saleable goods. No one corrects the men. Do any of you see us a people or just possessions?"

I started to sign then stopped as my thoughts caught up. I was going to say, "That's just the way it is." But had it always been that way or was it more the "Founder's Effect"? The culture of owning women and seeing them as property had started when the first biker clubs came together. They were basically boys clubs and the leaders set themselves up as kings, but they were no better than the other boys that joined them. Over time, things evened out, but the old beliefs that "boys will be boys" and women were nothing but sex toys and spoils of war stuck.

The Concrete Angels had been different. We had women members who had the same rights as the men because Loki wasn't a sexist little boy. He fucked with anyone—female, male, non-binary—in equal measure. But the human members had kept the old systems and Loki never saw a reason to change it.

Maybe Rochelle and the other old ladies need to give him a reason.

"I see you as a person."

"Oh yeah?" She dipped her chin. "Would you let me borrow your bike if I needed to go anywhere?"

I shrugged. "Not until I knew you could handle a bike."

"Why do you assume I can't handle a bike?"

"Because you're not a biker."

"Would you let a guy you knew who wasn't a biker use your bike if he needed it?"

I frowned, thinking of Eric, Karma's old man. Would I have let him use my bike if he'd asked? The immediate answer was yeah, of course. Because I'd known him longer and knew he could handle a bike, even though he wasn't technically a biker. The man drove a peacock green 1956 Chevy Corvette, for Goddess' sake.

"Your silence is *very* encouraging." Rochelle scowled. "Think about that. You're okay with a man riding your bike, and I'm sure you'd tell me that even if he has no previous skill, you'd expect him to be able to learn. Why wouldn't you naturally assume or expect a woman to be able to learn?"

Because women were delicate creatures to be coddled and cared for and most of them didn't like bikes or machinery or guy things. Except that didn't make sense when I thought about Karma, Viper, Calhoun, Chem, Dollhouse, Quan-Yin, Nessie, and Sith, our other mechanic and martial arts master. All those women were tough as nails, could ride as well or better than the men, and all worked on their own bikes without help, Sith especially.

"Errrrr."

Rochelle nodded. "And that's why I don't want to be your property."

Panic rose in my chest again. Did that mean she was walking away after all? I must have squeaked a sound because she patted my arm and sighed.

"Don't worry. I'm still going to sign the contract, but I want you to know now I'll never wear your property patch."

She let go and rose to get more tea. Mine sat on the table untouched while fear and frustration cascaded through me. How would I protect her if no one knew she was mine? Yes, the culture needed to change, but no one was going to start now just because she wanted them to. I had to wait for her to turn to look at me before I could demand anything and the waiting drove me nuts.

"I can't change everyone, Rochelle. But I won't leave you unprotected. Wearing my patch will keep the creeps away from you."

She raised an eyebrow. "Did you just call your brother bikers creeps?"

I growled. "That's not the point. Some of them believe and uphold the culture, and they won't change no matter what. I might be able to convince the Elder Race members, but the humans hold onto their bad habits even when shown a better way. How do I protect you from them?"

"I don't know, Flint. What would you suggest?"

She crossed her arms over her chest and I tried to rein in my anger. She wasn't asking questions that I wouldn't ask if I stood in her position.

"I'd beat the shit out of anyone to hurt you or came onto you after you told them no."

She nodded. "That's fine and warranted, but would anyone back me up when I tell a guy no the first time? Or would everyone just stand there and laugh when someone took liberties despite my objections?"

"They wouldn't if you were wearing my patch!"

"That's not the point!" I'd never heard her shout before and it surprised me. "I shouldn't have to wear your patch to be autonomous. I'm a full person, Flint. How many of your brother bikers hit on you? How many try to grab your dick, even after you warn them you don't want their attention?"

"None, because they're not attracted to me."

"Are you sure? Are you telling me there are no gay or

bi bikers out there? Because I'll bet you dollars to doughnuts that's not even remotely true."

I couldn't argue with her on that one. Both Attila and Michael were bisexual, and Samurai was gay. But they'd never hit on me or forced the issue with me. Most of them probably thought of me as Ace, and I'd never disabused them of the notion. I suspected Loki landed mostly on the Ace spectrum, but he never gave anyone a straight answer on anything personal, so it was hard to tell.

"No, there are gay bikers, they've just never hit on me."

"I'll bet it's not because they aren't attracted to you. You're sexy as hell. There's no way they haven't noticed." Rochelle rolled her eyes as I straightened my shoulders and pushed out my chest a little. "So really the only thing that keeps them from hitting on you and not pushing if you've said no is that you're male. Right? Because men are full people, full members, and once a man says no, the other men have to respect that. Right?"

I wanted to argue with her logic. I wanted to refute her statement that only males had autonomy and could deflect others with a single word. But my panic at her refusing my patch belied those arguments.

"Fuck."

She snorted. "Maybe later. At the moment, we have too much to discuss."

"Okay, you're right. The whole system is sexist and male-centric, but that still doesn't change the need to wear the patch." I met her gaze and bit my lip. "Please, Rochelle. It's for your safety, my piece of mind, and our overall peace in the club. I can't fight everyone, male or female, who might hit on you because you appear to be a honey. Please."

I'd never begged anyone for anything, not even from the Goddess, but this was a driving need. I belonged to her and she belonged with me, but how could I protect her if she wouldn't take my help?

Rochelle narrowed her eyes as she considered and my heartrate jumped up higher and higher the longer she took to decide.

"All right, I'll wear a patch, but not "property of Flint". I want it to say something else."

I gulped. "What?"

"Flint's Matron."

I damn near collapsed on the floor as the relief shot through me. "Thank the Goddess."

"Will that be enough to keep the creeps from treating me like free pussy?" Her voice was cold and her eyes hard as she crossed her hands over her chest.

I nodded. "That's enough."

"Good. And I expect the backup if I have to throat-punch anyone who doesn't take no for an answer."

"I will hold them still to get your blows in." Hell, I'd pay to see her kick some of the arrogant bikers' asses. And Loki would run a betting pool.

She sighed again and poured some more tea. "Okay, now that that's settled, how is your hand feeling?"

I'd totally forgotten about the burn and glanced down to check if it was still there. "Better. Doesn't hurt at all."

"Let me see." She returned to the table and lifted my hand into the light. "Wow, it looks like it's completely gone. Is that a virtue of your gargoyle skin?"

All of my tension and fear evaporated with her touch and calm replaced the unease tensing my shoulders. And a new sensation, something I'd only experienced with her, surged again. It was need, desire, comfort, calm, rightness, and serenity all rolled into one.

Yeah, the wise ones call that love.

The Goddess's voice intruded on my thoughts and made me freeze.

Love? I'd known we were bound mates, but I hadn't understood it would include love, the need to see

Rochelle's smile and feel her hands on me. The overwhelming desire to protect her from those who threatened her and to stand beside her as a guardian and partner.

Good glory, I am in love with her.

I heard the Goddess's laughter and tried not to grimace.

"I love you." I lifted one hand to sign to her while squeezing the one she held.

She blinked. "What?"

I took back my other hand. "I love you. Only you."

"You're just saying that because we're bound mates." She gave me a sad and indulgent smile.

I shook my head. "No, this is more than that. This is I want what's best for you and will do anything I can to see you get it. And if you had told me you'd never wear any patch, I would've fought for you anyway. I might have been pissed about it, but I would've done it. Wearing the "Flint's Matron" patch instead takes away my worries."

She bit her lip, vulnerability in her gaze. "So you really love me? As in, "I will live for you, my lady" sort of love?"

I raised an eyebrow. "Isn't the line usually, "I will die for you"?"

She rolled her eyes. "Heh, anyone can die. That's easy. Living for someone, especially if they're gone, now that's a trick."

"If it's all the same to you, I'd just as soon you don't die so I don't have to put that to the test. But yeah, I would live for you." I tugged her close and rested my forehead against hers. "I love you, Rochelle, and I want you to be my Matron, patch or no patch."

She laughed and her arms wrapped around my neck as she leaned into me. "If I'm completely honest, I want your patch. I just want you to acknowledge the problems with the system and help me work on changing it."

That made my heart flutter in ways I'd only heard

about in movies and love songs. It was a giddy, bubbly feeling that seemed at odds with anything associated with gargoyles, but I liked it and wanted more.

"So you will stay with me, here, and in the club wearing my patch, forever?" I'd never sounded so needy, but with her, I was.

She nodded with a smirk. "Someone has to do it, and I won't let another woman take the job. I don't share."

I growled. "Neither do I."

"Good. Now, that we've solved that, I'm starving."

"Let's eat and I'll tell you what I've learned about Creighton." I let her go and we returned to the kitchen to find something fit for a Yule's day celebration.

"You've been keeping an eye on Creighton? Why?" She helped me take food out of the refrigerator to decide what we'd make.

"Because I don't think he's going to stop coming after you and we have to make sure he's completely dissuaded from stepping up his game." I gave her my best evil smile.

"Oh? What exactly do you have in mind?"

"Let's get a meal together and I'll give you my ideas."

I already had a few I'd thought of and I'd share them, but I also needed to text the Friar and ask him to get a jacket for Rochelle. A smile curled my lips as I chopped vegetables for a salad. *Aw yeah, everything's coming together.*

CHAPTER FIFTEEN

Rochelle

I'd never had such a busy Yule weekend and I was exhausted. Or maybe it was excited. Or maybe I was just anxious. Whatever the emotion, I felt it all the way to my bones and it both tired me out and made me ready to move at a moment's notice.

Creighton had orchestrated my mother's murder and had burned down my home. None of us believed he would give up on his Wiccaphobia and stop coming after me, so Flint and Neo made plans for how to convince him I was no longer a target to be taken. It would require a kidnapping, a spell, and a little sleight-of-hand that would make our plan both amusing and beautiful.

Neo had kept us up-to-date on Creighton's movements as well as his purchases, of which he had very few given the holiday and his lack of credit cards. But his attendance of the Fort Collins Senior Center's Annual New Year's Fundraiser put him in an easy place to physically catch him. The Concrete Angels MC had a piece of property directly across from the church where the fundraiser would be held. We drove past it so I could see the property and I was impressed with both its size and its derelict appearance. No one would think to look for him there.

We'd snatch him after his speech and take him to the empty concrete shed hidden amongst the overgrown trees and vegetation, and spell him into leaving us alone. Me, especially. The only questions remaining were how were we going to get rid of his bodyguard Keith Grover and what spell I was going to use.

Despite my abilities of manipulating magic and earth energy, I'd never done a deterrent spell of this magnitude, and it worried me that I might cross a line I couldn't come back from. That was part of my nervousness. All magic came with a price, but dark magic used for harm, was too costly even for a witch of my caliber, and I wasn't about to tarnish my soul just to get Creighton off my back.

The other part of my nervousness stemmed from that damn contract I still hadn't seen. Apparently, Loki made it up on the fly, so with Joslyn's help, I could mitigate anything he threw at me. *But given that he's Captain Mischief, I really hope I'm smart enough.*

It took me a little while and a couple of conferences with Joslyn to nail down the right spell and all the ingredients I'd need to complete it, but by Tuesday morning, I had everything I needed. Flint took me to the concrete shed and let me set up the items I'd need for the spell.

I swept the floor with a hand broom so it would be clear of debris and set up my little brazier for burning herbs to ask the Goddess for her help and blessings. Beside that I added a folding TV tray table with a fresh white pillar candle, little bowls of salt, rosemary, and dried mint, a small paring knife, and an opal apple.

I took a piece of chalk and drew a large circle on the floor, big enough to contain a full grown man, and added salt, rosemary for cleansing and purification, and crushed mint for energy and healing. I hummed a prayer to the Goddess, letting the floor, walls, and ceiling absorb the vibrations of my song as I prayed. The concrete shed hummed with the power I called up from the ley line running beneath it, and though it was sort of sluggish due to being left unattended for a while, it still came when called. I lit a bundle of sage to smudge the whole space, walking around the outdoor perimeter to make sure all the energies within were aligned.

I chose five points equidistant around the circle to honor the five elements—Earth, Water, Fire, Air, and Ether—and set a black shorl tourmaline at each point to anchor my energy work and the circle. Black tourmaline was a protective stone to ward off bad energy, particularly electromagnetic energy of cell phones, radios, and computers. They would make it harder for Creighton to use his cell to call for help, though I was hoping Flint would remove the gadget, taking away the temptation entirely.

When everything was ready, I kissed Flint goodbye and settled down to meditate. He and his assistant, a white woman with reddish-gold hair and freckles across her nose named Nessie, left to wait Creighton out.

This is it. Please Goddess, help me get this right and not cross over into dark magic.

I'd been careful. I'd thought out my spell and though I would spit it at him like a curse, in reality, it was a healing and cleansing spell. It was powerful magic, but it would be more powerful because of Creighton's fear and belief in witches. I settled down and took deep breaths before closing my eyes to sink into the ley line below the shed.

Sinking down into magic energy was a little like settling into wet sand on the ocean floor. It surrounded me and held me, but wasn't particularly heavy. I liked the warm skirl of the energy sliding over my skin and I relaxed into it, like the moment of falling into a freshly made feather bed.

What I didn't expect was to meet someone there while I relaxed into the flow of the earth magic. At first, I saw merely a shadow. Then the image resolved itself into a cave with the sound of the ocean echoing through it and a tall woman in black leather leaned against the far wall, cleaning her nails with the tip of a dagger. She had long black hair tied into intricated braids reminiscent of a Viking warrior, and eyes full of stars against warm golden skin the color of beach sand.

"Looks like you're prepped and ready for this, Rochelle."

I shivered at Her voice and swallowed hard. I'd never been spoken to directly by the Goddess. Sure, I'd received Her messages, but they'd been visions, not Herself.

"Yes, my Lady. I think I am."

She scowled. "Either you are or you aren't. This is no time to 'think' about it."

"Yes, ma'am. I'm ready. I can't think of anything else I need to do and I trust Flint to bring Creighton to me, so I'm as ready as I'll ever be." I strengthened my voice and answered Her honestly. It didn't seem to be the time to vacillate when the Goddess visited in her Warrior visage.

"Good." The Goddess nodded decisively. "Now, about Flint. I'm pleased you're going to stick with him. He needs you to challenge his long held misconceptions and bring out the best in him. But you need him, too, m'dear. He will teach you about family having your back and asking for help. If a gargoyle can learn about that, certainly you can, too."

I giggle-snorted at Her words. Gargoyles seemed like solitary species for sure so to have Flint teach me about familial support seemed weird. But there was no question Flint valued his biker club enough to beg me to wear his patch.

Which still made me a little uncomfortable.

The Goddess snorted. "Oh, m'dear, you're going to knock that belief on its ear. Between you and Oriana, and the women members of the Concrete Angels, the old belief that men come before women is going to change. Not at first and maybe not as quickly as you'd like, but you're planting a seed that is going to grow tendrils and vines throughout the club, and before you know it, the whole culture will be unlike any other club. But it starts with you."

"Which means some of the members are going to hate me." Nothing like getting more enemies before I'd even started.

"Perhaps," the Goddess conceded. "But more of them will agree with you and all the women will be behind you. And that includes a Boobrie, a Fu Dog, and a *Morukai*, not to mention Karma."

"Wait, what?"

"I must be off." The Goddess shoved her knife in to a sheath at her hip and straightened off the rock wall. "You're going to do great. That little creep isn't gonna know what hit him. Just remember to keep your anger in check. He'll tempt you to do bad back to him, but you don't want Karma to notice, so it's best to keep with your original idea of a healing spell. It'll benefit everyone in the end, yeah?"

I opened my mouth to respond, but the Goddess and the cave disappeared. I found myself back in the concrete shed and darkness had set in. I shivered in my jacket and got off the floor, trying to rub feeling back into my ass.

I hadn't expected to be the agent of change for an entire culture, but I also hadn't expected to be mated to a gargoyle or join a biker club. Now I just had to figure out who was the Boobrie, the Fu Dog, and the *Morukai*.

I think I'll save that for Hogmanay. The Goddess's laughter floated on the wind rattling the door of the shed.

****

Flint

Bodyguard out of the way.

Neo's text made me grin. I'd been waiting for confirmation ever since Nessie and I arrived at the Willow Universalist Church on Ziegler Road. Apparently, Neo had falsified an email from Butler and the arsonist had bolted out of the church straight to his car. I wasn't sure what all the Friar, Luke, and Attila had planned for him, but it couldn't be good with the original fallen angel on the team.

And that's the end of Mr. Keith Grover.

I'm sure Haley, Michael's old lady, would have a story on him in the Fort Collins Bugle first thing tomorrow morning.

I waved at Nessie and showed her my phone. She nodded with her customary half-smile and trained her mismatched eyes back on the entrance of the church. I didn't know much about my Boobrie colleague, but I knew her heterochromia had made her an outcast in her homeland, and she'd joined the Concrete Angels in the mid-1970s after studying at Oxford University in mechanical engineering and robotics. Why she chose to be a simple security guard, I had no idea, but I didn't mind her quiet company.

Darkness shrouded the parking lot and the temperature had dropped to below freezing when the doors to the building opened. Earl Creighton stepped outside with an older man who looked to be an official of the church. They both hissed at the cold and Creighton buttoned up his black wool overcoat, turning up the collar.

"Colder than a witch's tit in a brass bra as my father used to say." The church official shook his head as he pulled out a cigarette and lighter, and I wondered if Rochelle wore bras at all.

Creighton shot him an uneasy look, but let it go as the older man lit up. Instead, he scanned the parking lot as if looking for someone.

Missing Mr. Grover, Creighton?

I grinned as I got into the van's driver seat and turned on the ignition, but left the lights off. Nessie climbed into the passenger seat and waited for my signal. As soon as the church official went back inside, we'd nab Creighton. She rolled down her window and we listened as the conversation continued.

"Ah yes, I remember one time at Christmas in Berlin, it was so cold, we had to wear masks to keep our throats from freezing. But they had a wondrous ice festival with tremendous ice sculptures, just tremendous, with every shape and style you could imagine."

Creighton's voice grated against my ears and I bit back a snarl. He was smarmy, obnoxious, and pretentious as if he hadn't grown up in the dirt poor tenements in Baton Rouge, Louisiana. He'd masked his accent pretty well, which was a surprise. Most people liked that slow, southern drawl and it made them less likely to see blackness under the polished veneer.

"That sounds marvelous."

"Oh, it was. It was. I hope to get back there soon, but alas, being a councilman has taken its toll on my free time."

I'd done my research on him when he started targeting Rochelle and found out while he feared all witches, the Voodoo variety made him shriek like a kid in a haunted house. Rochelle had told me she didn't have connection to Voodoo. Her specialty was earth magic, and it made sense given she was bound to me as my mate. Her favorite way of explaining was to talk like that big, russet creature from the movie Labyrinth. She said, "To quote him, rocks friends." I cracked a smile from the darkness of the van. The man speaking to Creighton finished his cigarette and stubbed out the butt, wrapping his own coat tighter around him.

"Well, thank you again for joining us tonight, Councilman. Your talk was inspired."

"Thank you very much for inviting me. It was a pleasure." Creighton smiled indulgently and shook hands with the official.

"Right, well, I'm going back in where it's warm. You have a good night, Councilman, and God bless you."

Oh, he'd have an exciting night, all right, and he'd be Goddess blessed for sure, but he probably wouldn't like it much.

After Rochelle's less-than-cordial meeting with Creighton at the swanky place in Fort Collins, Neo had been ferreting out all the ways Backlog had been funding and supporting Creighton. He'd gotten himself deep into money laundering, human trafficking, and political bribery. They then used his businesses as currency washing machines and his political standing to hide it.

And now we're coming for you, Creepy Creighton. It's time to turn the tables on your ass and show you what real power is.

The older man ducked back inside and Creighton scanned the parking lot again before digging out his phone. He started walking toward the road and I eased the van into gear. Nessie climbed into the back of the van and waited for my signal as I turned on the lights and floored it toward the man entering the second line of cars.

Like all adult humans, Creighton froze as the lights hit him and stared as the van screeched to a halt in front of him. Nessie threw the sliding door open and launched into the lot, grabbing Creighton by the lapels.

"What the f—!"

His exclamation shut off as soon as Nessie threw a black hood over his head and cinched it down tight on his throat. He squeaked his protest as she hauled him up bodily and tossed him in the van. She slammed the door and gave me a thumbs-up as I drove out of the parking lot. Whimpering came from behind me and I grinned, keeping my amusement silent.

Though the concrete shed was across the street, I took the time to text Rochelle to say we'd be there in fifteen minutes. Then I drove around Fort Collins to disorient Creighton in the back. I didn't want him to know where we took him should he try to remember back.

By the time we got to the shed across from the church, Creighton was whimpering like a beaten dog. I shut the van off and texted Neo to send Gopher with my bike. Our newest brother would go with Nessie to dump Creighton on his doorstep while I rode home with my witchy woman.

I shoved the phone in my pocket and got out as Nessie threw the side door open. We hauled the mewling man out of the van and I dragged his ass into the building. Nessie secured the van and followed, but stopped outside the door.

"I'll stay here." Her low voice made Creighton twitch as I nodded. I was glad to have her guard the shed just in case Grover actually showed up.

I jerked Creighton into the building as she closed the door behind us and marched him into the center of the circle drawn on the floor. I was careful not to scuff the lines with my own feet and I lifted the man high enough that he wouldn't either.

Rochelle nodded to me and threw herbs into her little brazier. The glowing coals flashed the dried bits into sweet scented smoke: sage, rosemary, and mint, all cleansing and purifying herbs meant to make the world a better place. She pulled out a hand fan made of wood carved in lacy delicacy, and wafted the smoke toward where I stood in the center of the circle.

"Ready?" I signed the word with one hand.

She nodded and gave me a thumbs-up.

I ripped the hood from Creighton's head and lifted him by the throat so he dangled in my grip as I bared my teeth at him. He yelped and grabbed my wrist as he struggled to get away. But his writhing barely registered as I tightened my grip.

"Who the fuck are you?" Panic laced his voice as fear blazed from his eyes.

"This is my assistant, Mr. Creighton. He doesn't like you very much." Rochelle's voice floated out of the darkness and he jerked his head toward it.

"Who the fuck are you and what the hell do you want?" He still struggled in my grip but he seemed less concerned with me than with Rochelle.

"I'm surprised you don't recognize me, Mr. Creighton. I did tell you I wanted reparations for the damage you've done to me and my family." She came to stand in his line of sight just outside the circle.

"You bitch!" He snarled and struggled until I squeezed him again and he whimpered into silence.

"I told you the more you put energy into taking me down, the faster the rebound of magic would be. Unless you made a deal with me." She shrugged and gave him indifferent grimace. "Since you didn't want to hear my terms and only insulted me, your first backlash of magic found you quickly."

"I knew it was you!"

"I'm glad I made an impression." She nodded. "But tonight, I want to make it absolutely clear that you need to leave me and my business alone, and if you don't, there will be rough consequences."

"Oh yeah? What are you gonna do? Throw some essential oils at me, bitch?"

My anger bubbled over and I shook Creighton enough to make him start whining in his throat. I wanted to throw him against the wall, but I couldn't break the circle Rochelle had worked so hard to prepare.

"That's enough, assistant." Her voice remained calm and I stopped shaking the man.

I held the sniveling miscreant up by his throat and growled at him. To my surprise, Creighton snarled back at me, a hopeless laugh rattling from his chest.

"What are you gonna do, big guy? Kill me? Fuck, get in line." He shifted his gaze to Rochelle where she calmly lit the candles around the circle in preparation for her spell. "Your evil won't get me, bitch. I'll take you down before you can do anything to me. I have a charm and the blessing of a priest. Your magic can't hurt me."

I wasn't sure who he was trying to convince because he sweated and his voice shook with fear. Of course, I had him by the throat so maybe that contributed to his shaky vocals.

"Blessings don't work if you don't believe in them, Mr. Creighton. And priests don't hold sway here at all." Rochelle continued until the last candle was lit then returned to her table to light the final pillar. He sweated more as she shook the match out. "I told you that if you continued to come after me and mine, there'd be consequences. So tonight, I'm going to make them real for you."

"Your mother tried the same thing, you know." He sneered, his feet dangling off the ground as I lifted him higher. "She had potions and spells and colored powders and shit, but once I knew what she was, she was marked for death. Hell, she was lucky to live as long as she did after she took her pictures and tried to show them to the Chamber of Commerce. But I rid the world of her and I'll do the same to you."

Rochelle shook her head. "You're in no position to make threats anymore, Earl. Besides, I'm not going to kill you."

She sounded calm and determined as I swung my gaze to her. I lifted my free hand to sign, "We're not?"

"You're not?" Creighton echoed, his eyes bulging. I loosened my grip a little and his eyes went back to normal.

"No. There's been enough death, and I'm not going to sully my hands or the Goddess with violence." She strode to me and held up her little paring knife. "I just need a little of your blood to get my point across."

She grasped his hand and nicked his palm, which made him shriek like an asthmatic banshee. She calmly gathered some of his blood in a little bowl. It wasn't much and he wouldn't lose consciousness over it, but he acted as if she'd cut off his arm. She stepped away and pointed to the chalk circle drawn on the ground. "Drop him inside, please."

I released the gasping man into the center and stepped quickly out as Rochelle added salt and rosemary to close the circle. Power rose in a column behind me, just a slight shimmer of light and a subtle click to show it had closed.

"What I'm doing is cursing you, your organization, and the organization for which you launder money. This ends your web now. First, it will untangle, bit by bit, the knots untying into loose strands." She raised her gaze to him as she tossed herbs into the brazier to add more fragrant smoke. "Then the tendrils will wither and die, and the panic will set in. Those in positions of power will start to lose control until the whole web unravels and falls into disarray. But the pieces will never be found to be resurrected. This I lay at your feet, Earl Creighton. The more you try to harm me by paying assassins and arsonists and thugs to come after me, the faster your networks will lose power and influence. If you should threaten my family, my associates, or my coven, the hate and threat will rebound and be visited upon you tenfold."

Creighton shrank back against the edge of the circle, trying to get away from her words, but the walls of magic held him secure. The light of the brazier flashed across his horrified face as she drizzled his blood onto the coals and a burnt metallic scent filled the room.

She met his gaze. "I curse you and yours, for all time. Your toxicity will infect your endeavors and projects, and your world will collapse around you. So I have said and so mote it be."

She took the knife and drove it into the apple, the

blood bright against the golden skin. Then she cut a sliver out of the apple and tossed it on the burning coals. A sweet, baked apple scent followed the blood and she finished with sage.

"I offer this to the Goddess. May She hear my spell and accept my offerings. Blessed be!"

Rochelle's voice thundered in the small space and all the color left Creighton's ruddy face. He started to shake and keen like someone had lit his clothes on fire. I raised my eyebrows as he thrashed in the circle as if trying to get away from something even I couldn't see. But when he rose to his feet and ran at the other side of the circle to get away, he slammed up against the magic and knocked his ass flat out. He collapsed into a boneless heap with a grunt and lay still.

I blinked and shot a look at Rochelle.

"I thought you said you didn't do black magic."

She grinned as she pulled out a little bottle of water to extinguish the brazier. "I don't. That was a healing spell to help those who've been hurt by his machinations and to drain the malignant energy from our community. It's a protective spell, too, to make sure he can't come after me, the Concrete Angels, and the coven. It's only a curse if he tries to continue his illegal activities or harm any of us. It's possible he could turn over a new leaf and heal." She spread her hands with a shrug.

I threw my head back and laughed at how clever my witchy woman was as she carefully extinguished all the candles and gathered them, walking around the circle clockwise. When she got back to the little table, she snuffed the pillar and stacked her little bowls before smudging the circle's lines. The magic hissed away and Creighton's body slumped onto the floor. She shook her head before meeting my gaze.

"You can ask your partners to come in now. Tell them to take him to his house and dump him on the front porch."

She waved her hand at Creighton's crumpled form.

"Are you sure you don't want us to drive him out to the National Forest and leave him there?" I raised an eyebrow.

She snorted. "It would be so easy to fuck up his life, but he'll fuck it up more if we deliver him home safely. We won't have to do a thing and acquire the karmic debt. I'd rather he did it to himself, thanks."

"Okay." I smirked as I opened the door to the outside where Nessie waited. Gopher stood near the van, his hands in his pockets and his shoulders hunched. "Come in and get him. Take him to his residence and leave him on the porch wrapped in his coat."

Gopher blew out a sharp breath. "Fuck, it's about time. My balls are fuckin' frozen."

I nodded and stepped out of the way for them to enter. Rochelle had already swept away the evidence of the circle. Nessie nodded to her and instructed Gopher to pick up Creighton's feet while she hooked her arms under his pits. I held the door open for them as Rochelle packed all her things in a rolling suitcase.

"I'm gonna sleep for a week." She rubbed her eyes as she followed me out to watch Gopher and Nessie load up Creighton's unconscious body into the van.

I glanced over at her as I locked the door. "Just sleeping? Are you sure I can't entice you to do something else?"

A sultry smile curled her lips. "It depends on what you had in mind. I might be persuaded."

I gave her some subtle but very explicit signs of what I wanted to do and her eyes lit up as she laughed.

"Take me home and show me what you've got, Flint."

She didn't have to tell me twice.

CHAPTER SIXTEEN

Rochelle

I didn't sleep for a week. It was more like three and a half days, but in that time Flint treated me like his favorite sex toy and his most valued partner. I was definitely okay with being both. Attila came by to help me go shopping for a new retail property and between him and Joslyn, we found a place located in a good neighborhood that was only about twenty minutes from Flint's home on the hill.

Attila flirted shamelessly with Joslyn, and I was glad Andre hadn't come with us because he wouldn't have understood Attila's efforts. But Joslyn blossomed and smiled more than I'd seen her do since her court case. Of course, that may have been because she was now spending all her free time with Andre, rather than Attila's flirting, but either way, the joy was palpable.

I'd learned that I had an online colleague in the Concrete Angels MC all along. Haley Michaels, Michael's old lady, was a reporter for the Fort Collins Bugle and she'd been working on gathering information on Backlog to expose the shadow organization that seemed to have fingers in every pie imaginable, and some I didn't want to imagine.

I gave her all I knew about Creighton, including his

efforts to kill me and burn my place down. Just before Hogmanay, she put the information everywhere she could and even shared stills from my home security cameras. She put the evidence together and made a very classy article in the Bugle condemning Councilman Creighton's involvement in trying to destroy the occult community in Fort Collins. She even alluded to my mother's letter and how it led me to nearly getting thrown off a cliff.

The article was well received and from what I could tell, already had thousands of hits on the online paper. It was a good thing I'd set my spell before Creighton saw the article or he'd come after me even harder. But each nefarious action would bring more of the dismantling energy, and his endeavors would fail. Not that I wouldn't be keeping an eye out for him, but he'd be one less worry.

Despite living with Flint, we were so busy that we didn't get much intimate time between the night we spelled Creighton and Hogmanay. I spent most of my time in the workshop, brewing and mixing product for when our shop reopened in January. Joslyn helped me when she wasn't designing flyers, blog posts, and social media announcements for the upcoming reopening. We'd never been so popular, but with the article on Creighton's manipulations and subsequent arson, the outpouring of support overwhelmed us.

Finally, New Year's Eve arrived and I could barely concentrate. Flint had been gone most of the day helping with security and set up at the Concrete Angels compound. But he did come home to drop off a garment bag with strict instructions to wear the contents that night. I hadn't been able to wait to see what he'd brought and unzipped the bag.

Inside lay a deep forest green crushed velvet dress with a scoop neck and a black leather bustier. *Sweet glory.* I pulled out the bustier first, turning it to take in all the details. A large decal of the Concrete Angels MC logo covered the back and it laced up the front with red satin ties.

I held the whole ensemble up to myself as I stood in front of the mirror and giggled. *We're gonna definitely deck my halls this evening.*

I zipped everything back up in the bag and set it on our bed as I went back to the workshop to finish the little swag bags I'd made for all the members and guests at the party that night. Jos and I had come up with a new hand cream we'd named The Concrete Angel because it helped keep the hands from getting all beat up after washing and drying in cold weather. It smelled of almond and coffee, and absorbed into the skin quickly so it wouldn't be greasy. We'd also thrown in some peppermint lip balm, chamomile tea, and a small keychain with the Herb Cabinette logo on it. All of it was contained in a hemp bag tied with a red, green, or gold ribbon.

Joslyn arrived an hour before we were supposed to attend the party and she helped me load up the little swag bags into the back of my car before we retired to the house to get dressed for the party. She'd brought a couple of dresses decide between since I'd told her the theme of the party that night was the Silver New Year's Celebration. I'd asked why they'd picked that theme and Flint had told me it was because this was the twenty fifth year they'd had a big party for the changing of the calendar.

"So are you ready for tonight?" Jos shot me a look as we headed into the bedroom.

I shrugged. "Yeah, I guess so. As I'll ever be, I suppose. I'm nervous about the contract."

"Hush, girl. I got you covered. You know we have all those terms wrapped up tight, right?"

I took a deep breath and blew it out. "Yeah, right. It's going to be fine." Even if I was signing a contract with Loki, Captain Mischief himself.

"Damn right it is. And you're gonna look fine, too. Me, on the other hand." She shook her head as she pulled out the dresses. "I just don't know which one would be best."

She held up a copper-colored long sleeved satin wrap dress in one hand and plum-purple strapless evening gown. I narrowed my eyes and looked at both of them as she laid them on the bed for better viewing.

I picked up the copper-colored dress. "Here. This one. It brings out your eyes and you'll look great."

"In this?" Joslyn raised an eyebrow as she took the dress. "Are you sure it's not too golden for tonight? Wasn't this supposed to be the Silver New Year's Celebration?"

"Silver refers to the years they've been having the party, not the color dress code." I rolled my eyes as I helped her lift the dress over her elegant braided chignon. "And the purple one, while pretty, won't keep you warm enough, and I want you to look hawwwt." I grinned as she settled the dress around her generous curves.

She laughed as she studied at her reflection in the floor-length mirror. "That's the wrong kind of hot."

"Heh, we'll see. Andre won't know what hit him. He'll be all over you like mist in the glen." I grinned at her as she rolled her eyes.

"I'm not sure I want that." But I caught the smile curling her lips before she turned to me. "So what are you going to wear?"

I shrugged as my cheeks heated. "Well…"

"Well what?" Her eyes narrowed. "What did you decide to wear?"

I ducked my head. "I didn't pick it, Flint did."

"Oh? Now I've seen it all. Rochelle Stone has finally let a man pick her outfit. I'd best make a note of this." I stuck my tongue out at her as she laughed. "So, what did Flint pick out for you?"

I shrugged but grabbed the black garment bag and unzipped it. Inside lay the forest green crushed velvet dress and the black leather bustier with the Concrete Angels MC logo on the back.

Joslyn whistled. "Damn, girl, you'll be the hottest witch there!"

"Hah! With you there? Not possible." I grinned as I pulled my shirt over my head and stepped out of my jeans.

"I admit, with all this caramel chocolate goodness right here they might be hard-pressed to notice anyone else, but you're sweet peppermint cream in spicy black leather. Um!"

She lifted the dress over my artfully ruffled curls and helped me into the bustier, tightening down the red satin ties while I held my boobs up to maintain the illusion of deep cleavage. When we were done, we turned to look at each other in the mirror.

"Damn! The bikers are in for a treat tonight." Jos grinned as she looked us up and down.

"We'll definitely make an impression. But I need one last thing."

"What's that?" She raised an eyebrow.

"It's Cinderella time. I need you to help me lace up my boots. I can't bend in half in this thing."

Joslyn barked out a laugh and nodded as she followed me to where I'd left my lace-up kitten heels. She helped me tie them then grabbed our long woolen coats to keep us warm in the drive down the hill. We'd been invited early so we could set up the swag bags for everyone coming to the party. Flint said he had to do security this evening but would catch a ride home with me at the end of the night. We'd convinced Andre to meet us at the compound and he'd take Joslyn home. I didn't ask if it was to his home or hers. She'd pick up her car at our place later.

"Ready?" Joslyn asked as we stepped out the door of the cabin.

"Hell no. You?" I locked the door behind me.

"Aw yeah. We're gonna rock this party."

I raised an eyebrow. "You're not nervous at all?"

"Of course I'm nervous. But fake it till you make it, sis, and we've got that hands down."

I laughed. "Got it. Head high, boobs up, and strut!" Which we did until we got our butts in the freezing cold pleather seats of my car. "Shit, it's cold! My ass is freezing to this seat."

I cranked the engine and let it warm up a bit before we headed to the compound, and texted Flint that we were on our way. My nervousness rose the closer we got, but I kept my thoughts to myself. Joslyn had given me all the help she could and we were prepared. I still felt like I was heading into an argument with the U.S. Supreme Court while woefully unprepared, but I tried to remind myself there was no use borrowing trouble. It would find me soon enough with Creighton still working with Backlog.

Flint stood waiting for us at the gate of the compound and waved us through before closing the gate behind us. I parked my car in the newly erected carport the club had put up for the members with vehicles, like Karma's old man who drove a 1956 Chevy Corvette in the summer and a midsize SUV in the winter. Haley drove a Subaru and commuted down into Fort Collins most days, and now I needed a place to store my car when I visited. We put up the windshield cover to keep any blowing snow off and hurried into the clubhouse and the heat there.

Though we were early for the official start time, many of the bikers were already in full party mode. Black leather, high heels, and glittering jewels were everywhere, and those were the men. The women came in a variety of colors and costumes ranging from incredibly elegant to downright kinky. Chemistry, the bartender, wore a beautiful high-collared red brocade dress with a high slit in the long skirt and her black hair in a simple braid down her back. Karma strode around in white leather, from her boots and tight pants, to her corset and half jacket with the club's logo on the back. Diamond drop earrings, a matching necklace and a tiara made up the rest of her outfit, and I was suitably impressed.

Most of the men wore clean jeans, their leather cuts or jackets with the club's logo, and heeled boots of one kind or another. Some had even bejeweled their beards and hair, and all of them wore fancy button-down shirts of metallic fabric in various colors – gold, silver, blue, red, green, and rusty orange. I noticed even Flint wore a dark green metallic shirt under his vest.

But the most spectacular costume was worn by Loki as he sauntered around the clubhouse, mingling with everyone. He wore a long tailored coat in royal blue with gold trim on collar, cuffs, and tails. It buttoned up the front to a high collar without lapels and looked like something I'd expect the members of some European royal family to wear. Black pants tucked into high black boots covered his legs and he carried an honest-to-Goddess tankard full of something steaming and mysterious.

He approached the table where we were arranging the swag bags and smiled his enigmatic smile. He made me nervous, but I did my best to smile back at him.

"Good evening, Ms. Stone. So good to have you here tonight. Big night, ja?"

I swallowed hard and set out more bags to give me some time gather my courage. "Yes, it is."

"And who is this?" He shifted his mysterious gaze to Joslyn. "A friend of yours, ja?"

"This is Joslyn, my business partner." I nodded to Jos. "Joslyn, this is Loki, President of the Concrete Angels MC."

Joslyn grinned. "Hahaha, Loki, great road name. Though I think you look more like the Thor character in the Marvel movies, personally."

I swallowed hard, remembering what the legends said about the sibling rivalry between Thor and Loki. But Loki laughed and shook his head.

"I hear this a lot. But Hollywood isn't always so on target, ja? It's the road name that stuck." He shrugged but his eyes flashed with amusement and I took a deep breath to keep from laughing nervously.

"Very nice to meet you, Loki." Jos's phone chimed and she fished it out of her little clutch purse. "Oh, it looks like my boyfriend is here. Excuse me." She smiled as she wrapped her coat around her shoulders and headed toward the entrance, leaving me alone with Loki.

"She is a good friend, ja?" Loki remarked as he watched her duck out the doors of the clubhouse.

I nodded. "The best of friends."

"And yet, you haven't told her who I am. Have you told her what Flint is?"

I met his unsettling gaze. "No. I've only known you all for a little more than a week."

He smirked as he shook his head. "Humans and their assumptions about time. It is confounding. How long did it take you to understand you're meant for Flint?"

I frowned and shrugged. "I don't know. I didn't keep track. Quick, I guess. Why?"

"You see? The length of time you have knowledge is irrelevant. Perhaps it's your comfort level with the knowledge that troubles you, ja?"

He winked as he sauntered away to visit with some of the other bikers and their partners, leaving me to wonder what the hell he had planned for tonight. I finished setting out all the swag bags and hoped Jos or Flint would come back soon. I wasn't sure where I fit in with the bikers yet and I didn't feel entitled to insert myself into random conversations. Still, I needed something to drink and I'd already met the bartender. I didn't think we were friends, but at least she knew who I was.

I caught her attention and nodded to her. "May I please have—"

"Let me guess. Virgin hot apple cider."

I nodded. "Yup. Gotta be sharp tonight."

"Is there ever a time when you don't have to be sharp?" This time she went to the back of the bar to get my cider.

I tilted my head, pretending to consider. "With this crowd? Nope."

To my surprise, she grinned. "Smartest answer I've heard all night. Your cider." She set an ornate goblet on the bar with steaming caramel-colored liquid in it.

"Thank you." I grasped the goblet just as someone's arms closed around my waist from behind. At first, I stiffened, but then the scent of petrichor filled my nose and I relaxed against the hard chest behind me. Life had been monochromatic before Flint came into it, and I realized, no matter what the contract said, I wanted to be with him enough that I'd make it work to my favor. And just like that, all my fear and nervousness was gone.

He turned me in his arms and growled with a grin. "You wore it. You look amazing." It was easy to read his signs because his expression showed the same admiration.

"Thank you. So do you. I love this color on you." I fingered the satiny material of his shirt sleeve. "Did you pick this dress to match?"

He nodded. "Thought it best to look like a couple."

"Aww, cute from the beginning." I winked.

He growled and pressed me up against the bar. "Not cute, hot." Then he cupped my face with his hands and kissed the hell out of me.

Wolf whistles and hoots of laughter filled the room as Flint plundered my mouth. I loved it and grinned when he let me up for air. By the time I looked around, Joslyn stood beside a handsome man in a three piece suit with short cropped hair, a goatee around his full lips, and skin the color of fine, dark suede. Andre Kinston was still as handsome as ever and I waved to him with a smile.

"I see you found your way here. Nice suit." I shot a

look at Jos with raised eyebrows. "Did you call him to tell him you chose the copper dress?"

"Now would I do that?" Jos widened her eyes and covered her mouth with her fingers, mock aghast.

I laughed. "Yeah, you're not fooling me." I turned to Andre. "But I was serious about the suit. The copper vest looks great with Jos's dress."

"A man likes to look his best for his lady." Andre's deep rich voice warmed me like melted fudge over ice cream. Absolutely delicious. He turned his attention to Flint and held out his hand. "Andre Kingston."

Flint took his hand and shook it gently as he nodded and signed with the other hand. "Nice to meet you."

"He says it's nice to meet you." I translated and Andre's eyes widened.

"I didn't realize he was deaf. I apologize." He made sure to be facing Flint when he said it.

"Oh, no, he's not deaf. Just mute. He can hear you just fine." I gave Andre a reassuring smile. Flint signed again. "He says your suit looks great on you and you and Joslyn are beautiful together."

I didn't expect the hardened lawyer to blush, but his cheeks grew rosy as he looked over at Joslyn. "She makes me want to look my best."

I grinned at my beaming best friend. "Mission accomplished."

Flint gestured to a quieter spot near the swag table and I nodded. "Why don't you folks get some drinks and join us after?"

"Sounds good." Andre took Jos's arm and guided her up to the bar.

She shot me an excited and delighted smile as I walked away and I gave her two thumbs-up. She'd gotten herself a very hot and kind man, and I was thrilled for her. Flint pulled me over to a semi-empty corner away from the pool table where Numbers was again holding court against the majority of the club. I thanked my lucky stars I wasn't into pool. That woman was a shark.

"How are you doing?" Flint settled me on a window seat looking out on the yard and stood in front of me, his expression watchful.

"I'm good, now that you're here. I was so nervous up to this point, but when you wrapped your arms around me, I knew everything would be fine and I'd be able to make the contract work for me." I tugged him closer to me. "How are you doing?"

He shrugged. "I'm good as long as you're good. Andre seems like a good man and a perfect match for Joslyn."

I blinked. "How would you know that? You just met him."

Flint gave me a half-smile. "Gut feeling."

Jos and Andre joined us and our conversation turned to how the year had gone and the coming New Year. Jos and I talked about the hunt for a new shop, and Andre mentioned that the spot we'd found was actually closer to his office. I shared a look of delighted surprise with Joslyn as bikers, honeys, Scooters, and other partygoers swarmed the table for the swag bags.

After the rush, Loki called everyone to come over by the huge holiday tree decked out in lights and ribbons and little motorcycle ornaments. I hadn't had a chance to look at them closely, but it turned out each one was of a current member. When Flint showed me his, I was astounded at the likeness.

"So it's the end of the year, ja? And it's time to get your resolutions or resignations in before the clock turns twelve." Loki winked and laughter rippled through the crowd of bikers and Scooters, what the club called the prospective members. "But before we party like it's going out of style, we have some business to take care of. Flint, you'll join me here, ja?"

Flint squeezed my hand and strode through the crowd a

good head taller than most of the men in the room with the exception of Michael, the VP, Attila, and Trigger, the cowboy biker who made me think he should be riding a real horse instead of an iron one. Loki smiled broadly at my lover and grasped his hand, bringing their chests together in a manly hug.

"Maybe you know, maybe you don't, but Flint is the first member of our club besides me." Loki spoke to the whole crowd, but his gaze rested on mine. "I asked him if he wanted to be the VP, but he said he wasn't much for speeches." The crowd laughed at his snark. "I asked him what he wanted to do and he said he was going to keep the rest of you hooligans in line as security. At first I was uncertain he'd fit the post so well, but have any of you come across him in the dark when you're perhaps choosing an unwise action?"

Laughter rippled through the crowd, some of it uneasy.

"Intimidating, ja?" Loki chuckled. "So he's very good at what he does." The president patted Flint's shoulder. "So when I heard my old friend had found a woman to keep him warm when he wasn't watching all of you, I said det er bra and hoped to meet her. We are in luck, brothers. Flint has brought his woman tonight. She's the lovely Rochelle Stone." His unusual gaze hit me and I took a deep breath to calm the butterflies. "And she wants to become part of the club. So you know what that means."

The crowd laughed and groaned at the same time.

"That's right, a contract needs to be written and signed."

Why did he sound so damn gleeful? A dark-haired, dark-eyed man with tablet and keyboard appeared on Loki's other side, wearing a traditional Indian man's outfit in black with gold embroidery on collar, cuffs, and hems of the long tunic over loose pants. The jacket illustrated his broad shoulders and narrow waist, and I wondered if there was an ugly man in this biker club.

"Here is Neo to write down our contract for us." Loki gestured to the tablet-toting man. "Now, we must decide on terms, ja? As is tradition, ladies first."

I stepped forward and licked my lips as I considered everything Joslyn and I had decided. "Before I dictate my terms, I need to know what my role in the club will be. I can't sign a contract if I don't know what's expected of me."

Hoots echoed around the room as the brothers made it clear they were impressed with my first parry to Loki's strike.

"That's a good question, Loki." The woman by the name of Numbers came forward leaning on her pool cue. "I remember having to sign a contract for a specific job. Now she's gotta sign a contract for what, exactly? Kissing the security guard? Hell, I've seen a lot more than that going on here."

Laughter rang out and Loki inclined his head with his amused smile firmly in place.

"You make good points, Ms. Stone. So what would we hire you to do for us?"

Though the laughter continued, I started to wonder if I'd gotten myself in too deep too fast. This was freakin' Loki I was dealing with and he played for keeps. But I wasn't about to offer my services unless asked specifically for them. I might have been crazy but I wasn't stupid.

"It is good to have a legitimate, visible business for the club, ja? I could see us getting into the occult business." Loki smiled and tapped his lip with one finger.

I shook my head. "My business isn't for sale. You'll have to start your own shop."

"Perhaps we should invest in your business, then. Like a silent partner, providing capital for all your shop's needs."

I narrowed my eyes. "In exchange for what?"

Loki narrowed his own eyes and his expression grew

shrewd. "I understand you have a gift in surveillance." He didn't say turning magical energy into data packets, but that was what he meant. "Perhaps we could hire you to set surveillance lines around our compound and other businesses that would allow us to keep them safe. We will provide the investment capital for your business, and the equipment you need to set up sensors around our other holdings, and you provide that surveillance."

"Investment capital…." I thought through his wording. "You mean you want to use my legitimate shop to launder your money where the cops, the government, and the IRS can't find it, correct?"

"I wouldn't call it laundering."

"Then what would you call it?" I raised my chin. "We need to be clear if we're going to sign a contract over this."

Loki laughed and I thought I heard some admiration in it. "Clarity is very important, ja? Very well. Let us call it scrubbing our currency of unwanted past actions. You agree to sift our funds through your shop and provide protective surveillance of our other properties, and you shall have your capital and any marketing and promotional help the club can provide, including our reach to other customers and suppliers of raw materials."

"Will this protection go both ways? For example, I'm providing my surveillance expertise on your other holdings. Will the club protect my new shop from vandalism and destruction, and my digital holdings such as blog, website, and social media accounts from hacking and ransomware?" I knew Neo was a hacker of epic proportions from what Flint told me and if he was on my side, other hackers wouldn't have a chance.

I shot a look at Neo, who'd been typing furiously on the keyboard connected to his tablet. *Looks like Flint was right and the terms would be typed on the fly.*

Loki nodded slowly as everyone's eyes shot back to him. It was like a ping pong match of attention.

"I believe that is doable. So we will provide capital for the Herb Cabinette, physical protection of the retail space, and digital protection of your digital footprint, i.e. blog, website, and social media accounts."

"Without censorship—I only agree to protection, not direction." I met Neo's eyes and he gave me a half smile with a nod.

"Very well. Shall we sign?" Loki smirked.

"Not quite yet. I have one more thing I want. If I'm going to…How did you say it? 'Scrub your currency of unwanted past actions,' I want fifteen percent of the profits to go to a social program of my choosing." I glanced over at Joslyn and she nodded, her face a beautiful stoic mask. This was the one thing that was near and dear to our hearts.

"Two and a half percent."

I raised an eyebrow. "Fifteen percent."

He tilted his head. "Five percent."

I took a sip of my cider. "Fifteen percent." I resisted the urge to explain why or to point out they had more money than most of the millionaires living in Denver and Fort Collins.

"Ten percent and that's as far as I'll go." Loki crossed his arms over his chest.

"Done." I nodded sharply, dancing on the inside. Joslyn and I had agreed we wouldn't go lower than ten percent, but would hold out until Loki made it his choice.

There were murmurs of surprise in the crowd and I overheard someone say, "Holy shit, she got Loki to give up money. Have you ever seen someone do that?" I didn't smirk. I wasn't willing to take the chance he wouldn't sign the mutual document if I did.

"Print that, Neo, and let us sign before the end of the year comes, ja?" Loki didn't lose his smirk, but intensity glittered in his eyes and I reminded myself who he truly was. "Please read it over, Ms. Stone, to be sure the terms are clear."

Neo printed the document and handed it to me. Joslyn stepped up beside me and we read it over together, making sure the terms we'd dictated were there in writing. I didn't see anything that I hadn't agreed to, but I raised my eyebrows at Joslyn. She kept reading but in the end, she shook her head. She hadn't seen anything changed either.

"Good, this looks fine to me. Do you have a pen?"

Loki's grin widened and I shivered. Why did he look so maniacal?

"We have just the pen." He pulled out what looked like a steampunk fountain pen with gold filagree over the black lacquered wood. "It's a special one of my design." He brought it to me and showed me how to hold it. "When you squeeze this lever, the ink comes out onto the page, ja?" Neo took the pen and cleaned it with an alcohol swab.

"Do you have ink in it already?"

He laughed and I swallowed hard. "Oh my dear Ms. Stone, you carry the ink within you. We sign in blood, ja? It makes the contract officially binding and unbreakable because it holds our DNA."

I wanted to be shocked, but many spells required a drop of the practitioner's blood to make them work properly, and this wasn't anything more than a binding spell.

"You mean to help me keep my word or to help you?" I let the pen prick my finger and waited for the blood to flow enough to sign my name.

"Both, but most especially me." He grinned and took the pen back for Neo to clean again, while handing me a small gauze pad. Then he pricked his own finger and signed his name with a flourish beneath mine.

"It is done." He clapped and a ripple of magic washed through the crowd, lifting hair and ruffling clothing as it passed. "Welcome to the Concrete Angels Motorcycle Club."

Damn, I guess it truly is official.

He blew on the contract to dry the blood and handed it to Neo.

"I'd like a copy of that, in color, for my files, please." I pointed at the document as the crowd cheered.

Neo grinned and nodded. "I'll have it for you when you're ready to take it."

"Way to go, girl!" Joslyn hugged me. "I knew you could do it. What are you going to use the money for when you get it?"

"I thought maybe you and Andre could help me decide. I was thinking something like legal aid for people battered and defrauded by the rich? You know, kind of a legal trust fund for when the wealthy think they can get away with anything because they're rich?"

Jos narrowed her eyes. "It's almost as if you've had some experience with that or something."

I grinned. "Or something. Maybe Andre might be willing to offer some hours? Just spit balling here."

"Hmm." She kissed the side of my head and hugged me. "Let's think on it in the new year."

"Done."

"All right, ye bastards, quiet down now. Flint has asked me to say a few words for him and ye canna hear them if ye're mawking about." Attila roared over the increased sounds of laughter and partying.

The celebratory noise settled down and everyone focused on Attila's impressive height. He wore a traditional formal jacket with his kilt complete with sporran and long socks with matching tartan flashes. I grinned at Jos, mouthing, *He's hot in his kilt.* She laughed.

"Right, so because Ms. Rochelle Stone is now part of our wee club, she'll need colors, aye? So Flint made sure to get her a jacket with his patch. So keep yer mitts off her, ye wee bastards. The hot witch is his." Attila snarled at everyone as I shot a look at Flint and rolled my eyes.

He lifted his hands. "Small changes, Rochelle, small

changes."

Flint grabbed some black leather off a nearby table and held it up as I met him in the center of the room. The black leather jacket had an elegant cut and flared below my hips to give the impression of a dress or skirt. But a slit broke the skirt into tails in the back below the waist. The Concrete Angels MC logo was stitched in the center back and the rocker read, "Flint's Matron."

He held it up so I could slip my arms into the armholes. Then he leaned forward and growled in my ear. "Sssexxy."

The jacket fit perfectly and was butter-soft to the touch. I loved the creaking sound as I raised my arms around his neck. "Thank you."

He nodded then kissed me soundly to wolf whistles and cheers from his brother bikers.

"Hey, y'all, it's time to count down to midnight!" The cowboy biker named Trigger raised his pint glass and looked at the big screen TV on the wall counting down the seconds.

"Ten…nine…eight…seven…six…five…four…three …two…one. Happy New Year!"

The cheer went up along with confetti and the grandfather clock near the door started chiming the twelve strokes. Voices rose with counting up the number of chimes until they reached twelve while everyone expectantly watched the front doors.

Michael stepped into the room just as the clock struck it's final chime. "Right then, are we late?"

The bikers roared with laughter and cheer, and a ripple of magic fluttered through the room. The Goddess had bestowed a blessing on the Concrete Angels MC when the dark-haired man stepped across the threshold just as the year turned over. *We're gonna have good luck this coming year.*

"Happy New Year." Flint wrapped me in his arms and

kissed me.

"Happy new beginnings," I whispered back to him. It was going to be a damn good year.

EPILOGUE

Viper

I wasn't a fan of most holidays, Christmas and Valentine's Day in particular made me want to puke. But I liked New Year's because it was the next opportunity to change things. To let go of the old and start life anew. I'd done it enough times to know what I was talking about.

It had been a shitty year for me, though nothing particularly bad had happened. It wasn't like my first marriage where my husband had looked perfect on the outside, but was into psychological and physical abuse at home. The year had just been meh, with a capital EH. But I'd watched my friends, Karma in particular, fall in love and find those perfect romances written in the books I loved.

I slid my gaze across the room where Karma and her old man were seated at one of the tables, talking with Attila, Piper, Attila's current boyfriend and boy-toy, the Friar, and one of our recent members, Trigger. Despite having been with the club now for about a year, I'd managed to avoid him for the most part. It was a habit I'd developed toward unknown men after my failed marriage, and I was a master at it.

It also helped that I was the AV security and surveillance expert of the club. I knew where most of the unattached men were at all times and I liked it that way. There were only four men I trusted and they were Michael, Loki, Luke, and Attila, in that order. They weren't really men in the traditional sense, since two of them were real angels, one was a god, and the last was a werewolf who turned into a glossy black wolf whenever he felt like running wild.

Yeah, most of the club didn't know what they were, but when my best friend in all the world was Karma—the real Karma, that made consequences come a lot sooner than expected—I'd learned long ago that humans weren't really the top critters out there anymore. I would argue that humans were more monstrous than the Elder Races were reputed to be.

Believe me, I'd met the real monsters.

No time for melancholy thoughts tonight, Viper.

I listened to my inner goddess and kicked the unhappy thoughts to the curb as I inhaled the general joy of the evening. Our newest member, Rochelle Stone, a real goddess-blessed witch, had just gotten her coat and patch as Flint's Matron, and their pleasure was palpable even to the casual observer.

I sighed. *The perfect romance novel.* I was a huge fan of hockey and cowboy romances, but biker romances were pretty damn good when they really happened.

Flint and Rochelle would get their happily-ever-after and I was pleased for them. I loved it when romance worked out for people. Just because it hadn't worked out for me didn't mean I begrudged them their HEA. They were happy and we'd have a new shop to launder some of our money to keep it out of the hands of the IRS. Win-win for everyone.

Pushing my hair behind my shoulders, I stopped by the

bar to grab a virgin hot apple cider. Ever since Rochelle had ordered one around the Christmas holiday, I'd made sure Grub produced it most nights. Apple cider was a favorite of mine and it gave me an opportunity to have something to drink that wasn't alcohol. I didn't trust people, even in the club, to let down my guard enough to get tipsy.

I made my way through the celebrating bikers to the table where Karma sat and let my mouth twisted into its usual sardonic smirk as the men I passed ogled my tits and ass. I wore my favorite black leather bustier with the hot red ties and my tight black leather pants. Normally, I wore heels, but the snow outside made them impractical should I need to make a quick escape. I never allowed myself to be vulnerable.

"Hey, Viper, pull up a chair, lassie." Attila waved to Piper, who jumped up to find another seat for me, but I shook my head.

"Thanks, Attila, but I just wanted to say my goodnights before I turn in." I raised my mug of hot apple cider. "I have a date with a cowboy romance."

"How about havin' a real cowboy romance, darlin'?" Trigger tipped his hat back and gave me the beginnings of a lazy smile.

Except when our gazes met, we both froze as stiff as the winter winds outside.

"Holy shit."

"Well, hell, darlin', I didn't expect to see you here."

That was an understatement. The last time I'd seen him in person, we'd been at his parents' swanky Back to School party just before he went off to college. We'd been boyfriend and girlfriend for all of high school, and while his parents expected him to get a degree, my parents expected me to get a husband. I didn't want to get married or wait around for a man to come back into my life, so I broke up with him. It had been painful and the end of my world, and I hadn't seen him since.

Until now.

Attila raised an eyebrow. "Ye know Trigger, lass? I dinna think ye'd met him more than in passin'."

I swallowed hard, desperately trying to put up a shield between me and the onslaught of memories from my life BM – Before Marriage. Truth be told, I hadn't ever really known the man with the road name of Trigger, although he'd been a strapping boy of 18 back then.

Paul Michael Whitmore III, heir to the Texas Whitmore Cattle Ranches and the new breed of Whitmore Whites cattle, was every bit the billionaire cowboy his parents had raised him to be. Except, now he was somehow one of the newest members of the Concrete Angels Motorcycle Club, and I was no longer the girl he'd known. I was too broken, too damaged, and too lost to be what he remembered.

"I hadn't." I faltered to a stop. How did I explain when I didn't want to dredge up the past?

"It's been, what, thirty years since that summer?" Teal-green eyes met mine as he leaned back in his chair, the goatee and sculpted golden brown beard a new addition since our last meeting.

Good glory, has it been that long?

"Viper, are you all right?" Karma rose to her feet, her expression both concerned and wary.

"Yeah, yeah, I'm good. I'm gonna go to bed. Good night."

I whirled away from their table, grateful I'd decided to wear practical boots that night. My breathing sped up as unusual panic welled in my chest. *Gotta get away. Gotta hide the ugly. He can't see me or tell my family.*

Too much history. Too much pain and humiliation. The Concrete Angels had been a safe haven because no one knew who I was. But now someone from my past had shown up and would expose the wounds again.

"Aeryn, wait!"

But I was already out the door into the howling winter night, running from my ghosts and the old love who'd somehow come back to life from the ashes of the past.

THE END

DUDE WITH A COOL CAR
CONCRETE ANGELS MC, BOOK 2
SNEEK PEEK

Bikers, Badge, and Backlog: Marshal DeVille always gets his man…and his Karma.

Cooper DeVille, US Marshal

Being undercover has its perks. I get to do stuff the day-to-day me would never experience. Like infiltrating the Concrete Angels Motorcycle Club and meeting Karma, the gorgeous Enforcer of the MC. Being handcuffed to her bed is a dream, but that's the problem with undercover work. Everything I'm doing here is only half true. The Concrete Angels—and Karma—are connected to Backlog, a shadow organization infiltrating law enforcement. The Fed undercover here before me was Backlog's bitch, and now he's dead. I have to determine which side of this fight the Concrete Angels are on… before Karma comes to bite me in ways I won't enjoy.

Karma, Concrete Angels' Enforcer

You bet your ass, I'm that karma, the one people pray never catches up to them. But my own karma has found me, seeing as the hunky P.I. who drove into the MC compound with his cool car is my Goddess-chosen true mate. But as my luck—and the Goddess' sense of humor—would have it, Cooper's an undercover US Marshal trying to ferret out our connection to a group called Backlog. Would've been nice to know before I took him to bed and discovered he's the best damn submissive this Madam could want, because I don't deal well with liars. And no one's happy when Karma's pissed. But Backlog has Cooper in its sights, and to survive… my mate might just have to die..

ANGEL INK
CONCRETE ANGELS MC, BOOK 3
SNEEK PEEK

Angels, Art, and Abduction: The magic of an angel's heart...is written on his skin.

Haley Michaels, Reporter

I was minding my own business, trying to escape a party, and walked straight into a murder. Which would've been the scoop of a lifetime if my phone hadn't died. And the door hadn't locked. Now I'm stuck in a cabin in the mountains with a hot guy who appeared on the street like my knight on shining motorcycle, and I should be more worried than attracted. I mean, he's covered in tattoos and is VP from the notorious Concrete Angels MC, the same group I'm investigating. Because I know they're involved with the deaths of a U.S. Marshal and two FBI agents. My love life luck sucks.

Michael, Concrete Angels' VP

Love isn't something that archangels ever expect to feel. At least not the all-consuming, no-holds-barred kind of love spoken about in films and songs. But that's what I felt the moment I laid eyes on Haley. She doesn't know I'm not human, or just how inhuman the rest of my MC is, but I can't stay away from her if I tried. Now I have to protect her – not only from the men hunting her, but also from the truth. The question is: will she stay when she finds out what I really am? Because if she can't be trusted with the truth, Loki will make sure she can't pass on the information. Permanently.

OTHER BOOKS BY SIOBHAN MUIR

Her Devoted Vampire
Queen Bitch of the Callowwood Pack
Second Chance Succubus
Darwin's Evolution

Bad Boys of Beta Squad Series
Bronco's Rough Ride
The Navy's Ghost
Rimshot's Hard Target
Bam-Bam's Inked Hart
Deli's Take out

Cloudburst Colorado Series
A Hell Hound's Fire
The Beltane Witch
Christmas I.C.E. Magic
Cloudburst Ice Magic
Cloudburst Coffee & Spa
Courting the Dragon Widow

Concrete Angels MC Series
My Forever Cocky Biker Encounter
Dude With a Cool Car
Angel Ink
The Concrete Angel

Elemental Hearts Series
Wildfire's Heart
A Timeless Heart

Rifts Series
Take the Reins
A Centaur's Solstice Wish
In Death's Shadow

The Ivory Road
A Walk in the Sand
Outback Dreams

Triple Star Ranch Series
Rope a Falling Star
Star Light, Star Bright
Star Spangled Banner

Warbler Peninsula Series
Order of the Dragon
The Valkyrie's Sword
Burning Yuletide

Coming Soon
Sorceress of Song & Flame
Running from the Texas Millionaire (Concrete Angels MC #5)
The Siren and the Scientist (Sirens, Inc. #1)

ABOUT THE AUTHOR

Siobhan Muir lives in Cheyenne, Wyoming, with her husband, two daughters, a kitten who thinks he's a dog, a cat who's not impressed with him, and the dog who just wants to go for a walk.

In previous lives, Siobhan has been an actor at the Colorado Renaissance Festival, a field geologist in the Aleutian Islands, and restored inter-planetary imagery at the USGS. She's hiked to the top of Mount St. Helens and to the bottom of Meteor Crater.

Siobhan writes kick-ass adventure with hot sex for men and women to enjoy. She believes in happily ever after, redemption, and communication, all of which you will find in her paranormal romance and dauntless romance stories.

Connect with Siobhan online at:
https://www.siobhanmuir.com
https://www.facebook.com/siobhan.muir.35
https://twitter.com/SiobhanMuir
https://www.siobhanmuir.com/siobhans-blog
https://pinterest.com/siobhanmuir.35

www.ingramcontent.com/pod-product-compliance
Lightning Source LLC
Chambersburg PA
CBHW050417260626
47156CB00003B/1046